SMART MOVES

SMART MOVES

Adrian Magson

THE
DOME
PRESS

Published by The Dome Press, 2018
Copyright © 2018 Adrian Magson
The moral right of Adrian Magson to be recognised as the author
of this work has been asserted in accordance with the
Copyright, Designs and Patents Act 1988.

A CIP catalogue record for this book is available from the British Library

ISBN 9781912534012

The Dome Press
23 Cecil Court
London WC2N 4EZ

www.thedomepress.com

Printed and bound in Great Britain by Clays Ltd, Elcograf S.p.A.

Typeset in Garamond by Elaine Sharples

For Ann. My own Lilly-Mae
who makes me believe in myself.

ONE

I never thought of guys having bad hair days.

Bad razor days, sure. Relentless stubble and scraped skin is no joke – try kissing my grandmother. Bad head days, too, from too much of the wrong kind of booze. But that's commonplace for anybody with a real life. Some problems, though, can't be overcome with a slap of skin balm or a handful of pills.

'You're laying me off?' The words dropped into the room like a stun grenade and rolled across the carpet. I stared at my boss, Niall Dunckley, in disbelief.

'Sign of the times, Jake,' he replied flatly. 'Sorry.' I wondered if that was the beginning of a smile threatening to edge past his bloodless lips. They went well with his fish eyes and the strands of lank hair carefully arranged over his balding head. The overall effect gave him the appearance of an undertaker's assistant. The kind who stays late at work for all the wrong reasons.

'Why?'

Pathetic response, I know. But being laid off is having someone say, 'We don't need you.' Or, 'Get the fuck out of here.' Or, 'We found someone we like better.'

Even in this business – what am I saying, *especially* in this business

1

– it's akin to a death sentence. A bullet behind the ear. A quiet visit from a bad person on a dark night. I mean, I didn't know for sure if that had ever happened, but people talk. You hear stuff.

I should explain. I have this oddball kind of job; I work for a sideline operation in a multi-divisional business called HP&P. Nobody knows or cares what the initials stand for, or precisely what the company's core business is. But I know it has its fingers in a great many pies from civil engineering to shipping to nightclubs – and allegedly, a few things in between.

It's the in-betweens which we're encouraged not to ask about.

Not that I'm in that sector. I'm a project troubleshooter, and it's my job to solve problems in faraway places. A gentle talk here, a nudge there, a discreet payment if something gets stuck in the pipeline, that kind of thing. The company operates on a time-sensitive schedule, and delays are unhelpful to the bottom line. As are glitches caused by local officials trying to muscle in and cause problems for their own ends.

Don't get me wrong; I don't use physical pressure – I don't have to. A sweetener with a local regional governor or a union boss usually does the trick, from Azerbaijan to Zambia. If that doesn't work, I make a report to Niall Dunckley at HQ in London, and that's the last I hear of it. Because by then all the talking and offers and mild threats of layoffs will have been exhausted and it's time to call in the big guns and for me to catch a plane out. I don't actually know what the big guns are, but that's where I'm encouraged to turn and look the other way.

The job pays well and I rarely get to follow up on a previous visit. If I do, it's usually bad news because the project got canned and there's a lot of name-calling going on. I'm just there to see that everybody knows whose fault it really is: theirs.

Over the three years I've been doing this I've managed to refrain from asking too many questions. It's one of the main requirements of my job description. Come to think of it, it's the only requirement. Don't ask, don't nose, don't look.

And because I find it easier to take the money and not rock the boat, I've gone along with it. My bad, as the kids say. Still not sure what that means but it sounds about right. It doesn't mean I'm dead from the neck up and haven't occasionally put two and two together and made seven. Being suspicious and doing something about it isn't always that simple. Or wise.

My job might, at least in some parts of the civilized world, be regarded as slightly unethical. The use of money – slush funds as some people like to call it – to solve problems is never on the up-and-up. Sure, it's been going on since time began and will continue. Bungs, bribes, emoluments, skims, unscheduled performance bonuses – call them whatever the hell you want – do serve a purpose. They oil the wheels.

In that sense, I'm a bag man.

The first time I thought my job was a little unusual was a year ago. Until then it had been pretty much the routine: get on a plane, talk to people, find out what the problems are and look for a solution. It meant asking questions of local representatives and negotiating our end of the argument to get things moving. If I couldn't get agreement there and then, I'd make a POH – project-on-hold – report and head for home. The rest was up to Dunckley and his management team. The big guns.

But I'd never been asked to deliver a package before.

This was an envelope to go to Denver, Colorado. Actually, I never made Denver city itself, just the airport arrivals hall. I'd been met by a sweaty guy in a suit, clutching a shiny briefcase. He looked stressed. A lawyer, I figured, since most lawyers wear stress like a second skin and these were the people I seemed to meet a lot: men in suits and shiny cars, with that money smell mixed with a vague hint of effluent. He handed me a business card which matched the photocopy in my pocket and, in return, I gave him an envelope, before making my way up the stairs to the departures lounge for the return trip, as per instructions.

As I turned to look back down the stairs, I caught a flash view of Sweaty Suit being hustled away by two police officers, one on each arm. He didn't look happy. For some reason I was relieved he didn't look back and shout, 'There he goes!'

When I got back to the office I relayed this incident to Dunckley. He listened, made a note or two on a lined pad, then gave me a sideways look before saying it was probably a private or local issue and to forget all about it. End of.

Strange stuff like that had happened on a few other occasions, and each time I'd come close without being picked up. It was like I was charmed. Eventually I came to the conclusion that, whereas delivering these documents seemed to be an OK job, collecting them was a whole other issue.

Then a guy doing a similar job in another division disappeared. Just like that. His name was John Baddeley and we'd met a few times like ships in transit, one of us leaving, one arriving. It took me a few days to realise I hadn't seen him for a couple of weeks, although that wasn't surprising because he travelled as extensively as I did. When his desk was taken over by another suit I asked where Baddeley was, but the new guy shrugged and said he didn't know and looked at me like I should go away. I asked around, but nobody knew a thing – not even the people he worked with. In fact, it was obvious that lips had been zipped and I should stop poking my nose in.

Two days later, I chanced on a news item about a body found floating in the river by Tower Bridge. A suicide, it was speculated, or a drunk who'd wandered too close to the embankment. It happens all the time along that stretch of London's waterway; once in, with the cold and the currents, people don't always come out alive.

It was John Baddeley.

I asked around some more, and before I knew it I was being marched into Dunckley's office and being told to mind my own. Accidents, he'd said heavily, sometimes happened, and Baddeley had been reportedly stressed of late and must have found it all too much.

'It's a dangerous place, the river,' he'd pointed out unnecessarily, 'especially with a gutful of booze and a confused state of mind.' He made it sound no worse than tripping and falling into a puddle on a wet Friday night.

'Confused?'

'You know what I mean.' Dunckley's voice was a snap, and he gave me his best fish-eyed look. His demeanour took on a whole new level of cold, and I sensed something I hadn't really associated with him before: he might look like a creep but there was something about him that suddenly told me he'd be a dangerous man to cross. I don't know how I hadn't noticed it before. Maybe I'd never had cause to. As if to reinforce the message, a stranger came in and stood by the door. I hadn't seen Dunckley call anyone, so I guessed he had a panic button beneath his desk. A quick flick of the foot sideways and help was on the way. The newcomer wore a smart, purple-toned security uniform but that was the only civilized thing about him. The rest was all bunched muscle and scar tissue and a wave of aggression coming off him like electricity.

'Actually, I don't.' I turned back to Dunckley; it was easier on the nerves than looking at King Kong. I nodded backwards. 'Who's this?'

Dunckley sighed and ignored my question. 'You do good work for us, Jake. Always on time, never any issues, no questions asked. Until now, anyway.' He leaned on his desk and stared hard at me. 'Don't go spoiling a fine record.' He pointed at the door. 'Now go about your business – our business – and forget the rest.'

The suited primate held the door open for me, and I took it as my signal to leave. But the way he leaned towards me and sniffed the air as I passed was the scariest thing I'd ever experienced.

It hadn't taken a genius to confirm that this weird division I worked for was connected with something very unusual and not entirely above board.

And now I'd discovered they didn't need me.

TWO

'You're not the only one,' Dunckley said, bringing me back to the present. 'Other divisions have had to lose personnel, too.' He shuffled some papers into a folder. My personnel folder, I read upside-down. He must have been going through it in the moments before giving me the deep six.

'So what's the problem?' I queried, waiting for some sign of regret, a tiny glimmer of conscience which might help us both overlook the times we hadn't seen eye to eye, when the grit of corporate life had insinuated itself between us and worked up a sore spot of cold-eyed politeness. It hadn't been often, but it had happened.

It was like trying to outstare a dead sheep. He shifted his gaze to somewhere above my right shoulder and cleared his throat. 'It's the economic downturn, I'm afraid. It's hit us all.'

Economic what? Now, I might play three wise monkeys and spend my time sitting in airport lounges waiting for flights to God knows where, and therefore be slightly divorced from the day-to-day business, but even I knew HP&P was rolling in cash. Strike that: Dunckley and his business partners were rolling in it. Financially speaking, the business was shitting banknotes. True, I didn't know where it was all coming from, but then, I knew not to ask.

'We're restructuring,' he continued smoothly. 'I'm afraid your job is no longer seen as viable. All that travelling around the world... Computers are taking over and face-to-face is no longer the way to go.'

'It's not?' That was news to me. Hadn't he said not long ago that they were pleased with my work? Besides, how could a computer deal with a local union boss in the Lower Amazon, for heaven's sake? Or face down a chieftain in the Upper Niger river basin who was threatening to bring out his workers on strike if they – meaning he – didn't get a nice fat bung? Some of the places I had to visit didn't even have electricity most of the time, and any computers left lying around pretty soon went missing, courtesy of the local bad boys.

'No. Lower costs, faster turnaround, that's the new maxim,' he blathered on. 'Speedier solutions are needed these days to keep ahead of the competition.' He stood up and marched over to the window, on the outside of which hung a box filled with a line of tulips, where he rocked back and forth on his heels like a general reviewing his troops. 'We're moving over to secure servers and encrypted systems, and we've decided to invest in a big video conferencing facility. It should be up and running within three weeks.' He turned and smiled as if he knew one end of a video conferencing facility from the other, and stretched his neck out from his collar trying to make himself appear taller. 'As for your job, we're going over to local agents; they're cheaper and... well, less concerned about project-on-hold reports, if you know what I mean. It's a new world, Jake, and we need to take a tougher line with contractors and local officials or we lose business. And we can't afford to do that. What can I say?'

Sorry, Jake, might have been a start. I take it all back, Jake. Just kidding, Jake. We'd be completely screwed without you, Jake.

I don't believe you, was what I wanted to yell at him. But I did believe him, which was the problem. I could sense it in Dunckley's voice and see it in his face. Somewhere along the line I'd asked one too many questions, voiced one too many concerns and, as far as Dunckley and HP&P were concerned, my time was up. I consoled myself with the thought that I was at least being offered a free walk out of the building rather than a swim in the river.

'What do I tell Susan?' I managed to mutter. It was more to myself than him. I mean, how do you tell your wife that you've hit the buffers, job-wise? Some might take it reasonably well, after the initial shock. Pick up the pieces and soldier on. But Susan didn't do soldiering, on or otherwise. She had a predilection for order and 'everything in its place' verging on the obsessive, and that included our individual jobs: mine with HP&P and hers as co-owner of two – or was it three now? – high-end shops catering to the wealthy fashionistas of West London. She'd been doing it since before we met, and was clearly successful and enjoyed it. What she didn't quite enjoy was my job, which had caused the occasional grit in the ointment.

I wasn't one for unnecessary change and my job hadn't been a major issue, most of the time, as far as I could recall. Well, apart from one time when I'd arrived home a day late, and she'd swung round to continue a defensive argument I should never have started. A meat tenderizer was something never to bring to a dispute, not unless you were an underworld gang enforcer. But Susan's arm had swung out under the weight of the implement, and centrifugal force had done the rest. Explaining away the grid-pattern bruise on my face to clients had been a week-long nightmare of embarrassment.

Now this. How would I confront her with such a bombshell? There sure as hell wasn't an easy way, short of lobbing a message tied to a brick through the front window. Whatever I did, she'd go ape-shit.

Dunckley said nothing, but began to look shifty, as though this was a topic he didn't want to get into. He clearly preferred to be on the more secure ground of economic restructuring and downsizing, of corporate planning and system implementation or even sending big guns into dark places to unstick projects-on-hold. Much more his cup of tea than giving some poor sap the elbow and having his wife and kids with no roof over their heads. Not that I had kids – but the principle was the same.

It reminded me that he wasn't without problems of his own, family-wise. Office gossip had it that not long ago his eighteen-year-old daughter, Melanie, had gone over the wire one night to live life to the full in sunny California. A week later his wife had scarpered to Ireland with her night-school art teacher to join a retro-Sixties hippie commune. Sensible woman, in my view; fancy waking up every morning to see Dunckley's comb-over crawling across the pillow towards you.

'I don't need to stress how important it is that you remember the confidentiality agreement you signed when you joined us,' he reminded me. To make certain, he held up a copy. It promised fire, brimstone and blood if I ever breathed a syllable about my work. I'd thought it a bit over the top at the time, but hardly worth worrying about, so I'd never questioned it. I wasn't in the habit of discussing work outside the office, anyway.

But now things were different. I knew stuff. And Dunckley was reminding me of the dangers of talking out of school. Jesus, I'd been dumb. And now it had come back to bite me where it hurt most.

'I'll try to remember,' I said grudgingly, my mind on the gorilla in the suit.

'Don't just try, Jake – do it.' The bloodless lips snapped together, and I felt a chill touch the room. Dunckley could do sinister at the drop of a hat, and I wondered if he'd ever had to carry through with a threat himself. He wasn't big but he had the look of someone who could be mean if he chose. I decided I didn't want to find out. I was turning to leave when he added, 'Don't be a smart-arse, Jake. Don't even think of blabbing about what you did for us. Especially to the authorities.'

Bloody hell that was a wide field. 'I was an errand-boy, that's all. Why should the authorities be interested?'

He rolled his eyes. It gave him the platform he'd been waiting for. 'Don't pretend,' he said, 'that you didn't ever wonder what happened once you put in a POH report.'

'I didn't.' I had, of course, but beyond reporting one it had never been my problem.

'Right. So you think if someone started throwing their weight around and making demands above what we'd agreed they got a mild telling-off? A strongly-worded letter?' His mouth curled in derision at my apparent innocence.

'Sure. I mean, legal action, I suppose. What else?'

'Get real, for God's sake. You saw the places the projects were in. Our costs rocketed the moment they downed tools. The people who let us down got canned or dumped… or worse.'

'Worse?'

He didn't say anything to that and, for a second, he looked as if he could have bitten through his bottom lip. I realised that 'worse' meant some people found themselves handed a brown paper envelope by a messenger who'd promptly disappeared as instructed, leaving them to be picked up by the police – most likely following a careful tip-off. Worse still would have been punishment meted out by those further up the local food chain who'd felt cheated out of their share of the contract payments. Some of the local politicians I'd met were no more than warlords in cheap suits and branded trainers, whose idea of man-management might well have come out of the barrel of a gun.

'I didn't know any of that.'

'Rubbish. You chose not to see it.'

He was right, of course. I'd been kidding myself. I thought everything I did was above board and legal, resolving problems where I could, advising others where it seemed intractable. Hands clean at the end of the day.

He waited for the penny to drop, then nodded. 'Good man. Now we know where we stand. Just keep your mouth shut and you'll be fine.'

Where the hell was this going? He was coming across like a third-rate mafia don. But I, of course, had to push it. After all, to make an effective threat you have to have something to hold over someone. 'And if I don't?'

He sighed and studied his fingernails. 'I didn't want to do this, but let me enlighten you.' He spoke slowly, like he would to someone who was mentally defective. 'During the last eighteen months you've been a party to breaking the laws of at least seven different countries by delivering illicit disbursements to a number of government and other officials. You've also delivered unauthorized bonds, bank documents and other financial papers on at least ten occasions.' He held up a hand to stop me saying anything. Not that I was going to; I was dumbstruck. 'Not all of those papers reached their intended destinations, and not all of them were meant to.'

The guys who'd been picked up. I already got that; they'd been set up for a fall. Payback for failure.

'That wasn't my fault. How was I to know what was in the packages?'

'Ignorance is no defence.'

'What does that mean? What's going to happen?'

12

'Nothing.'

'So why are you telling me this?'

'For your own good. We have no ill intentions towards you, Jake. You did a good job for us, which is why you're being paid to go. But circumstances can change.'

'Like how?'

'I'm not prepared to say. You keep quiet and you'll be fine. You talk about any of it, and you'll find yourself in all kinds of trouble.'

Now we were getting somewhere. What he meant was, if I started talking, who knew what it might unearth. The last thing HP&P wanted was a whistleblower opening a can of worms. The pay-off was seen as the better option. But better than what?

'But I don't know anything,' I protested. 'How can I talk about stuff I don't know?'

'Makes no odds. You'll be the first to go down.'

'Down?'

'Prison.' His eyes went dull. 'That's if they don't come after you.'

'They?'

'There are people above me who don't share my confidence in your ability to stay silent, Jake. Powerful people, they play by different rules and want to do things their own way. They're ready, on my say-so, to give you the benefit of the doubt. However...'

God, I hate howevers. They rate even lower on the scale of scary clauses than buts. 'Go on.'

'They'll be watching you. Never forget that.'

I turned and walked out, clutching an envelope containing my severance details and with his words ringing in my ears. He was kidding me, surely. But no, Dunckley didn't know how to kid; he'd never been taught.

The office downstairs, where I had been assigned a desk and terminal which I rarely used on account of always being on a plane to somewhere, was empty and silent, the computers all switched off except for one with a rainbow-coloured screensaver telling everyone to stay the hell away from the keyboard. I guessed the rest of the staff were at a separate meeting being informed of the changes, one of which was that the weird guy in the corner – the one they used to look at and wonder what he did all the time, jetting off overseas – had received a higher calling, work-wise.

As I was clearing out my desk, a security guard in the starched purple uniform and big boots marched into the room. He had tattoos down each arm and a haircut a Royal Marine recruiting sergeant would have been proud of. He stood by the door and watched unemotionally as I filled a box with my meagre belongings: some travel wipes, a spare shirt and socks, a broken iPod, a flight bag, travel kit, miniatures of scotch and gin, a travel mug… and sundry other examples of how life has a habit of spilling over from home to the office until sometimes one becomes a carbon-copy of the other.

The guard was yet another cog in the machine, oiled to ease my passage from the now into the future – whatever that might be – with the minimum of fuss. I had no doubts that if I'd kicked off, he'd have had me pinned to the wall within seconds before carrying me outside like an old suitcase and dumping me in the gutter.

I surrendered my company phone and credit cards, along with my electronic entry-card. He bent this between fingers like bananas and tore it into confetti, never taking his eyes off me. Then he escorted me to the front entrance and watched as I drove out of the car park for the last time.

Three years. Three years of my life devoted to my tiny corner of HP&P, otherwise builders of roads, dams and sewage-treatment plants, among other things less explainable and clearly not entirely legitimate. Three years of foreign airports, trains, buses and indifferent food; of waiting hours for contacts to come out of meetings with other wily, slush-funded competitors; of days spent wandering through fly-infested, roach-ridden corners of the globe where not even satellite phones could be arsed to work properly; of regular turbulence, occasional dysentery and tracking down lost laundry in backwater fleapit hotels.

And now I was out on my feet without so much as a by-your-leave.

A troubleshooter with troubles of my own.

While I drove, I used my teeth to rip open the envelope. It contained a cheque for £30,000, a letter of regret confirming my release from the portals of HP&P and a careful reminder of the considerable legal penalties that would fall my way if I ever disclosed details of the company's business.

What it didn't contain was any hints on how to break the news to Susan.

Or any kind of warning that my bad hair day had only just begun.

THREE

It felt wrong arriving home in the middle of a weekday. That was for kids playing hooky or reps working from home. No doubt the neighbours would notice, in which case the jungle drums would put two and two together and build a rumour which would circulate the area within the hour. Something new to discuss alongside who had just bought a new Range Rover Evoque or a cottage in Normandy.

I didn't trouble with keys at the front door, remembering that Susan had said she'd be working at home all day. It didn't often happen, but it should be a nice surprise… until I told her my bad news, anyway. She didn't like bad news, especially if she figured I was to blame, in which case the sky would cloud over and crows would gather on the roof to pick my bones.

'Bugger and damn!' I reeled back, clutching my right hand under my arm and dropping my briefcase on the gravel. The door was locked.

'Susan!' I yelled testily, as the upstairs curtain at number 40 next door twitched in the late morning sun. Mrs Tree was in her observation tower again. Not a bird parped in the neighbourhood without Mrs Tree being aware, and strangers were catalogued and surveyed as if she were a one-woman Neighbourhood Watch. I often wondered if she'd been a member of the Stasi, the East German secret police. No way the Berlin Wall would have come down on her watch.

I went to the back door and looked under the grating where we kept a spare key. Not there. Sod and damnation. I returned to the front and looked in the kitchen window.

Bare as a badger's eyeball. No kettle, no microwave, no crockery, no gin bottle on the side, no fridge magnets, no fridge.

No fridge?

We'd been burgled. I ran to the garage. Susan's GTi was gone.

It took a tour of the outside of the house to see that, other than the moth-eaten La-Z-Boy armchair I'd inherited from my father and a pile of books tossed into a heap in the hallway, the lower floor of the house had been cleaned out.

Lock, stock and bin liners.

Bastards! Was this part of the redundancy package, too? Take my job and leave me without a stick of furniture just to rub it in?

Susan. She had to be somewhere. Maybe the police station. Yes, of course. Filling in endless forms for the insurance claim. God – what if she'd been attacked and was even now lying battered and broken in casualty? It didn't bear thinking about.

'Mr Foreman?' It was Mrs Tree, leaning over the fence with a fixed smile on her grizzled face, an ancient cardigan pulled around her shoulders. Seeing her reminded me of driving across a patch of the Namib desert and spotting vultures circling over the remains of a dead zebra. I knew how the zebra must have felt.

'Have you seen Susan?' It was a stupid question. If it moved, had a pulse or made a sound, Mrs Tree would have it logged and timed. Among her many accomplishments was a regular stream of letters to the local council, complaining of everything from the speed of traffic bouncing wilfully over the speed bumps in the street to the amount of water used by neighbours each Sunday washing their cars. Even the vicar had been reported for wearing a leather jacket off duty.

'Yes, I have,' she said, and jumped back smartly as if I was going to assault her. God, I'd have to be desperate or mad. She was ninety if she was a day and reeked of mothballs. The last time she'd have been fanciable would have been when Crippen was a boy. 'She's gone.'

'Gone where?'

She pointed a bony finger at my feet, as if the answer lay in the soil. I looked down and saw a deep rut in the gravel of the drive. It was normally raked smooth. Tyre tracks. Big ones – the sort a truck would make.

Poirot, eat your heart out. So there had been thieves!

'In a big removal lorry,' Mrs Tree confirmed cheerfully. 'About ten minutes after you left this morning.' She sniffed disapprovingly. 'Great big thing belching filthy blue smoke all over my washing. Four men, there were.'

A gang? My God, the callous bastards. What had they done to Susan? Then I remembered: there had been a removal lorry parked along the road when I drove out this morning. Not that it was unusual; people came and went regularly in this neck of the woods, driven in by ambition and out by debt and failure. I hadn't given it a thought, too intent on switching into work mode.

'They were very efficient. Your wife seemed pleased, anyway.' This was delivered with a slight toss of the head, as if being pleased with anything was a sign of a deviant nature. 'She was having a jolly good laugh with them, I can tell you that.' This was followed by an arch look that no doubt spoke volumes among her equally aged mates about what a jolly good laugh really meant.

'Did she say anything?' I asked faintly. This was surreal. Any minute now and this ancient pony express would be telling me what they'd been wearing and how many sugars they'd had in their tea.

'Goodbye, I think.' She gave it some thought, then nodded. 'Yes, definitely goodbye. She stuck two fingers in the air at the house and went off in her little car. It was all done very quickly, I must say. You must have been packing for days... although I suppose those men do it for you now, don't they? Not like in my day, when you had to find your own tea-chests and collect papers to wrap your china. I didn't realise you were moving, Mr Foreman.'

Fuck me sideways. I know I'm forgetful, but neither did I. I marched across the drive, leaving Mrs Tree wittering away, and stooped to pick up a brick from the flower border. It made enough noise going through the front door panel to wake the dead. Glass and wood showered everywhere, and the brick bounced around in the hallway with that uniquely hollow sound made by deserted buildings.

That was when I discovered Susan had switched on the burglar alarm before she left. The same burglar alarm which we'd deliberately stopped using because it kept going off for no reason and annoying the neighbours. Neat touch.

I tore through the house, ignoring the clanging bell, until the message finally sank home. I'd been left with the empty shell of a house, a wardrobe full of my clothes, a stack of overdue bills, a few books, a mortgage the size of the Senegalese national debt and a lumpy old armchair.

I sat down on the stairs and stared around in confusion. This couldn't be happening.

Five minutes later there was the crunch of tyres on the front drive and a flash of blue and yellow. The cops.

Footsteps pounded up to the front door egged on by an excited Mrs Tree, who broke off from giving a commentary to one of her friends by mobile long enough to tell the officer there was a lunatic on the loose inside. She must have phoned the local nick before patching into half of southern England on a conference call.

'*He arrived home in a right strop, I can tell you…*'

The first one inside was a young, pencil-thin PC. He looked about sixteen and as nervous as a kitten, as if he thought I was about to start foaming at the mouth and barking like a sea lion.

'Are you the owner of this property?'

'Yes,' I snarled. 'What about it?' I was feeling less amiable by the second. If junior Robocop here was paying any attention to my duplicitous neighbour, he'd already have built up a lurid picture of a homicidal maniac looking for blood. I was surprised he hadn't already got out his pepper spray and telescopic baton.

A small box under his chin emitted a squawk of static, and he lifted a black-gloved hand to flick a switch. He was dressed more like a trooper than a constable, with an array of sinister-looking pouches and holsters attached to his person. I wondered how he managed to stand upright weighed down by that lot. God help him if he ever fell over; he'd lie there like an inverted turtle until someone flipped him upright again.

'*For a second, there, Doris, I thought he was going to attack me… that my time on this earth had finally come.*' Mrs Tree again, her shrill voice rising above the sound of the alarm bell.

'Oh, if only!' I snapped, before junior cop waved a warning hand.

'There's no need for that, sir. Did you know your alarm was going off?'

I cocked an ear towards the bell-casing on the front of the house, which was doing its level best to jump off the wall. 'Of course I do – I'm not bloody deaf.'

'You don't have to take that tone.' The constable gave me a stern look, straight out of the police training book, guaranteed to intimidate violent thugs into making instant apologies for being boisterous. Right at that moment it had all the impact of being hit with a cottonbud, even if he had dropped the 'sir'.

'Bollocks,' I told him, and went to the wall and hit the kill switch. The silence was almost as deafening, but a vast improvement.

'*He picked up a brick and heaved it right through the front door. I think he's deranged, I really do. His wife left him – and can you blame her with that sort of carry-on?*'

The constable took a look at the empty rooms; at the layer of dust and debris, the holes left by the carpet nails and the bare patches on the walls where the sun hadn't shone for years. The noise of his boots on the floorboards and the static from his radio was suddenly far too loud in the silence. He tactfully didn't comment on the broken glass from the front door or the large scar made by the brick down the wallpaper.

'You moving in, sir – or out?' I think he was being genuinely tactful, but in my fragile state of mind, his serving-the-community smile merely came across as taking the piss.

'Actually, you young arse,' I told him, finally losing the thread, 'I've just finished robbing the place of all the furniture and fixings, which I've packed into the tiny boot of my car. I'm now going to get a box of matches and a can of petrol and firebomb the bloody lot!'

There then followed what is commonly called a heated exchange of words, which I lost on account of the constable having called up two larger colleagues who must have been loitering nearby. I was then invited to visit their nice police station for a chat.

As I was escorted to the police car, I heard Mrs Tree describing in cheerful detail to her friend Doris what an arm lock looked like.

FOUR

'You're a twerp, Jake,' said Hugo Palmerston in his plummy, public school voice as he escorted me from the police station six depressing hours later. Just what I needed after being ticked off by the desk sergeant.

'Thanks a lot,' I muttered. 'What it is to have the support of a friend.'

As if being arrested for breaking into my own house wasn't enough, I'd been further stressed by being locked for the best part of the day in a small, airless room in the company of a toothless, grubby, religious vagrant. For some reason he'd insisted on reciting obscure psalms at me as if I was in need of salvation and succour. He'd smelled worse than an old, wet cocker spaniel and his halitosis had reached out across the space between us like a guided missile, making me gag each time I breathed in.

'Ingrate,' said Hugo vaguely, opening his car door. It was a shiny, new executive Lexus and after old dog-breath back in the nick, the aroma of leather and plastic was like nectar. 'I'm amazed at you, Jake. Why on earth pick a fight with the police? It stands to reason you were going to lose.'

Hugo can be boringly logical at times. Also employed – still employed, furthermore – at one of the more legitimate divisions of

HP&P, who were unashamedly in awe of his old school tie and city connections. We'd been friends for years, by some odd mixture of chemistry, and he was the first person I'd thought of when the desk sergeant had listened to my tale of woe and suggested I get someone to come and collect me before they decided to transport me in chains to a penal colony on the Isle of Wight.

'It sounds like you've had enough dumped on you for one day,' he'd added sympathetically, and handed me a phone. 'Why not call a friend and get out of here?'

I'd called Hugo at the office, where he worked in international finance. He'd immediately dropped what he was doing to come and take me home.

Now he was trying to talk reason?

'At the time,' I reminded him tersely, 'I'd just found out my wife had done a bunk with all the furniture, locked me out of the house and set the burglar alarm just to piss me off. And all on top of being made redundant. So tell me where bloody reason comes into it.'

He said nothing and I sensed it wasn't because he lacked a quick retort. Snappy comebacks were Hugo's stock-in-trade, as useful for sealing deals as putting uppity employees in their place or breaking the ice at boring corporate gatherings.

'Sorry,' I said after we'd covered a few hundred yards in silence. 'It caught me on the hop.'

He nodded. 'No problem, old chap. Perfectly understandable under the circs. I um...'

'What?' I asked, as he hesitated.

'Pardon?'

'You were going to say something.'

'Was I?' He feigned surprise and scowled through the windscreen in furious concentration. It was enough to set my alarm bells ringing. He didn't normally concentrate on the road – he had the reactions and spatial awareness of a slug and drove so slowly everyone else gave him plenty of room. He was also a terrible liar.

'You know something, don't you?' I muttered, and poked him in the arm. There was a blast of a horn as he veered off course and narrowly missed demolishing a traffic island.

'Hey – cut that out!' he said reproachfully, rubbing his arm. 'There's no need for violence, otherwise I'll take you back to your cell and leave you there to rot with that vagrant fellow.'

There was no fighting that, so we sat in silence until we arrived back at the house. My car was where I had left it. I climbed out and retrieved the keys, then led Hugo across to the front door under the gaze of Mrs Tree and three of her old cronies from along the road who'd gathered to watch the fun. All it needed was a hot sun and the flapping of wings and we could have been in the Serengeti.

'Friends of yours?' asked Hugo.

'Ignore them. They're waiting for an injured wildebeest to limp into view so they can have their daily feed.'

'Looks like they've already got it,' he pointed out, and gave them a friendly wave.

I pushed open the ruins of the front door and stepped inside, crunching through broken glass and splintered wood. I stopped. I could hear music playing.

Susan?

I ran upstairs and into the main bedroom... and found two complete strangers in combat trousers and tie-died T-shirts going through my wardrobe as if they were at a jumble sale. On the windowsill a plastic ghetto-blaster was giving out a thump-thump beat of something vaguely African in style. There was already a sizeable pile of my clothes on the floor around the two intruders and, by the sour expressions on their faces, none of it was fit to die in.

'What are you doing?' I demanded incredulously. Christ, what else could the day throw at me – part of the MIR space station landing on the roof?

The male half of the duo didn't even bother looking round, but waved a dismissive hand. 'Get lost, mate – we were here first.' He was built like a brick outhouse and had several silver studs through one ear and purple-streaked blond hair hanging down to his shoulders. Huge Doc Martens were planted on my tweed sports jacket, while my favourite tie was around his waist holding his trousers in place.

The girl with him was a smaller, thinner copy, with orange hair and a large silver stud in her lower lip. She blinked when she peered round him and saw that I wasn't another khaki-clad eco-warrior looking for somewhere to doss, and nudged the man until he turned and looked at me.

'This is my house,' I said indignantly. 'Who said you could come in here?'

'Fuck off,' he said pleasantly, and tossed a pair of my slacks on the floor with a sniff of derision. 'Wouldn't give this shit to a refugee.' He looked around at the bare room, then peered through the window into the back garden. 'Still, not a bad gaff. Do us okay for a couple of weeks. What d'you say, Dot?'

Dot giggled excitedly and put her arms round him, completely ignoring my presence. She had a tattoo of a dragon on her shoulder and a thick collection of bangles on her arms. 'You mean it, Dash?' she said in a kittenish voice, as if he'd given her the keys to the Savoy. 'You mean we can stay here?'

There was a strong southern-hemisphere twang to their words with an upward lilt at the end of each sentence. It was like stepping onto the set of *Neighbours*.

Dash looked down at her and smiled, showing a row of surprisingly white, even teeth. 'Course we can,' he said magnanimously. 'No worries.'

'Can you buggery!' I yelled. 'This is my house!'

Dash stared at me as if it had finally sunk in that I was serious. 'Jeez, mate, no way. Where's all the stuff, then – the furniture and that? You a bit strapped for cash?'

'My – no! If you must know my wife took it and... left.' I wondered why I was telling this travelling moron my private woes. 'That doesn't mean it's open house for a bunch of drop-outs from Alice Springs.'

'Watch your fuckin' mouth, mate,' Dash said mildly, and stuck a muscular finger under my nose. 'We come from Wellington, ya Pommie twat.'

Just then Hugo appeared, puffing up the stairs behind me. He was followed by a cloud of cigarette smoke.

'Friends, Jake?' he grunted.

For all his soft-looking, middle-class executive appearance, Hugo exudes a certain presence. He has pale skin, puppy-dog eyes and a heavy lock of blond hair falling across his forehead. On a bad day he gets mistaken for Boris Johnson, which he hates. But he still manages to impress by aura alone. Something in his genes, probably. Whatever it was, it wasn't lost on the Morse Code twins, who stared at him as if he'd metamorphosed from under the floorboards. I doubt they came across too many Hugos in Wellington.

'They're squatters,' I said, glaring at the intruders. 'Have you got your phone on you, Hugo?'

'Sure. Why?'

'Call the police.'

Hugo looked at me and shook his head. 'I wouldn't bother, old chap. They won't come unless there's a threat to life and limb.'

We both stared at the giant Kiwi, entrenched in our own thoughts. He looked as if threatening life and limb was something he did when he got bored with tearing the legs of spiders. Our faces must have been easy to read.

'Hey, we wouldn't do that,' he protested with a friendly grin. It transformed him instantly into someone marginally less threatening than a big kid. 'Me and Dot are peaceful, man. Mind, I can't say the same for the rest of them toe-rags, know what I mean?'

A noise came from downstairs, and when I glanced at Hugo, he turned and studied the ceiling with deliberate concentration.

'There are more of you?'

I walked through to the front bedroom with a faint feeling of unreality, and stared down into the drive. An ancient Red Rover bus had spluttered to a halt across my flower border and was disgorging people like day-trippers at Stonehenge. Mrs Tree was staring from her upstairs window, her jaw hanging open like a bear-trap. It was almost enough to cheer me up.

'It's the rest of the commune,' explained Dash helpfully, whipping out a smartphone. 'We travel together, see. One finds a place to crash and the rest pile in. It works a treat.' He came across and slapped me on the shoulder with enough force to make my teeth rattle. 'So, mate, whereabouts d'ya keep the fusebox?'

FIVE

'You knew, didn't you?' I said, staring into one of Hugo's crystal whisky glasses. 'You knew Susan was going to leave me.'

We'd left my former home, now a Kiwi-laden squat, and driven to Hugo's elegant Kensington house to assess the situation. I'd decided to leave my car in the garage and collect it later, when I felt less of a liability to other road users.

'I knew she wasn't happy,' Hugo countered judicially. 'But not that she was actually going to up sticks.'

'Why didn't you tell me?' Yes, it was unreasonable, but that's how I was feeling. When life kicks me unfairly in the scrotum, I tend to look for someone to blame. It was far easier than thinking any of it might have been my fault.

'Because you should have noticed, you dimwit,' he responded testily. 'Honestly, Jake, you must be the only man I know who didn't realise his wife was chea–' He stopped dead and stared at me, his face draining of colour. Then he bounded up to refill his glass from a crystal decanter on the walnut and rosewood-veneered sideboard which he'd once told me was inherited from a titled uncle.

'What?' I said stupidly. 'She was what?'

Whatever he was about to say was cut short by a noise from the

29

front door and the faint blare of passing traffic. Like a drowning man seeing a lifebelt bobbing towards him, Hugo turned and fairly sprinted from the room to greet his wife, Juliette.

Cheap? Was that what he'd been about to say – my wife was cheap? Or cheesy? Christ, he might be a friend, but that was a bit much, even now.

Judging by the furious whispering in the hallway, Juliette wasn't impressed by finding me there. She was a friend of Susan's and we normally got on reasonably well, providing our meetings were brief. Truthfully, given a choice of having me or Hannibal Lecter in the house, I always suspected Juliette would have plumped for the psychopath.

She finally peered round the living-room door, waving a Prada bag. She wasn't showing off – merely acting in character. Shopping was a major part of her day, so why not ensure everyone knew it?

'Jake.' Her impossibly cultured voice usually trailed my name out like a mild cuss-word. But not this time. There was no peck on the cheek, no witty exchange about the state of the country's economy. In fact, no sharing the same breathable airspace. But that was normal. Yet something about her looked almost… sympathetic.

Odder and odder.

'Hello, Juliette,' I replied, and wondered what was going on. She was tall and willowy, and habitually wore sunglasses on top of her head, indoors and out. A genuine Sloane with years of practice behind her, she carried a permanent air of disdain for anyone not 'in the circle' of approved friends and acquaintances. Shop assistants, traffic wardens and utility people – gas men and the like – were to be seen and not heard. Even Susan had once wondered aloud whether Hugo would have been acceptable if he hadn't had a private income and shares in half of Gloucestershire.

Susan. Juliette must have spoken to Susan. It was the only explanation, since they were usually joined by hip or smartphone. But before I could ask her, she disappeared at speed. Hugo followed, reacting to a look which had the same effect as a whistle to a sheepdog.

When he finally trailed back into the room he looked a little subdued. I guessed he'd been given some kind of ultimatum: me out or he could bed down in the spare room.

'Jake,' he said uncomfortably, and waved a hand in the air like someone about to impart bad news.

'No need,' I said, heading for the door. I knew the signs of marital thumbscrews having been applied. 'It's time I was going, anyway.'

'What are you going to do? I mean, where will you go?' He looked genuinely pained, if a little relieved, and I felt guilty for having dragged him into my mess. On the other hand, the more I thought about it, the more I realised Hugo was one of my few options. It was a sobering thought. I'd spent so much time out of the country over the years, I knew the security teams at Heathrow airport better than my neighbours.

Even so, I'd been thinking about it on the way over. Instinct had warned me I might not be able to count on bunking down with Hugo, and the idea of sharing my own empty house with a bunch of squatters was definitely out. That left a hotel or finding somebody else to lean on. Now I'd finished trawling my mental address book for lean-able friends and come up with a disappointing and fairly scary zero, it was another sad pointer to the fact that I was screwed.

'I'll camp out with Marcus. He's got plenty of room.' Desperationville, Arizona, I thought grimly. Marcus was my kid brother. Well, hardly a kid. Aged thirty-one going on eighteen, he

31

was the co-founder of a start-up dating site and video game production unit in London's Old Street, where techies gather like flies on a digital jam sandwich. He wore the permanent other-worldly look of someone whose brain was in another dimension, and I'd heard it said he was on target to becoming a millionaire any day now. Not that his appearance supported the notion. He shared a foetid pad with a couple of ex-college roomies he'd known for years, and claimed it kept him on his toes and 'connected', whatever that meant. Even though there weren't more than ten years between us, I'd never pretended to 'get' Marcus fully, and he seemed quite happy looking on me in the same fashion. As long as we left politics, drugs, sex and religion out of discussions, we got on pretty well. Silence was usually the safest bet.

'Ah. Good idea, old chap,' Hugo offered. 'Of course, you can stay here if pressed. You do know that, don't you?' This last would have been better had it not come with a faint whiff of reluctance, like someone inviting the family alcoholic to a Christening.

I shook my head and stepped out into the street. The haunted look as he said it told me he was being kind but hoping I'd say no. 'I appreciate that, Hugo. But honestly, not to worry.'

Hugo's townhouse was on an elegant street in the northern quarter of Kensington. The kind of street where trees loom overhead to give an impression of verdant splendour and to complement the neat brickwork and classic columns of the buildings. According to Hugo, someone on the local council had once suggested that streets with trees attracted a lower level of crime than those without. He should try telling that to people who get mugged on Clapham Common. Follow that kind of thinking and we could disband every rural police force in the country and stick another tree in the ground.

Verdant or not, the trees here served to block out the sickly glare of the street lights. They also dumped large areas of shadow every few yards, mysterious dark pockets of impenetrable gloom concealing who knew what.

I was halfway down the street, sticking as closely as I could to the edge of the pavement – whatever street-savvy instincts I possessed were at work in spite of my brain being in under-drive – when I heard the pad of heavy footsteps coming up behind me. Oh, buggeration. After everything else, I'm about to find out the man on the council was talking bollocks. I stopped and turned, balling my fists and steeling myself. After everything I'd been through today, if this was a mugger he was going to wish he'd never set eyes on me.

It was Hugo, panting like an old washing machine with a saggy belt, and struggling into a wrinkled green Barbour that had seen better days. Behind him came remnants of Juliette's voice raised in anger followed by the sound of the front door slamming. Dry rations for Hugo tonight, then.

'Jake,' he wheezed, and clutched my arm. 'Please, mate… hold up.'

I waited while he patted down his pockets for a cigarette and got his breath back. Being office-bound most of his working days and generally inert the rest of the time, Hugo is about as unfit as a man is capable of being without being on life support. Added to that, while he didn't smoke indoors as a concession to Juliette and his two children, he rarely let an opportunity go by without lighting up everywhere else. He'd even threatened to resign one day when someone at HP&P had suggested bringing in a smoking ban within fifty yards of the premises. It also explained why he persistently refused to take his children to Disneyland, Florida, where he'd have been locked up within ten minutes of touchdown.

He puffed away happily in the gloom, then nodded towards the far end of the street where I was hoping to pick up a passing cab. 'Fancy a drink, old boy?' he offered companionably. 'And a chat?'

'Sure. Why not.' In truth, I was glad he'd come after me. Whatever he knew about Susan's departure, it was a whole lot more than I did. And he might have some goss on why I'd been selected by HP&P to join the great unwashed. Maybe over a drink or two I'd find out why my life had suddenly gone into freefall.

We walked along together while I let Hugo marshal his thoughts and inhale more nicotine into his system. I knew him well enough to know he had something on his mind, and in his own good time he'd come out with it. Either that or I'd lose patience and brain him with one of the many 'no parking' cones lining the street.

He led the way into a small pub containing a handful of customers. It was one of those rare old places which seemed to have survived the developers and avoided being turned into an Irish theme pub filled to the ceiling with harps, shillelaghs and fishing tackle. The clientele consisted of solitary drinkers staring into their glasses as if there lay the answers to the mysteries of life.

Hugo ordered pints and whisky chasers. It was a bad sign; he only drank chasers when he had to face something particularly unpleasant or shocking. The last time had been when he'd lost a packet during an illicit visit to Epsom, only to turn round and bump into his next-door neighbour, a noted blabbermouth. Apparently Juliette rated gambling on horses on a par with being a wife-beater or a socialist.

'Bad business, this,' he said, after inhaling half his pint. I was struggling to keep up, too entombed in my own thoughts about Susan's departure.

'Which specific bit of bad business are we talking about?' I asked, keen to remind him that it had been a bad day in more ways than one.

'Why, Susan's leaving, of course. I – oh… you thought I meant the other. Sorry. Listen, I promise I knew nothing about that, Jake. God's honour. A bolt out of the blue, I promise. I may work for HP&P but they don't tell me what they're planning to do. It's all the new owners' doing, I suspect.'

I waved away his protestations. I knew he wouldn't have been involved; I'd worked for HP&P long enough to know that they operated a strict left-hand/right-hand policy. The kind which meant neither hand operated as if it were joined to the same body. It was a corporate nightmare but hardly uncommon.

'Are you going to let me in on it or not?' I finally prompted him, staring at his reflection in the bar mirror. It seemed easier than looking at him full-on; a bit like a confessional, although imagining Hugo as a priest was stretching things a bit.

'It was Juliette who first told me,' he said slowly. 'She and Susan, they get on, you see. They talk about things. Always have. They trade secrets and… well, I suppose Susan needed someone to confide in.' He looked at me in the bar mirror with a spaniel-eyed expression of regret, as if it was his fault for knowing more about my personal life than I did. 'Like a bloody sponge, my wife,' he continued dolefully. 'She knows the secrets of half the married women in West London. I'd make a fortune if I could get her to write it all down. Why, there's a merchant banker's wife over in Ealing who–'

'What did she tell you?' I interrupted him, before he launched into a long story about someone neither of us knew or cared about. 'Did she say why Susan left – or where she is?'

'I don't know why, other than what Juliette told me – which might or might not be reliable info, you understand. You see, Juliette hates anyone associated with HP&P, for some reason. You included, I'm

35

afraid.' He grinned nervously and sucked in more beer. 'Come to think of it, I don't think she likes me much at the moment.'

I sighed and took a sip of whisky. Its warmth burned all the way down. That was all it did, though, and if there was any answer in the bottom of my glass, it wasn't in any format that I could decipher. Maybe one of the other drinkers would be able to translate it for me. Roll up, roll up… come and read my glass and tell me the secrets of where I've gone wrong.

'Come on, Hugo,' I said tiredly. 'In the absence of Susan being here to tell me herself, it's all I've got. So shoot, will you? I'm a big boy now – I think I can take it.'

'Yes, I suppose so.' He took a deep breath. 'I'm afraid – Susan left you because… well, she was bored.'

SIX

As the words left his mouth, the landlady, a woman of advanced years with a blue rinse and smoker's cough was standing nearby, carefully pulling a pint of the black stuff. Her meaty hand stopped in mid pull and she gave me a look guaranteed to strip varnish. I wondered what she would have done if I'd been accused of serial adultery or molesting sheep. Hawked into my pint, probably.

'What?'

'Bored,' Hugo repeated, unaware that the landlady was all ears. 'She said you ignored her and spent all your time working.'

'But I didn't,' I protested, as much for the landlady's benefit as Hugo's. Something told me she might be a hard-core feminist. 'I never ignored Susan in my life. How could I?' I didn't dare, was the truth, since doing so carried an automatic health warning.

The fact was, Susan, attractive, auburn-haired and slim, bore inactivity badly. Whenever more than five uneventful minutes passed by, she became fretful, anxious to be up and doing. It wasn't that she was hyperactive – she was just a born do-er and socialiser with a contacts list to rival Mark Zuckerberg's. It was what I'd initially found so attractive about her: that she didn't want to settle into a life of dull domestic ritual and produce a stream of kids like flicking peas from a pod until she slipped into matronly middle age years before her time. We'd talked around the subject of family a couple of times, in the early days and sometimes when one of her fecund pals announced yet another addition to the backseat of the family 4WD. We'd finally concluded that the usual two-point-four wasn't for us, and left it at that. Susan seemed happy to be involved in the retail ventures, which took her to endless events all over the city and, in the absence of any further reports, I'd concluded that must be fulfilling enough for her.

'You were never here,' Hugo pointed out, by way of explanation. 'She complained to Juliette that you spent too much time overseas, always flying off to some remote spot for days or weeks at a time. She said she knows the British Airways flight schedules better than they do, and had to book sex with you so you could take a run-up from Kazakhstan or some such God-awful place.' He sighed and turned to face me. 'You've got to admit, you have spent more time out of the country than in it, Jake. I'm amazed they haven't put you in a special tax category all your own. You should ask for a rebate.' He took another sip. 'Did it never occur to you to throttle back a bit – or take her with you?'

I shook my head, amazed and ashamed all at once by a kaleidoscope of images spinning in front of my eyes: a pictorial list of evidence against me. It was a bit like what they claim happens when you're in a moment of mortal peril. Only these images were somehow malevolent. Damning. Accusing. And unfair.

Most of the images were of me working in foreign parts… with few of Susan until I thought hard about it. And I realised that over the years the travelling had built up, increasing inexorably to meet the demand, extending from a couple of days to whole weeks at a time – easier to stay on a few more days rather than face another return trip. And taking Susan simply hadn't been an option. One thing I'd learned very early in our relationship was that Susan didn't do rough. Her idea of an adventure holiday was having to switch on the air-con herself.

'But I was doing it–' I stopped, about to come out with something horribly trite. I ordered another round instead.

'You were doing it for Susan?' Hugo nodded as his drink arrived and sank it in one go. Mine was slammed down unceremoniously by the landlady into a puddle on the bar, spattering me with stale beer. 'Of course you were. We all do… or so we kid ourselves. But really it's for us, isn't it? The old career ladder. The treadmill. The corporate battlefield. But our wives need more, d'you see? They need the constancy.' He peered distantly at the mirror like an old Greek sage.

'Constancy? Is that even a word? Anyway, since when did you become so bloody wise in the ways of women? You're the progeny of centuries of male chauvinist porkers.'

He looked almost hurt at that. 'It means unchanging and dependable, you peasant. And I know women, believe me. They're all the same, even Juliette. Although God knows, she's the most independent woman I've ever met, bless her heart. Even sex takes a poor second place to a session at her beauty clinic or whatever it's called. D'you know, she's the only woman I know who can sleep deliberately?'

I must have looked blank, because he continued, 'If she's annoyed with me, she sleeps like a dead donkey: completely comatose. At least, that's how it seems. I can't wake her up for a kiss and cuddle – I've tried. It's like trying it on with a corpse. I've often wondered if there are any other women like that.'

'Only dead ones,' I said bitterly, and wondered whether Susan had ever deliberately fallen asleep on me. If she had it had passed me by – evidently like so many other things in our relationship.

39

Hugo reached for his whisky and shook his head at my offer of a refill. 'I'd better be going. Don't want to leave it to fester, eh? Probably been relegated to the spare room as it is.'

'Hang on. You still haven't told me where Susan is.'

He pulled a face and I guessed he'd been hoping to get away without having to answer that question. He stared up at the greasy, smoke-yellowed ceiling, then down at his feet, before putting a hand on my shoulder. 'She's, um…' He shook his head and looked genuinely saddened. 'Oh, God, how do I do this? She's found someone else, Jake. Sorry.'

'Found some–?' My voice sounded faint even to me, and I had a sudden image of Susan in a tangle of naked arms and legs with another man and enjoying every minute of it. 'Already?'

'Sorry.' He looked embarrassed.

'Who? Do I know him?' Could I take him in a fight, I began to wonder, before being stunned into silence by the sheer shock of finding I'd become the third wheel on a two-wheeled bike. Why do people always ask if they know the third party in a deception? Is it because when they hear of the unthinkable, they instantly lose all trust in their friends? I took another slug of whisky and tried to think of all the men I knew who might have looked even mildly covetously at Susan. In the end I gave up; there were too many. She was slim and beautiful and got noticed wherever she went. I reached across and finished off Hugo's drink as well. If it burned on the way down I didn't feel it.

'Yes, you know him,' said Hugo quietly. He gestured towards the bar. 'Perhaps we should have another.'

'No!' I shouted, louder than I'd intended. The landlady glared at me. She'd obviously marked me down as a troublemaker as well as a wife-ignorer, and was on the look out for something kicking off. The other customers looked across in the hope, no doubt, of witnessing something exciting to finish off their uneventful evening's glass-staring. 'Who is it?'

Hugo ordered another round anyway, and I was forced to wait while he had a stiff jolt before continuing. 'She met him at the office Christmas party last year,' he said finally. 'The one you missed.'

I remembered. I'd missed my flight from Bahrain – along with pretty much the whole of Christmas. It was an air traffic controllers' strike, I recalled. Idle bastards. Clearly idle bastards who'd cost me my marriage. It's always easier sharing the blame.

'You go anyway,' I remembered telling Susan on the phone from the departure lounge, anxious that she meet more of my colleagues and knowing that Juliette would look after her, vitriol dripping into her ear at every turn. It was a small price to pay for peace of mind, even if I'd have to do some damage limitation, involving a serious visit to the duty-free shop.

I also remembered a terse comment Susan had made about the party when I'd finally arrived home, jet-lagged and rumpled after the journey from hell, and asked her how it had gone. 'I thought she was complaining about the party,' I told Hugo, re-running her words in my head. 'She told me she'd been bored rigid.'

He choked on his whisky and I had to pound his back with the flat of my hand before escorting him outside. It was then that he told me what had happened.

Susan had indeed been bored rigid, he said regretfully.

On a table in the computer room.

By my former boss, HP&P's Operations Director, Niall bloody Dunckley.

By the time I'd got all the gruesome details we were halfway back to Hugo's house. In spite of my deep shock and immediate, instinctive desire to search out Dunckley and erase his cod-like face from the earth, I was having to hold Hugo upright to stop him from pitching headlong into the gutter – something Juliette would never have forgiven or forgotten.

'I can't believe it,' I kept muttering, as he drifted across the pavement. He'd lost control of his legs and was dragging me with him as he lurched from side to side like a great, fat trawler in heaving seas.

'Can't believe it meself,' he muttered, a slurred echo. 'But I saw 'em with me own eyes.'

'But... *Dunckley*?' I wailed. 'How could she?'

'Maybe because she–'

Whatever he was about to say was interrupted by the sight of two figures emerging from a pocket of shadow. They moved across the pavement and stood menacingly in our way. Both were tall and dressed in leather jackets and jeans, and neither looked like members of the Salvation Army's pick-up-a-drunk patrol.

'Oopsh,' Hugo said, and breathed a disgusting mixture of tobacco and alcohol in my face. Then he focussed on the two dark strangers and wagged his finger angrily in their direction. 'Treesh... we've got bloody treesh in thish shtreet, y'know.'

Plainly neither of the men had heard of the anti-crime concept mooted by the local councillor. They stared at Hugo with the tired look of men without patience or pity who desperately needed someone to punch lumps out of to make the night worthwhile.

'Spare some change?' said the one on the left with heavy sarcasm. He was holding a length of metal pipe down by his leg, the street lights glinting off the metal. I didn't think he was a plumber touting for business.

His colleague glanced around, checking the scenery, then nodded and held out his hand. 'Give us your wallets. Now.'

'What for?' I asked, some deep instinct making me search for a way out and realising that flight was not an option. To flee, you need two things: the ability to run and a sense of direction. And right at that moment, Hugo and I had neither.

'We want your money, *twat!*' the pipe man said savagely, and whirled his weapon through the air, swishing it like we were in a bad martial arts movie.

The thought made me burst out laughing and I nearly dropped Hugo in the process.

'Oi – what's so bloody funny?' demanded the other man. He'd clearly never mugged two idiot drunks before.

Then Hugo joined in and we stood leaning against each other like two precariously-balanced statues, braying like a pair of jackasses.

'They're nuts,' the pipe man said. He was looking twitchy, and even in my inebriated state, I could tell he was gearing up to do something nasty.

Hugo must have noticed, too, because he waggled his finger again.

'D'you think,' he mumbled seriously, 'd'you fellas seris– serisly think… that if we had 'ny spare change we'd be in this cond… ondit – as sober as this?'

For a split second he stared at them, then howled with laughter. It was enough to set me off as well and we both hooted, tears streaming down our faces as we staggered across the pavement towards the road. I glanced over my shoulder in time to see the two muggers shake their heads despairingly and disappear into the gloom.

We eventually arrived at the bottom of the flight of steps leading up to Hugo's shiny black front door. At least I think it was his; with every door in the street looking the same it was hard to tell.

'Did you bring a key?' I asked him.

He shook his head, seemingly unconcerned by the wrath he was going to face inside. Always assuming he got back inside. At least since our confrontation with the two muggers he'd sobered up quite a bit and sounded almost lucid. 'No. Forgot. Don't worry, old boy. One of the kids'll let me in. Withhold all pocket money for a month, otherwise. Say, would you like to come in fr'a wee drinkie?'

'No thanks.' I turned him towards the house before he lost direction and stepped away. Apart from feeling over-stocked already, I didn't fancy getting a close-up of Juliette waiting inside. I'd had enough excitement for one night.

'Wait,' I said, remembering he'd been about to tell me something before we were rudely interrupted by the two footpads. Something about Susan and Dunckley?

'What?'

'I said "How could she?" and you said, "Maybe because she"… something or other. But you didn't finish. Maybe because what?'

'Christ, I don't know,' he breathed, and began to lean sideways at an alarming angle.

I grabbed him and he hauled himself upright, but it was the last effort of a nearly comatose drunk.

'Go to bed,' I said, and he launched himself up the steps in a rush and pounded on the large, brass door-knocker with enough enthusiasm to wake half of West London, let alone a deliberately-sleeping Juliette.

I waited until a light came on, then turned and slipped away, avoiding shadows until I found a late-night café where I sank three strong Americanos in quick succession. If I was going to face my kid brother, I might as well do it as sober as I could manage.

SEVEN

Brotherly love was clearly in short supply because Marcus didn't look very pleased to see me. I could tell by the way he stuck his head out of the window and asked why I was trying to effing break down his effing door. He also called me a knob, which I thought was unnecessary.

It was accidental, I tried to explain. The front door of the cesspit he shared with his mates was, like Hugo's, up a flight of steps bordered by iron railings. Unlike Hugo's des and expensive res, Marcus's steps were crumbling through neglect, carpeted in a green, moss-like substance, and the top slab had a loose segment just waiting for the unwary. I hit it dead centre and was hurled headlong into the front door with a crash, sending a dozen empty beer bottles skittering sideways into the basement moat below with the sound of a collapsing greenhouse.

It was hardly my fault that two of Marcus's mates, thinking it was the local drugs squad, did a bunk through the back window. I told him later that they should start leading more blameless lives – or invest in a CCTV system.

'What do you want?' he asked, finally letting me in. I got the impression this was out of embarrassment rather than brotherly concern.

His long, gangling figure was barely covered by a T-shirt bearing a pink angel fish and the name of a dive centre in the Maldives. His hair was rumpled from sleep and his breath could have killed a cactus at fifteen paces. If anything, he looked worse than I felt, which was why, when he started lecturing me about turning up at this time of night drunk and incapable, I got a little snarky.

'I am not drunk,' I told him. 'I've had a drink or two, I admit – but incapable I'm not.' Unfortunately, this argument fell over at the same moment as I did, when I discovered an aluminium briefcase someone had left lying in the middle of the hallway.

'I'll make coffee,' he said, looking at me in disgust. 'You'd better not have dented that – it cost me a fortune.' With that he turned and disappeared towards the kitchen while I picked myself up.

'Tea!' I called out. 'I've had enough coffee to float a Japanese whaling fleet.' Even as the words left my mouth I looked up and saw a huge poster on the wall, extolling the work of Greenpeace in their fight to stop the Japanese sticking harpoons into Moby Dick's cousins.

Oh, balls…

The living-room was a bombsite of DVDs, clothes, magazines, books, bottles and electronic equipment. I recalled Marcus once saying that a couple of his roomies were in the retail marketing business and spent their leisure hours testing the latest gizmos to come on the market. Judging by the state of some of the gear, the testing must have included impact-resistance as well as the content.

'So what do you want?' He crept up on me while I was examining a wristwatch with email capability. It looked like the kind of toy I used to get with Cornflakes coupons as a boy. I took the mug of tea and thought about how to tell him the bad news.

He looked a lot like me, I realised, studying him. He was taller and thinner, and could occasionally brush up rather well. Right now, though, he looked like a train wreck. On the other hand, I had dragged him out of bed, so given a haircut, shave, shower and some personal grooming, he'd be – God, listen to me. I sound like his father. Our father.

'Susan's gone,' I said, pitching right in. The direct approach is usually best – if sometimes the most painful. But Marcus was a big boy and I figured he could handle it. Shows how much I know.

He flopped down on the settee. 'I know. She told me.' I could see a muscle moving in the side of his jaw, but his expression was blank, like he'd just heard it might rain next week.

Oh, boy. 'When?'

'Earlier today.'

I wondered why Susan had called him. It's not as if they'd ever been especially close. She'd always looked on him as an inconvenient oik who turned up occasionally looking for a handout, and he'd always seemed polite but distant. 'What did she say?'

'Nothing much. Just that she was leaving and she'd be in touch. She wanted to let me know, I guess, although I'm not sure why.'

'Dotting the i's and crossing the t's, I expect,' I said. 'She's good like that.' It came out snarkier than I meant it.

'You don't seem too cut up about it,' Marcus suggested. 'Or guilty.'

I bit back a sharp retort. 'What's to get guilty about? She left me, don't forget.'

'Right. Like she didn't have good reason.' He scowled at me and muttered, 'Sorry – low blow.' I watched the flicker of expressions crossing his face. There was accusation and resentment, but also an underlying vulnerability. Like when he was younger and disappointment had come calling and stamped on his foot, the way

47

it does from time to time just when you think you've got life all figured out.

'You, too?' I muttered. The tea was strong and full of tannin, laying a gritty coating over my teeth. It did nothing to improve the taste in my mouth, which was beginning to backfire on me. My kingdom for a toothbrush, I thought, before remembering I didn't have a kingdom to trade, much less anything else.

'What does that mean?'

I waved a hand, suddenly too weary to argue. I didn't want to drag Marcus any deeper into the whys and wherefores, and falling out with him was the last thing I needed. Besides, there are some things you don't air in public, even with your brother.

But he didn't want to let it go.

'What? You said me too.' He jumped up from the settee, a wild glint in his eye. The picture of manly outrage was spoiled by his T-shirt lifting and exposing his nether regions, and I nodded downwards with raised eyebrows. He hastily covered himself while trying to remain dignified. 'What did you mean?'

'Okay.' I put down the mug and stood up. It was better than getting an eyeful of his groin and a cricked neck. 'If you're sure you can handle it. She left,' I announced, 'not because I've been playing bash the beaver with anything that has a pulse; not because I beat her black and blue every Saturday night after coming home nuked from the pub; not because I treated her like a slave or suddenly announced I was gay and wanted to shack up with an interior designer named Darryl from San Francisco. She left me because – so I'm told – I committed the cardinal sin of ignoring her. In other words she was bored.'

'Well, you did. She was.'

'Unfortunately,' I soldiered on, waving that aside, 'my mistake was spending too much time working when I should have been at home. Only somehow we didn't get round to talking about it like mature adults until it was too late – for which I plead guilty. My fault. Now, I don't know if it's true or not, since I haven't had a word from her on the subject, but that's what she's been telling people and I suppose it's as good a reason as any. Boredom, I mean. The only thing I can't figure out is why she had to clear out the house. I didn't realise she was so attached to the furniture she couldn't bear to leave it behind.'

As speeches go it was probably the longest he'd ever heard me make. It wasn't the sort of speech brothers usually go in for, as far as I know. In this new age we're supposed to reason with our siblings, treat them like equals and give them their platform so they can air their opinions in a mature and equitable fashion and get in touch with their inner beings.

To my surprise it worked, because he sank back down again and stared at me. 'Sorry,' he said. 'Didn't mean to judge. It's a bit of shock, that's all. I thought you two were solid.'

'Yes, me too.'

'Thing is… I'm not sure what you want me to do.'

I shrugged. 'Not a lot. I need to crash on your sofa for the night, that's all.'

He scowled, probably worried in case I was going to settle in and never leave. 'One night?'

'Maybe two, until I sort something out.'

I left him to mull it over and went into the kitchen and rooted around in the fridge until I found a can of beer. I tossed it to him, figuring it would probably do him more good than tea, or any of those remedies our mothers recommend in times of crisis.

'Well, that's a new one,' he said finally, after sinking half the can.

I waited, expecting an outburst at what he plainly thought was a pile of bullshit to cover my many failings as a husband. 'What is?'

'"Bash the beaver".' Then he smiled in spite of himself. It reminded me that he'd always had a good sense of humour, but I hadn't had much chance to see it lately. 'D'you mind if I borrow it?'

'Help yourself. It's a free world. I'm sure I can come up with a few more if you need them.'

I woke up the following morning with a weak sun filtering through the curtains and my head throbbing like a bass drum. Around me was the same debris I'd seen the night before, which did nothing for my spirits. Waking up with a hangover is bad enough; waking up in a tip which looks as if it had been bulldozed didn't help.

I swung my feet to the floor and stumbled into the kitchen, where I hunted round until I found a clean mug and brewed some tea. While the kettle hissed I stared at the piles of plates, cups, pans and takeaway packets piled up on every surface like a submission for the Turner Prize in the making. It wasn't pretty and I steered well clear of the layer of grease on the breakfast surface, wondering how much dedicated effort it took to get a place in this state.

Actually, I knew; I'd lived in one just like it once, way back when I could plead I didn't know any better.

I sat and sipped my tea, listening to the house tick and trying to decide on a course of action. One thing was sure – I couldn't or shouldn't rely on staying there too long. I may have lived like this once, when I was spotty and free of encumbrances, but too long with this disorder and I'd end up hiring a large skip and an industrial flame-thrower. Anyway, it was Marcus's mess, not mine.

There was also the question of Susan. I had to speak to her. Whatever had happened, we had to talk. It's what civilised people did before they threw in the towel, wasn't it?

I heard movement from upstairs and hoped it was Marcus. He hadn't said much last night after my lengthy outburst. 'Are you going to get back together?' he'd asked at one point, overlooking the degree to which Susan had left. Leaving in a huff and slamming the door is one thing; it implies the person leaving might come back at some point. When someone takes the furniture and fittings as well, it's a pretty safe bet their trip out is strictly one-way.

'No idea. I doubt it.'

'That's it? No arguments… no discussion?'

'Marcus, it's difficult to argue or discuss anything when my other half's gone AWOL. I don't even know where she is.'

'Have you tried calling her?'

Damn. I hadn't. So obvious. 'Not recently.'

'Okay. But what if she offered?'

I saw a packet of cigarettes and a lighter on the side and took one. It had been years since I'd smoked, a habit I'd dropped when I met Susan. But I suddenly had the need; Marcus's question was the one I had been dreading having to face. What if she wanted to come back? What if she wanted us to start out all over again and let bygones be bygones?

Right then I knew what my answer would be, but I didn't trust myself to be rational.

'You don't smoke,' Marcus pointed out, suddenly looking alarmed as I lit it.

'Watch me,' I said, and took a puff. It didn't draw well and I wondered if cigarettes were being packed tighter these days. Or maybe

I'd lost some of my puff since my feckless youth. Then I noticed a small slit in the paper halfway down, so I clamped the tip of one finger over it and tried again. This time I got a serious mouthful of smoke. It tasted hot and foul but I wasn't about to give up. Some things you just have to work at. Dead relationships being the exception, I told myself.

After a couple of minutes I noticed Marcus was looking a bit fuzzy around the edges. At first I figured it was because smoking after a long lay-off always has that effect, inducing dizziness and nausea, nature's warning that you're being a dick. Then he began to wobble and recede, and I was just wondering if tobacco had got stronger when I noticed he was grinning at me, as if I'd missed out on a secret joke.

Then the penny dropped and I stared at the cigarette in awe. It seemed to be smoking fiercely all by itself, giving off little spits like an angry cat in a cardboard box.

'Zzz… this got thomething in it?' I asked. My tongue was tangled round my teeth and I felt a giggle beginning to well up from somewhere down by my navel. I sighed and felt my body sag in my chair like a de-stringed puppet, my head way too heavy for my neck. Oh, boy. What a time to tune in, switch on and… whatever the rest of it was.

Marcus leaned over and took the joint from between my fingers before I dropped it on the carpet, and mashed it in an ashtray. I shook my head and waited while the dizziness began to recede and his face settled back into something I remembered. It wasn't perfect – a bit like seeing him underwater – but it would do until I got to the surface and back on the beach. Or wherever.

'Is that your first one?' he asked. He was looking at me with a sly grin and I realised this was the first time in years we'd been so relaxed with each other, even if it had taken a joint to get there.

'Of course not,' I said, feeling ridiculously defensive but unable to understand why. 'You think your generation invented having a good time? Let me tell you, I've been around the block a few times. They think it was back in the Sixties when it was all love and free drugs – I mean, free love and… but some of us have done our share since then, believe me.' I was talking rubbish, I knew that. Among the temptations over the years, anything stronger than aspirin had always seemed to me to be something best avoided because deep down inside I wasn't sure I could resist the lure. Alcohol, fair enough. But weed, pills and powder were a fast track to hell.

'Yeah, right.' He didn't believe me but I let it lie. At least my head was beginning to clear, which was a relief.

'How about you?'

He shook his head. 'Tried it once – never bothered since.' He laughed suddenly, unconcerned, as I shook my head to restore some order to my skewed vision. 'Wait 'til I tell Susan. Oh… sorry. Bad idea.'

We looked at each other until I broke the silence. 'I need to call Susan,' I said, before remembering that Dunckley's man had taken back my company mobile.

He handed one over from a side table. 'Help yourself.'

I dialled. Unobtainable. Great start: she'd changed her number.

I felt ridiculous having to ask him, but there was no way round it. 'Do you know how I can get in touch with her?'

He scribbled a phone number on a scrap of paper, then headed for the door. 'She said not to give it to you, but I'm not getting caught in the middle. Sort it out yourselves.' He hesitated, and I was sure he was going to resurrect the question about whether I would take Susan back if she asked. But he shook his head. 'I'm going back to bed. I've got a meeting with some investors in the morning.'

Now, in the cold light of day (natural), the aftermath of drink (intentional) and hash (accidental), taking the step towards calling Susan didn't seem quite so simple. To be honest, I think I was scared of the reaction. I fished out the slip of paper, but the number didn't give me any clues as to where she might be. No doubt wherever she was, if Hugo's Juliette had been right, Dunckley wouldn't be very far away, God rot his socks.

I took a turn around the debris-strewn room, trying to decide what to do. It was an odd state to be in. I was accustomed to dealing with temperamental types who looked ready to take off your arm at the shoulder if you squinted at them a bit wrong, since being a troubleshooter placed indecision at a very low pitch on one's set of skills. But handing over iffy packages in back streets and faceless hotels was no match for this kind of problem.

The first thing was to wash and get some clean clothes. I might have been in the kaka with my job and relationship, but I was buggered if I was going to go round smelling like it. After that I'd do what I'd so often resorted to when everything else had failed.

I'd play it by ear and stay on the move.

EIGHT

At least the house was still standing.

I edged past the decrepit old bus which had brought the rest of Dot and Dash's shifting commune, and was now an eye-catching garden feature in my flower bed. Its original Corporation red had been thickly overlaid with a variety of other hand-painted colours and dotted with flowers and symbols extolling peace and earthly love – although whether that meant love on the earth or of it, wasn't quite clear. The windows were hung with curtains and beady things, and inside the seats had been ripped out and replaced with fitted furniture and hanging lamps. I pounded on the front door of the house.

Someone had nailed some plywood across the damaged section and cleared up the bits of broken wood and glass. Through a small hole in the glass I could see the brick had gone from the hallway. A dog began barking inside and someone shouted for me to wait. Next thing a bedroom window opened above me and Dot's orange mop of hair appeared.

'Oh, hi.' She grinned in recognition. 'Hang on – I'll come down.'

I waited while her footsteps pounded down the stairs. It sounded loud. Then I remembered Susan had taken the carpets.

'Mr Foreman. I say.' It was Mrs Tree, leaning over the fence and waving at me, the poor demented soul. She was looking strained, probably with all the letters she'd fired off at the local council for allowing undesirables to come into the street.

Just then Dot unlocked the door and I dived inside. I really couldn't take any more of my neighbour's carry-on.

'Sorry,' I explained. 'Nearly got caught by the local witch-finder.'

'She had a go at Dash earlier. Said we had no right to be here, we should all go out and get jobs. Oh, and we were unwholesome. I've never been called unwholesome before.'

I wasn't surprised; she may have been dressed like a disaster zone but she looked clean and scrubbed.

'I need a shower and some fresh clothes,' I told her, heading for the stairs. That's if there are any of my clothes left, I thought, recalling Dash's caustic comments.

'Sure,' she said as if it was the most natural thing in the world for me to ask her permission to get some possessions from my own home. 'I made Dash put them all back tidily. Do you want tea or coffee? We don't have anything stronger.'

I nodded, thrown by her air of open friendliness. By rights she should have been on the defensive and expecting me to come marching in backed up by a private firm of storm troopers. Yet here she was offering me refreshments like we were old buddies.

I stopped two steps up, aware of a strange quietness. 'Where is everybody?' The place should have been heaving, with bodies covered in tattoos and safety pins lying around doing drugs and burning the door frames. Instead there was an almost deathly hush.

Dot popped her head round the kitchen door. 'Working. They'll be back later – those that aren't doing double shifts, anyway. I'm on the sick until tomorrow – I've got a belly like Vesuvius erupting. Me periods are playing up.'

'Sorry to hear it,' I said, and continued up to my room, where the floor was wall-to-wall with sleeping bags and mattresses. Alongside each one was a collection of clothing, the common colour a muddy green. It looked like a bring-and-buy at the local army surplus store.

I found my wardrobe closed and marked with a sticker saying 'DO NOT TOUCH'. Inside, all my clothes were neatly arranged on the shelves and hangers. Even my tie was on the rail, looking none the worse for its brief stay round Dash's waist.

I picked out everything I needed, including and especially a leather jacket I'd had for years and which Susan had tried many times to slip to the Salvation Army. She claimed it made me look like a second-hand car dealer. I shrugged it on with a satisfied smile; there's nothing like a busted marriage to make you revel in the things you wanted to do over the years but were rarely allowed to.

I packed a few things in a holdall and decided that anything else I needed, I'd buy along the way. I could hardly keep coming back there for a change of clothing, and instinct told me a few new things would be good therapy. Then I dived into the bathroom and had a quick shower, surrounded by other people's toothbrushes, soap and tubes.

I went down to the kitchen, where the work surfaces were strewn with a collection of mugs and plates. Every item was different and, by the looks of it, hand-thrown to individual requirements. It was a colourful collection.

'Thanks for putting everything straight,' I said.

Dot smiled and handed me a mug of coffee. 'S'all right. Dash really did think the place was deserted at first, otherwise he'd never have gone through your stuff. He's a bit impetuous sometimes. It's Jake, right?' She pointed a blood-red fingernail at the other side of the mug and I turned it round and found my name inscribed in the glaze.

'Dash had Molly make this for you. She's our resident potter. She can make anything as long as it's clay. D'you like it?'

There couldn't be many things left that could throw me after the events of the last couple of days, but this one did. For some reason I found it difficult to speak for a few seconds.

'It's… brilliant. But why?'

Dot shrugged. 'We crashed your place – it's the least we could do. Especially after your wife took off the way she did. I mean, shit happens, but there's no need for complete strangers to pile it on as well, is there?' She peered at me as I sipped my coffee. 'Say, did you know someone damaged your front door? It wasn't us, I promise. We don't do that sort of thing. Dash fixed it for you so you wouldn't get anyone barging in. Well, except us, that is.'

'It was me.' I explained about not having a key and how I'd ended up at the local nick for being rude to a policeman. Dot seemed to find that impressive, her eyes widening like saucers as I described my stay in the pokey.

'No way!' she cried cheerfully. 'Jeez, you're a deep sort, Jake… for a guy who looks so square, I mean.' She managed to conceal the criticism with a big grin and a matey punch on my upper arm. 'Good on yer! I've been busted plenty of times. Nothin' serious, though – the odd bit of weed, some trespass and that sort of thing. I went on a protest once, too, against whaling. It got a bit heavy when they called out the riot cops – that was in Auckland. Luckily they didn't have room for all of us in the jail and they had to let us go with a slap on the wrist. Say, are you sure you're okay about us being here? You ain't gonna get us bounced by the cops are you?'

I shook my head. For some reason, since stepping back in the house and being greeted by the effervescent Dot, my mood had lifted.

'No need. I won't be staying here for the time being. I'll probably have to sell the place eventually. Stay as long as you like.'

'Cool. Thanks.' She jumped up and sat on the work surface, staring at me. 'So, what do you do, Jake? You look like a solicitor or something. My dad's a solicitor in Auckland.' She pulled a face. 'He thinks I'm a wastrel – d'you believe that? I mean, who uses words like that these days?'

'Solicitors, usually,' I told her. 'I'm a troubleshooter. I sort out problems. Well, I did until yesterday. I got laid off.'

'Ouch. Bad luck. Still,' she grinned with the irrepressible attitude of someone happy with her lot, 'there's always something out there if you look. You just gotta be ready to change direction, my dad always says.' She looked suddenly soft-eyed. 'He's okay, my dad.'

I thanked Dot for the coffee and the personalised mug, and told her I had to be going. Things to do, people to see. Life to live. Like I'd got it all planned out.

'No worries. You can leave the mug with us if you like. Most of the others do, even if they're gone months. Some of them we've been carryin' around for ages.'

'Really? Why?'

'So they've got something to come back to.' She looked wistful for a moment. 'Man, I'd hate that – not havin' something to go back to.'

'What if you move on? How do they catch up with you?'

She pointed to a laptop sitting on the end of the work surface. 'Internet – how do you think? All they have to do is find a cyber café and drop us a note. We tell 'em where we are. Dead easy. You should try it. Here, I'll give you our email.' She scribbled out the details on a piece of paper and handed it to me. 'There. You're now part of a worldwide family of travellers. If ever you need to crash somewhere, hook up and shout. Someone'll get back to you. We know loads of places.'

I was amazed. Yet why not? That's what technology was for, surely. 'Anywhere?'

'Pretty near.' She rolled her eyes and laughed. 'Well, we haven't got anybody in Moscow yet, but give it time, eh?'

I left the new and bubbly occupant of my house and managed to avoid Mrs Tree while she was complaining loudly to her neighbour on the other side about the hippie invasion. I had no doubt she'd try to get some action taken against them, but since I wasn't about to file an official complaint, I guessed she'd have her work cut out.

On the way back to see Marcus I called in at the bank to present my severance cheque and draw some cash. If I was going to set about getting another job and deciding if there was any mileage left to my relationship with Susan, I'd need a fighting fund.

News of Susan's leaving had evidently spread like a bush fire. As I stepped through the door of the bank, I met Andrew and Lynne Kossof. Lynne was one of Susan's wolf pack and Andrew was someone who always seemed to be in the background even when he was by himself.

'How could you!' Lynne snapped, giving me the kind of look normally reserved for dog owners who failed to scoop the poop. Her wrist was heavy with a collection of bangles, and they shook and clanked as she waved an accusatory finger at me. 'How you can even show your face I don't know! That poor woman…'

Since she chose to yell this at me, every syllable was heard by customers and staff alike, who each put their own interpretation on what she meant. I suddenly knew how it must have felt to be on the way to the guillotine in Paris during the French Revolution.

'I didn't–' I began, but she didn't want to hear.

'Andrew, come away. Now.' With that, she swept out of the door, dragging her docile mate after her. He threw me a sympathetic glance, but it was like being tossed a chocolate teapot.

I sighed and waited for the first available cashier, ignoring the looks coming my way. It was clear that Susan had done a damage-extension job on me, convincing her friends that her leaving and taking every stick of furniture was all my fault. I shouldn't have been surprised; whatever her failings, communication delays among her mates wasn't one of them.

'Mr Foreman,' said the cashier, her eyes frosting over ominously. 'We've been expecting you.'

'You have?' I didn't like the sound of that. Banks don't expect customers to do anything but pay in money and stay out of the red, and I hadn't spoken to an employee there for as long as I could remember. Instinct told me I should leave the severance cheque in my pocket.

She guided me to a booth at the far end, where a chirpy youth in Day-Glo braces and hair gel smiled at me as if I'd won first prize in their customer of the year contest. Then he set about stamping all over my face, personal-banker style.

'Mr Foreman,' he said cheerfully. 'We have a problem.'

'You do?' He could have fooled me. Anyone that cheerful obviously didn't know what problems were. He needed to get out more.

'Uh-huh. Your account doesn't have sufficient funds to pay your outgoings, I'm afraid. And you've exceeded your maximum credit limit.'

I stared at him, my belly turning to liquid. 'That can't be right. My salary only went in last week – and I haven't been down to the pub for my weekly ration of twenty pints and a hundred fags yet.'

As a joke it would have been weak after several pints of vodka. Early on a weekday morning, and to Junior Banker, it didn't stand a chance. He dropped his smile like knicker elastic snapping, suddenly all serious and cool.

Susan. It had to be.

'You don't understand,' he said, speaking slowly as if to a halfwit. 'All available funds up to the limit have been withdrawn. You haven't had your cash card or chequebook stolen, have you?'

Actually, he wasn't too far off the mark.

'As good as,' I told him. 'I think I've discovered another way of being mugged.'

NINE

I left the bank and went to a shop round the corner, where I armed myself with a new mobile phone. It was one of those throwaway models and would do me for the time being. With everything that had happened I had a feeling that being off the grid for a while might be a good thing. I found a quiet corner in a coffee bar and called the number Marcus had given me. I had to sort this out. It rang several times before being picked up. I fancied I recognised Susan's breathing and decided to launch in before I lost my nerve.

'We need to talk,' I said, surprised at how calm I felt. Lost job, wife bunked off, empty house, ditto bank account, cold shoulder from friends... I should have been drunk, drugged or sitting on a high building somewhere, contemplating the pavement below. Instead, I felt remarkably sanguine. I wondered how long sanguine lasted.

'Is there any point?' Her voice was cold, like a digital answering machine. It was her coping-with-stress voice. I'd heard it many times, usually aimed at shop assistants who couldn't add up fast enough or call centre operators who wouldn't take no for an answer.

'We can hardly leave things the way they are, can we?'

'All right.' She sounded unnaturally calm, but I could tell she was nervous. Susan had a way of holding her breath when she was tense which, during the first row we ever had, had me wondering if she was suddenly going to keel over from oxygen starvation. I'd often wondered if it was a hangover from when she was a child, and was something she resorted to when all other avenues had been explored and she could see she obviously wasn't going to get her own way. 'Where?'

I thought quickly and suggested a fake tapas bar near Piccadilly which, due to its low atmosphere and extortionate prices, was always quiet. The last thing I needed was a shouting match in the company of a hundred or so hearty lunchtime drinkers eager for a bit of entertainment.

I dropped my things off at Marcus's place and left him a note, then legged it for Piccadilly, where I found the bar with its usual sparse clientele. I ordered a glass of dry white, took a corner table, and waited for doom to drop in.

Susan arrived forty minutes and two glasses later. She was followed closely by an overweight, sweaty individual in an expensive suit who blinked in the gloomy atmosphere and took another corner table across the room, his eyes on her all the way and not in a lascivious manner. Susan came across and sat down, elegant as usual in a pale cream suit and gold blouse, her auburn hair cut shorter than I remembered and expensively glossy. It made her look younger, and I wondered if it was our current situation which made me think how attractive she looked and if only…

But she soon nipped that in the bud.

'You're wearing that old thing just to annoy me,' she said coolly, sniffing at the sight of my leather jacket.

I grinned, in spite of the situation, and silently thanked her for reminding me what this was all about. Had she come in all sweetness and light, I doubt I'd have been able to remain objective about her. She really was very attractive.

'If that was all I wanted to do,' I pointed out, 'I'd have been late.'

Her expression darkened and I mentally awarded myself a point. Childish perhaps, but I had the feeling I was going to have to take whatever small consolation I could from this meeting.

'I don't want any trouble,' she said frostily, and peered at my glass. 'Is that medium dry? I'll have the same.'

I ordered another glass, then changed it to a bottle. If our meeting didn't last more than a couple of minutes, I could always finish it off myself before going round to Dunckley's house and lobbing the empty through one of his windows.

'There won't be any trouble,' I said calmly. 'Not unless Dunckley's outside and comes within fifty feet of my right fist. I suppose he's told you he made me redundant?' It must have been the icing on the cake for him, screwing both of us, I wanted to say, but didn't.

'That's your answer to everything, is it – violence?' Her voice was tight and I realised this was going to be harder than I'd thought. It suddenly felt as if I was talking to a complete stranger. I decided I couldn't let that crack pass without comment.

'Since when have you ever known me be violent?'

'I haven't,' she conceded reluctantly. 'But there's always a first time.' She glanced across to where Mr Sweaty was deliberating over the wine list as if he expected to find a bargain-priced Chateau d'Yquem. I was amazed by her attitude. How could she have cleared out the house and the account and be so calm about it?

'Is this how it's going to be?'

She frowned. 'I don't know what you mean.'

'Invention. Exaggeration… suggesting things happened which never did. Is that how you're going to justify what you've done?' My voice began creeping upwards in volume, drawing a look from Mr

Sweaty. I lowered it again to little more than a murmur. 'In case you've suffered an acute case of amnesia, Susan, you walked out on me and took all the furniture *and* emptied the bank account. What was it you said to Marcus – that I'm unstable? Have you done a hatchet job on me with your friends, too, like the Kossoffs and Juliette?'

For a second she looked uncomfortable. As reasons for desertion go it was hardly one to stand up to close scrutiny; plenty of men spend too much time at work, but it was unlikely grounds for divorce. Golf courses, on the other hand, or pubs or the bookies – even other women – were different. But since I was innocent on all fronts, and hadn't done anything more ambitious than look at another woman over the edges of an in-flight magazine, none of them applied.

She sipped her drink. 'It was the only way I could see of having any kind of life. Did you ever think of me stuck back here while you were off on one of your jollies?'

That was a new one. I'd described my trips to fly-blown corners of the globe in lots of different ways, but none of them could have been characterised as jollies. I might have been inconsiderate but taking Susan with me to those hell holes would have bordered on cruelty.

'So it's true,' I said resignedly, and wondered if Susan could hear what she sounded like.

'True?'

'What you told Juliette – that I didn't pay you enough attention. That you were bored. I assume that's what you meant? Or was there something else I didn't do to make our life complete?'

'I don't know what you mean.'

I took a deep breath. 'Children.'

She looked surprised and said, 'God, no. We talked about that, remember? It was never on the cards for either of us, I think we agreed on that. Anyway, isn't boredom enough of a reason?'

Aware that I was going to sound like an inconsiderate dick, I said, 'But you never said. I thought you liked the way we had things.' As game-changing ripostes go it was pretty pathetic, but I was caught on the back foot. Show me a backwater troublemaker stirring the pot in search of a pay-off and I'm your man. Faced with a grasping local politician trying to shaft his workforce to his own benefit and I'm in like Flint. But this?

She tossed her head back, showing me a smooth expanse of throat. It reminded me of what her skin felt like, and the way she used to shiver with pleasure when I nuzzled into the crook of her neck. For a second I even harboured thoughts of a strictly libidinous nature, the kind that had me wondering where the nearest hotel might be. Then I recognised the body language for what it was. She was waiting for me to make the first move; a grand gesture which would include an apology of the self-abasing kind, preferably involving my knees touching the floor seconds before my forehead. I'd seen it before when things had been less than harmonious – usually over money. Or maybe it had always been this, disguised as something else. 'Is that all you can say?' she muttered, and I swear I heard the wine in our glasses begin to ice over.

I felt a tightness in my chest, like a volcano about to erupt. 'Why clear the house? Bit extreme, wasn't it?'

'I did it on impulse.' Her voice at least sounded faintly sheepish. 'I've put everything in storage, so you don't have to worry – I'm not going to set fire to it. Anyway, by all accounts it's a good job I did take everything, with that crowd of God-awful hippies you've allowed to move in. You realise we'll have to get the place fumigated.'

'They're rather a nice bunch, actually,' I said defensively, and remembered the smiling Dot and the mug she'd given me. Somewhere to go back to.

Susan looked directly at me for the first time, like the owner of a puppy which, if it performed as instructed, would get a suitable reward. 'Well, you'll just have to get them out again, won't you, or I'll call the police. Let's hope the neighbourhood forgives you. In any case, now you no longer work for that horrid company, you won't be travelling anywhere and we can put the place on the market. As for a job, I'm sure we can find you something suitable locally.'

I couldn't believe it. One minute I was being hauled over razor blades and broken glass for being a callous, absent bastard, and the next she was saying everything could go back to the way it had been. With conditions.

'You mean you'll come back – and bring all the furniture?'

She nodded with the beginnings of a smile edging her very kissable lips. 'Of course.' I almost wavered, looking at those lips, and remembering when– Then I felt as if I was supposed to leap on my chair with my tongue hanging out ready to catch a biscuit.

'And everything goes back to the way it was? Including letting me have access to some of the money I earn?' I couldn't help the last bit, which fizzed out like steam under pressure.

'Why not?' she said calmly. 'Which reminds me, if you want to give me your redundancy cheque I'll pay it in for you.' She held out her hand.

It was the last straw. I wondered if she could see the steam coming from my ears. She'd got everything bar the clothes on my back and now she wanted my severance cheque? Did she really think I was that dumb? And that wasn't all: she either didn't know Hugo had told me about Dunckley… or she did know and was conveniently managing to overlook it while she fleeced me for everything I had.

Unless Hugo had been lying.

I decided to put it to the test, as painful as it might be to my pride and sanity.

'So you'll forget about all the time I spent away?'

'Of course. We'll start again… a new leaf. Lots of people do, you know. Perhaps we can have a long holiday to catch up on where we used to be, rekindle what we had. Thirty thousand, wasn't it, the pay-off?' The segue from future promise to hard-nosed business came without a break in her voice.

'And the way I ignored you?'

'All in the past.' She smiled grandly, her forgiveness a prize I was supposed to appreciate and savour like a fine wine.

'And you'll forget all the time you've had to amuse yourself while I wasn't around?'

A frown fluttered across her brow. It might have been the first suspicion she had that I was actually going somewhere with this. 'Jake, I said yes. Please don't be tiresome. Now, the cheque?' The hand edged further across the table, the fingers beckoning, like a mother demanding a child hand over a forbidden toy.

'Because you know, don't you,' I continued, somehow maintaining a calm tone of voice when I actually wanted to explode all over the fucking place, 'that although I may have been too… wrapped up in my work, I've never been unfaithful? Ever.'

'Of course I do, silly.' She showed me her even, white teeth, and reached out to touch my arm with a painted fingertip, as if bestowing a blessing. The contact sent a ripple up my arm which wasn't altogether unpleasant. 'That's the one thing I always could count on,

69

Jake: you being faithful. It was that darned job that became your mistress. But that's all done with now, isn't it? It's over. I want us to start again.'

Ruff. I experienced the good-doggy moment again, and felt a mixture of humiliation and anger. And sadness.

'In that case,' I said calmly, 'since all you've got to forgive *me* for is working too hard, perhaps you'll tell me how I'm supposed to forgive *you*.'

She put down her glass and looked at me. This time there was a flash of the old steel I remembered, which was my signal for putting on my tin hat. 'Forgive me? What on earth do I have to be forgiven for? For walking out because you were never there for me?' She looked away with a sharp intake of breath; the picture of someone bravely holding back tears in the face of trying odds. I noticed Mr Sweaty was watching with close attention, and the barman was shifting towards the hatch as if expecting trouble. The vibes in the air must have been crackling with negative energy.

Too late, I felt like announcing. Trouble was already here.

'No,' I said. 'Not that. What I mean is, how can I forgive you for screwing Niall Dunckley?'

Her mouth fell open and the colour drained from her face like a cistern emptying of water. In that instant, I knew Hugo hadn't been lying. She sat back, evidently groping to find words, and snatched her hand away from my arm as if a cockroach had strolled out of my sleeve. Then she turned and glanced helplessly at Mr Sweaty, as if she realised this had gone as far as it could.

'Who's the big guy?' I asked, as he rose from his table and lumbered towards us. I noticed he'd ordered a drink but hadn't touched it. 'Lawyer, bodyguard... or the next in line?'

'Nothing. He's—' Susan stood up, knocking her glass over and drawing the attention of everyone in the room. 'I don't know what you're talking about. How dare you accuse me of… of such a horrible thing!' In case they misunderstood what was going on she stepped back from the table and glared at me, her beautiful eyes full of venom. 'You sanctimonious prick!' she spat loud enough for the people outside to hear. For good measure her lower lip wobbled like a half-set jelly and she dabbed at her eyes. 'I'm going to sue you for desertion – and you'd better get that ghastly crowd of street riffraff out of the house, because from now on it's going to be mine! I put money into it, too, remember.'

'Really? Remind me.'

She went red instead. 'Niall was right about you – you're not worth it.'

In that instant, whatever feelings I might have had for her disappeared. Betrayal, I decided with a sick feeling, was the kindest word I could think of. And the most painful.

'You knew!' I said, in a moment of clear realisation. It was like a punch to the gut. 'You knew I was going to lose my job!' Dunckley must have told her everything, and I couldn't help wondering if it had been while they were at it on the table in the HP&P computer room.

Susan tried to speak, but in the end she gave up and looked past me, unable to meet my eyes. It was just as well, because suddenly I'd gone past the point where I was prepared to believe anything she said. As well as the physical betrayal, she had watched as I'd had my job stripped from me, and without a hint of warning. God, they must have had a laugh at that one. Poor, stupid Jake. Doesn't know what's going to hit him.

'Was that why you left on the same day?' I said softly, cheating the crowd of nosey bastards of my response. 'Was it the coup de grâce? Kick the dog while he's down? Or was it your own guilt?'

She shrugged in a particularly childish way which made me want to rage at her, futile though it would have been. Then she turned away, leaving Mr Sweaty standing there with a business card in his hand. He dropped it on the table in front of me.

'I think that confirms Mrs Foreman will be taking out divorce proceedings against you,' he said. He leaned closer, bringing a wave of aftershave with him. 'Look, Mr Foreman, just a friendly word: she's got a watertight case and she will win, you know.' He gave a shark-like grin, showing perfect teeth. 'Just so you know, I never lose.' Then he turned on his heel and lumbered out after his client.

'Bollocks,' I said to his departing back, and poured another glass of wine. I'd been put through the wringer and done over like a kipper, as an old engineer I'd once worked with used to say. Yeah, clichés, I know; but when you're feeling wounded, you reach for something familiar.

All in all, as days went, I'd experienced better.

TEN

'What you need to do, old son, is to review your options,' suggested Hugo knowingly, like the sage and worldly soul that he was. Somehow I doubted that owning large chunks of the shire counties – which Hugo did – involved the need for reviewing options other than deciding how many more acres to buy and how many tenants to evict if things got tight. Still, he meant well, which after my meeting with Susan, came as a welcome relief.

We were back at the drinker's pub, where I was once more under the cold scrutiny of the landlady. She evidently hadn't made up her mind whether or not my money was good enough to make up for my crimes against womankind, or perhaps she was considering gathering some of the locals together to tar and feather me and roll me down the nearest hill in a barrel.

'What options? No wife, no house, no money, friends blanking me in public and now she's going to sue for divorce.' I'd given him the bare bones of Susan's response after our meeting, and how the door to matrimonial harmony had been slammed shut unless I was prepared to prostrate myself before her and become her whipping-boy for past hurts.

'Put like that, no,' he agreed calmly. 'But what's the point wallowing in self-pity? It's not your usual trait, is it?'

He had a point there. God, I hate arguing with Hugo. He knows me too well.

'Okay, so what would you do?' I challenged him. A management trick: turn the question back on the questioner.

'Simple. Find yourself a girl with the sexual instincts and appetite of a starved mongoose and go for it. Everything will seem unimportant after that.'

I stared at him, hardly recognising my friend of several years. This wasn't the boring old logical Hugo: of the home counties cardigans and the traditional values, anxious to gallop home to Juliette in case he was cast into the outer darkness. This was a monster I hardly recognised, peeling back his outer layer like a snake shedding its skin.

'Apart from the sex bit,' I finally managed to tell him, 'you make this whole getting back on your feet bit sound like an exercise in better management. Is that all you've got to offer? Thanks a lot!'

'Maybe it is.' If he was offended by my ingratitude, he didn't show it. He finished his pint and signalled for a refill. The landlady smiled at him and ignored me. 'Thank Christ for all those boring sessions at the MBA classes I went to. Learned bugger all about business management, but I've never been so expertly shagged in all my life. You remember Lorraine from Executive Accounts?'

How could I forget Lorraine? I'd have to have been blind to forget HP&P's resident beauty. She had looks, brains, ambition and an earthy sense of humour, and Daddy was well connected in the city. She had, as I also recalled, been sent on the same MBA course as Hugo.

I felt my jaw drop as if on hinges. 'What? You mean *you*?' I couldn't believe it. Rumour had it that no-one had ever got to first base with Lorraine because she was so stand-offish and wrapped up in her career. Not that I'd ever ventured to try; but I knew the names of some of the fallen who were whispered about in the corridors. And now this paragon of virtue was admitting to having been there.

'Three times, actually,' confirmed Hugo happily, before I could ask. 'All in one night. Couldn't keep up in the end, literally or otherwise. Jesus, I dunno what she was on, but she could go like a train and still have enough energy for an early-morning swim. I was so buggered I overslept on the third morning and missed two sessions. Pruitt was furious. Still,' he stared dreamily into his glass like an old soldier remembering past campaigns, 'it was worth the bollocking just to see the look on his face when he realised what we'd been up to. Letchy old bastard had been trying to get into her knickers since day one.'

I was staggered. Pruitt was HP&P's Finance Director and someone more seemingly straitlaced you couldn't get. He probably had the Institute of Chartered Accountants logo embroidered on his underpants. I wondered how much he knew about the less salubrious side of the business. As FD, surely he'd have seen any wrongdoings first-hand in the figures. Although it was possible that, as with Hugo, they had taken care to ensure there were several faces around the place who could present an outwardly law-abiding image to the general public, just for show. And that meant making sure the public saw only what they wanted them to see.

As for Lorraine, all I could picture was an image of starched blouses, power suits and the kind of 'invade-my-space-and-I'll-kick-you-in-the-balls' look which stopped most chat-up lines dead in their tracks.

'But she was always so forbidding.' I was desperate to believe he was kidding me.

'You're dead right, mate. Kept forbidding me to slow down and forbidding me to stop.' He laughed wickedly, pleased by his own coarse wit.

'Very funny. And since then?'

'Not a look.' He frowned. 'I've dropped the odd hint, you know, suggested drinkies and so forth. But she's blanked me every time. Must have been the mood of the moment, I suppose. Still, can't say I'm sorry, to be honest; it'd be hell on wheels if she decided she wanted a re-match. You can only keep up that sort of pretence for a while. Juliette would skin my balls and feed 'em to the dogs if she ever found out. Not that they're much use to me these days, anyway.'

'Bloody cheek,' I muttered heavily, and sank some more beer. Hugo was sounding as if Lorraine hadn't been his first away match.

He looked surprised. 'Well, I dunno about that. She'd have a point I suppose.'

'Not her, you pious, double-dealing arse,' I said angrily. 'You rattle on about me not being around enough to give Susan more time, but at least I haven't slept with anyone else. God, I've a good mind to tell Juliette.'

Hugo stared at me, the blood draining from his face. 'I say, that's low, old boy. You won't, will you?' He grabbed hold of my arm, suddenly the one on the defensive. 'Christ on a broomstick, Jake – come on. I was only telling you by way of trying to help lighten the atmosphere.'

I grinned, enjoying his discomfort. Served him right. 'Actually, I wouldn't. But just remember: now I know who and I know when.'

We drank some more, with him shooting me nervous glances. Then I said, 'Actually, you're right. It's about time I got back on the bike and started riding again. I suppose I have been wallowing a bit. It all came as such a shock, though. I let it get to me. Sorry.' Christ, I almost sounded as if I meant it, even to myself. Maybe I was getting there after all.

'Good for you, old boy.' A look of relief passed across his brow now I wasn't going to drop him in it. 'You need to get away for a while.

Let the atmosphere settle. As for the girl thing, well, you're not past it, are you?'

'After the last couple of days I bloody well feel past it. First thing is to get a job.'

'D'you have any ideas in the pot?'

'Not really. I was hoping you might be able to help.' I'd had a quick trawl online for jobs, but unless I fancied teaching English to school kids in New Guinea, packing rubber boots in a factory in Park Royal or wearing a dark uniform and making sure no-one ran off with bottles of sherry from the local supermarket, there wasn't much about.

'I might.' He gave it some thought for a moment, then finished off his pint. 'Tell you what, I'll ring a couple of pals and see what's about. That do you? I suppose you're not too fussed about what, are you?'

'Anything,' I said gamely, remembering Hugo had friends in some very exotic places. 'Just something to get me back on my feet and keep me solvent. I need to get away from here for a while. Overseas would be nice. Somewhere sunny, perhaps – but not the Foreign Legion; I've developed a sudden aversion to sand and camels. And if you can think of a way of cashing my severance cheque without using my bank account, that would help. Susan's got her sights on it already.'

He nodded. 'Okay. But, umm... one thing, old boy: did you mean it earlier on, about never having strayed? I mean, not even once? Hell, I mean, it's not as if anyone – Susan – would have found out, is it?'

'Never.' I repeated firmly. 'I told you. Maybe I should have put in for the MBA course you were on.'

'Come off it, Jake.' He gave a wry snicker. 'You'd have got nowhere, I promise you.'

'Maybe not with Lorraine,' I said. 'But I might have got an MBA certificate.'

Marcus's electronic product tester mates were slouched in the living-room when I got back, wearing what looked like over-sized crash helmets and visors, with the sounds of pitched battle coming from the earpieces. If they were aware of me from within their virtual reality zones, they made no signs, and I guessed I could have stripped naked and done the conga and they wouldn't have turned a hair.

When Marcus came in, he nodded with more civility than I'd expected, and hovered in the background like a spare part. It was a familiar sign: he had something to say but wasn't sure how to go about it. It didn't really go with the smart suit and aluminium briefcase, no doubt his kit for meetings with investors, but that was business; this was closer to home.

'What's up?' I said, making it easier for him. At this rate we'd still be there at midnight and he'd never get it out. It reminded me of when he was younger and needed some pocket money for something urgent. He'd hover around me, hopping from foot to foot, looking as though he was about to speak but never quite getting there. In the end I'd got used to asking him how much he needed; it saved us both a lot of time and embarrassment.

'I wondered if you fancied coming to a football match tomorrow,' he said quickly. 'Only if you'd like to, of course.'

ELEVEN

On top of the shock of being invited to share leisure time with my brother – quite something after all the recent years of distance between us – I realised with surprise that tomorrow was Saturday. One of the consequences, I guessed, of being without a job to go to: lose the routine, you lose track of the days. Only in my case I'd lost track of a few other things as well.

'Not much,' I replied instinctively. Football has never been a passion, any more than cricket, darts, rugby and most other sporting pastimes. But the look on Marcus's face was enough to convince me it was about time I showed an interest. In any case, I was intrigued by the invitation. Was this some kind of white flag of peace? 'But if it includes a pint or two and a pie afterwards, I'd love to.'

'Cool,' he said, and smiled with an awkward look of relief which made me glad I'd accepted.

The following day, I joined him and a couple of his mates at a minor league ground where we stood and rooted for the team in blue. They seemed quite good – not that I was any kind of judge – and, after they'd managed to thrash the opposition comprehensively, who responded by kicking lumps out of their striker, we found a pub and sank some celebratory pints amid a heaving mass of genial drunks.

'I spoke to Susan yesterday,' I told Marcus, when I sensed the atmosphere was right between us and his mates had gone. I hadn't bothered telling him the previous evening, mostly because I was still spitting nails and hadn't been able to trust myself to remain calm.

'Yeah?' He sank some beer and looked warily at me. 'How did it go?'

'It didn't. We met, we spoke, we parted. She's filing for divorce.'

'She said that?'

'No. She had a legal gorilla along to say it for her.'

He surprised me by shrugging and saying, 'That's okay. I guessed she would, I suppose. What will you do?'

'Get a job. Start again.' It sounded easy if I said it quickly enough.

'Do you think you can?'

I narrowed my eyes at him in mock warning. 'Watch it, kid. I may be older and more careworn than you, but I'm not finished yet. It's called getting back on the bike, in case you've never heard of it.'

'Right. Like, if you fall off, get back on before you lose your nerve.'

'Sort of. It's been a long time since I was last on a bike, but I'm sure I can remember how it goes.'

'Any ideas what you'll do?'

'None at the moment. Trying some smart moves for a change would be good.'

'Smart?'

I didn't want to burden him with the possibility that Dunckley might be keeping tabs on me through Susan. It was only just hitting me that the fish-eyed git must have had more on his mind than simply lusting after my wife to have decided to get rid of me. Had I somehow tripped over something I shouldn't see? Blundered into something he'd rather I didn't talk about? Otherwise why the threats about confidentiality agreements and not talking to the authorities? God knows what he thought I might know, though. All I'd been interested in was doing my job and staying out of trouble in hostile places. But staying out of Dunckley's way would be a wise course of action – even if my instinct was to nail him to a tree and let the birds pick his bones.

'Jake?' Marcus was looking at me with a worried expression, and I realised I must have zoned out for a moment.

'Sorry,' I said. 'Just looking at the way I've been doing things. I've blundered along in the past, gone from one thing to another. I can't afford to do that any more. I need to think smarter. You know what they say about moving targets.'

'They're harder to hit?'

'Exactly.'

We drank another couple of rounds and talked generalities, and even did some catching up on things which had fallen between the gaps of our relationship over the past few years. It proved more interesting than I'd expected, and I found myself admiring what he was doing and how serious he was about his business.

After a while he put down his glass and said casually, 'Would you like to come to a party this evening?'

'Do what?' I nearly choked.

'I'm serious,' he said, at my evident scepticism. 'I got an invite from the guy who's throwing it. He's a new contact looking to get into the gaming and VR field.'

VR. I knew that meant virtual reality, and nodded wisely. 'VR. Right.'

'He's reportedly got a ton of cash to invest and I'd like to ease a little of it our way. He wants me and a few others to make a pitch.'

I gave him a sideways look. I didn't know much about the investment field, but I figured anyone who had to go round telling people they had a ton of cash was not exactly on the up and up. 'Do you know this guy?'

'We've spoken on the phone, and he seems a good bloke. A bit Jason Statham, if you know what I mean. Anyway, I thought it might help.' He stopped and shrugged. 'The party. Help you, I mean.'

I was having trouble reconciling this new side to Marcus. Along with the suit and briefcase it was like meeting a stranger, and another indication of how much we'd lost touch over the years. 'Help take me out of myself? No, thanks. I should be job-hunting not partying. Anyway, I'm not sure I'm ready to regress that much. My partying years were a long time ago and I'm not sure I enjoyed them much even then.'

'Why not? Come on – you said about getting back on the bike. It's got to start somewhere. What's the harm in a couple of drinks? You can start looking for a job tomorrow... or Monday, I should say.'

He *was* serious; he actually wanted me to accept. I thought about it under cover of going to the toilet, and thought back to parties I'd gone to in the days when leaving with the person you arrived with was considered subversive, and if you remained sensible you obviously weren't enjoying yourself properly. It came as a shock to realise that I hadn't been to a party in about fifteen years – and then they were those anodyne, civilised suburban affairs where everyone is terribly polite, watchful as hawks, and the only shag on the premises is the pile of the carpet.

But Marcus was right: what harm could it do? It wasn't as if I had any prior engagements, and the only thing I was risking was enjoying myself.

'All right,' I said, rejoining him at the bar. 'Party it is. As long as you can stand the embarrassment of having your big brother in tow.'

He laughed. 'Forget it. I might be inviting you along, but if you think we are about to hang together or that I'm telling anyone we're related, dream on.'

The first thing I had to do was get myself some new clothes. I'd come to the conclusion that the ones I had were beyond their wear-by date. They certainly weren't designed for boogying the night away. Okay, I was being optimistic in assuming there would be any boogying, but hope was beginning to spring eternal in the breast, and even I could see that my current kit had a certain middle-aged quality about it.

The trouble was, buying clothes had never been my favourite occupation. I hate the whole rigmarole of trying on stiff new clothes in a tiny booth built for a rabbit, and finding my already low expectations of what I might look like being fully met.

I headed for Regent Street and trawled through some of the stores in search of something suitable. I ended up in one, gulped at the inevitably high prices, and, as they had a few options on offer, I forged ahead. 'Good afternoon, sir.' The first assistant to spot me performed a deceptively lazy gallop across the thick carpet, abandoning a pair of French tourists who were fingering the goods with a look of disdain. He looked to be in his forties though could have been older, but he moved like a dancer. Along with his fake tan and elegantly combed hair, his pinstriped suit and pink shirt gave him the air of someone about to break into a routine from a Fred Astaire movie.

Two other slim young things who had started forward from further back in the shop gave up halfway out of their blocks and went back to folding jumpers and discussing the price of property. Business was clearly a bit slow.

'Looking for something specific, sir?' he ventured. I could feel him running his eyes over my clothes and totting up the potential bill.

Though all my instincts were to bug out of there and go with what I'd got, I gritted my teeth and nodded. Might as well get it over and done with.

'I'm going to a party,' I told him. 'I need something respectable but casual.'

'Mmm.' He fingered my leather jacket and stood back for a moment. Alongside his tailored elegance, I felt like something the cat had dragged in. 'What sort of party, may I ask?'

'I'm not sure. Younger business people, mostly. In IT.'

He nodded, zeroing in on a type. 'Ah. That's where all the fun is, so they say. Any older people?'

I looked at him, trying to spot any meaning in his question, but he stared back without a flicker. Something told me he was treading a well-worn and tactful path.

'Older than me? Probably not. But I don't want to kid myself or look out of place.' He nodded and led me past racks of perfectly suitable clothes – the type I would have gone for if he hadn't buttonholed me – into the rear of the store where they kept their changing booths and a scattering of comfortable chairs. Shades of *Pretty Woman* – only I wasn't the Richard Gere type.

He managed to ease me out of my jacket and place it carefully on a hanger with what I thought was undue reverence. He even brushed a hand across one lapel to remove a trace of dust. This man took his job seriously.

He squinted at me in the manner of an undertaker and wandered away with a faint smile and a casual wave to indicate he wouldn't be long. He came back with a pair of tan chinos and held them up for me to see.

'I was thinking of something a little–' I floundered, feeling unaccountably faint-hearted now I was faced by the need to make the first decision. Given my own head, I'd have plucked something simple from the rack and got him to wrap it up, then beaten a rapid retreat. Later I would have found it either didn't fit or was somehow unsuitable and quietly slid it to the back of the wardrobe. Then I remembered I didn't have a wardrobe. Which meant whatever I took had better be right.

Thus dresses the modern man.

'Smarter?' he finished for me. 'More formal?'

'Yes. I suppose.'

He shook his head and pursed his lips. He may have moved like Fred Astaire, but he reminded me of my old history teacher when given a wrong answer in the weekly quiz. Harold Bleech, bless his socks. The more lamentable the answer, the more Bleech pursed his lips and shook his head. If the head shaking lasted longer than five seconds the class would fall deathly silent as we all waited. Out of nowhere, like an old western gunfighter, Bleech would produce a wooden blackboard rubber, the missile catching the slow-thinking a swat on the side of the head with a faint thud and a cloud of white chalk dust. It was considered almost an honour to be caught out by him, so dazzling was the speed of his draw and the accuracy of his aim. Ah, the good old days. They don't make them like they used to.

'Not necessary, you'll find, sir,' the assistant advised me. 'The only people who wear ties to parties are the police officers who arrive to break them up. Casual is a great leveller, you see; people don't like to be pigeonholed. Much better to hide behind a vague hint of style, and that way nobody knows if you're a dotcom millionaire or a dustman. May I ask, sir, how long it is since you went to one of these... parties?'

'For ever,' I said. It had probably been fifteen years, but somehow for ever seemed less personally damaging than admitting to a specific and possibly huge number.

'I see. A tad out of practice, then.'

'I'm forty-one, not twenty-one, if that's any guide.' It felt somehow safe breaking the news to a complete stranger I'd probably never see again. I was tempted to tell him I'd never been in practice, but made do with a nod. No reason for me to confess all my failings to him. I snatched the trousers and headed for the changing booth, where I was serenaded by a poor copy of Simon and Garfunkel while I wrestled with my clothes. When I came out I was sweaty, irritated, uncomfortable and self-conscious. More so when I saw the assistant's two colleagues had abandoned their folding and had drifted across to watch their colleague attempting the impossible.

'Oh, goodness, what a nice fit,' the Fred Astaire move-alike murmured, without a trace of irony. He plucked at my shirt, which was white and plain, and turned to the taller of his two colleagues, who were both standing with hands clasped before them like a pair of pantomime dames. 'Chris – I think the charcoal polo, don't you?'

Chris made a pretence of eyeing up my size by pursing his lips, but I could tell he was only playing. He drifted languidly away and returned moments later with a lightweight sports shirt wrapped in tissue paper. He handed it to Fred, who carefully unwrapped it and held it up before me.

'Try this on, sir. So much more a statement than white, I think you'll find.'

'And slimming,' murmured Chris, as if bestowing a blessing.

I disappeared into the booth again and put on the charcoal polo. It was a good fit and I was surprised by the effect. When I stepped outside again, the three stooges were waiting wordlessly. They all nodded approvingly.

Fred was holding out my leather jacket.

'I was thinking of a new jacket, actually,' I told him. Mine wasn't too bad, even among all this brand-new finery, but it had seen better days and had been dragged around the world more times than a ship's rudder. Maybe it was time to consign it to a better life somewhere else.

To my amazement, they all shook their heads.

'Stick with the leather,' said Fred, finally managing to sound camp, and looked to his colleagues for support. 'Don't you think, boys?'

The boys oohed and aahed in unison and fingered my jacket, and before I knew where I was, it was back on me and I was standing before a long mirror, their faces smiling encouragingly in the background like ghosts at a wake. Even I had to admit I looked a hundred per cent better. Well, maybe eighty per cent.

'You can't get leather jackets like that now,' Chris explained wistfully. 'Cheap crap, most of them. I bet you got that one abroad, didn't you?' He fluttered his eyelashes in what I was sure was a piss-take. 'Gran Canaria, was it? Tunisia?' His eyes went big and round and he said softly, 'Don't tell me – Rabat in Morocco!'

'No way,' the third one finally joined in, pulling in his cheeks and shaking his head as if he had a wasp in one ear. 'That's a Kos number, if ever I saw one. Hell, I should know, I've seen enough of 'em.' He smirked knowingly, attracting a warning look from Fred.

'Actually,' I muttered, deciding to bring the Bluebells show to a close before they got carried away and broke out the tap shoes, top hats and tails, 'it was Cape Town. And you lot are kidding me, right?'

Fred smiled and adjusted my collar. 'If you mean about the jacket, sir, not a bit. You look great, I promise. Believe me, no-one will know what you do or – forgive me – how long you've been doing it. But they'll have a good time guessing.' He patted my arm. 'Just don't leave it lying around or you'll never see it again.'

'Thanks,' I told him, and meant it. He could have oversold me twice over and I wouldn't have known. I asked him to wrap up a second pair of trousers and a couple more shirts, and handed him my credit card. Might as well hit it while I could.

'Thank you, sir,' he said, handing me my purchases, and glanced towards the other two, now dismissed back to folding jumpers. 'Sorry about the display. The boys like to have some harmless fun when things are quiet. Enjoy your party.'

TWELVE

'Well, this is it,' said Marcus, eyeing a broad expanse of front garden with a couple of girls standing under a tree sharing a bottle. 'I'm off.'

We'd left his place half an hour earlier and travelled by taxi into the depths of the Kingston/Richmond jungle, finally fetching up at a large house close to the river. The location of the party was marked by an obscenely-arranged bunch of balloons on the lamppost outside and a heavy beat of music pounding through the pavement. The surrounding properties were equally expensive-looking, and I wondered what the neighbours thought of the din. If the people throwing the party had any clue, they'd have issued a street-wide invitation to head off any complaints.

'What do you mean, you're off? We're here to have a good time, aren't we?'

'Too right we are. But not in the same airspace.' Marcus rolled his eyes. It made me feel like his younger, dorkish brother rather than the other way round. 'You're on your own, Jake,' he continued, and glanced at my new trousers and shirt with a look of approval. 'Cut loose, explore. Do your own thing – you're dressed for it.'

'My God, you approve?' I was shocked. Football matches, party invitations, enthusiasm for my clothes: this was breaking new ground.

'Sure. Why not?' He looked at my jacket. 'I thought you were going to buy a new one.'

'I was. But I was persuaded this one has a few miles left on the hip, cool and trendy clock.'

'Shame. I was going to nab it, otherwise. I bags first refusal when you go back to wearing boring suits.'

'Bags all you like, but don't hold your breath. Experts in the trade say this jacket is about as able as it gets.' And for a fashion dropout like me, I thought, that's like being a born-again Christian.

'Yeah, right.' He turned away, barely able to resist flapping his hand as if telling me to get lost before anyone noticed we'd arrived together. 'Anyway, I've got to find this new guy and see if I can squeeze some finance out of him. See you tomorrow.'

'At home?'

'Of course at home.' He laughed, suddenly, sensing my nerves. 'You haven't forgotten how it works, have you?'

I had, actually. There was I, advanced in mind if not entirely in age, like a novice on his first day out from the monastery being offered the freedom of the city. Did I simply charge in, spreading bonhomie and conversation like confetti, or was it cool to slide in and absorb the atmosphere before striking up some idle chit-chat with the first person I saw looking as out of place as I did?

I nearly turned around and went home. I may have been dressed with the unconditional approval of Fred and his boys in Regent Street, but I was still the same person inside and consequently didn't feel right. If it hadn't been for Marcus eyeing my clothes the way he had, I would have bolted for the nearest pub and made do with a stiff drink before I caught a bus back.

Moments later I saw Marcus watching me from a downstairs

window and decided I couldn't let him down. Not without trying, anyway. So with family honour in mind and feeling supremely out of place, I trudged across the threshold and into a world I'd forgotten existed.

The music was loud enough to break eggs.

As I pushed my way through the crowd, I nearly lost it again, fighting a desire to turn and run. Then I saw Marcus through a doorway raising a can of lager in my direction. He was standing in the shadow of a towering, thickset, physical-looking character in a rugby shirt with a face like a punch-bag. I wondered if that was his investor. I waved back and went in search of the kitchen.

As any seasoned partygoer and fan of Jona Lewie knows, in the kitchen at parties is where it all happens.

After helping myself to a drink or two and listening to three blokes with yah-yah accents dishing the sleaze on some unsuspecting acquaintance, I decided to mingle before I lost whatever bottle I'd come in with. I tried three vague and unsuccessful attempts at conversation, repelled one obvious gay youth and finally wound up in what looked like a study, which was as far from the head-thumping music as I could get without being in the street.

'You look bored. Aren't you having a good time?' I spun round from examining the contents of a bookcase and found myself looking at a pretty woman with long, frizzy ginger hair. She had pale skin and the barest trace of make-up, and was wearing a dark green, floaty number which looked as if it was made of silk.

'No, not really,' I said, and felt the temperature of the room zoom up a few notches. Underneath the green dress, which was clinging to parts of her body like a second skin, was a disturbing amount of detail I was trying hard not to notice. And it had been a long time since anyone as attractive as this had asked me whether I was having a good time or not.

'I'm Jane,' she said, and offered me a slim hand with green fingernails to complement the fabric of her dress. Her skin was cool and soft.

'Jake,' I replied, thinking, was it really this easy? It never used to be, and I looked around in case she was confusing me with someone else. Experience had taught me long ago that rarely does the best-looking woman at a party come up and introduce themselves unless they are (a) smashed out of their brains (b) desperate (c) trying to score a point off their boyfriend who will shortly come over and beat you to a pulp or (d) short-sighted to the point of blindness. 'Sorry – I always go through bookcases when I'm anywhere strange. Terrible habit.'

'Not at all,' she said winningly. 'I do the same. I've been through this one already. Nothing much to write home about, I'm afraid.' She drained a glass of what looked like white wine, and I tried not to stare as the dress slithered over the outline of her nipples and down the gentle swell of her tummy. God, I couldn't recall being as aware as this, so close to a woman for... how long? Years. Decades, almost.

'Can I?' I nodded towards her glass, assuming a veneer of cool. A pity my voice ruined it by coming out as a squeak.

'I'd love some.' Her voice was deep, even husky, and with a hint of the Surrey belt about it. Someone's wife? Girlfriend? Significant other? I wondered what she was doing there. And who she was with. 'Dry white, if they have any left.'

I dived into the kitchen, brushed aside the three yah-yahs shouting at each other, slammed in another two glasses of white and was back alongside Jane before the bubbles had time to settle. Unseemly haste, but I blame it on history; I could still remember the pain of what it was like going to replenish someone's glass, someone I thought I'd clicked with, only to find on my return that some other oily git had slipped in while I was gone. In circumstances like that, I'd found, there were no second chances.

'You don't hang about, do you?' She smiled over the rim of her glass with eyes a similar colour to the dress.

'I used to be a waiter,' I said casually, and made a throwaway gesture which pitched half the wine in my glass onto a highly-polished occasional table. If she noticed, she gave no sign and I instantly loved her for it.

'Really?'

'No. I made that up.'

She nodded and studied my face for a few seconds, which I found disconcerting. I wasn't sure I shouldn't whinny and paw the ground.

'How old are you, Jake?' she asked.

And here, I thought, is where it all goes downhill. She's already decided I'm one bottle short of a crate and now she's checking if I'm old enough to be on the registered senility chart. Age. Why does it all come down to that? I'm hardly leaning on a Zimmer-frame, I've got all my own teeth, a good head of hair and I don't have to sit down to pee.

'Forty-one.' Might as well be honest in case Marcus had split on me. Anyway, it was out before I could stop it.

'I'm thirty-five,' she said with a twinkle. 'So what do you do, Jake, when you're not browsing bookshelves at parties?'

'Well, I'd like to say I was an airline pilot or a brain surgeon, but I can't. I usually work in the construction business.' It was sort of true and would do for now. I sank some more wine and wondered how long it would take for her to get bored and wander away. If she did, I decided there and then that I'd probably grab her by the leg to restrain her.

'Usually?'

'Temporarily resting,' I said, 'as actors would say. Redundant and looking.'

She nodded and reached out to flick something off my jacket. It was an oddly intimate gesture, and I suddenly divined that she wasn't about to run off anywhere. 'Snap. I'm in the same position,' she said. 'I just got fired from my job in an art gallery near Bond Street.'

'What did you do – hang a Picasso upside down? I mean, how would one know?'

Someone brushed past and forced her to move towards me, and I felt a firm nipple brush my hand. I nearly dropped my glass and stopped breathing. Who needs to breathe at moments like that? When the other person had gone, Jane stayed where she was, close enough for a trace of warm perfume to invade my senses and close enough for me to see a tiny gleam of moisture on her top lip.

I wondered what she would do if I leaned forward and licked it off, and from down below felt a stirring which I hadn't in any way been prepared for.

'Nothing so mundane,' she replied, looking up at me. 'One of the artists exhibiting there thought I came as part of the facilities. He kept pushing against me, and when he stuck his hand inside my blouse and stroked my breasts, I showed him where he could shove his brushes. The boss decided he could afford to lose me more than he could the artist.'

'Bad luck,' I croaked, trying desperately not to think about hands stroking breasts. Specifically her breasts. The imagery won over, however, and whatever had been in the background – music included – sank into a haze.

She shrugged, an elegant lifting of the shoulders, only this time she was so close I felt, rather than saw, her body move inside the green silk dress.

'Could be worse,' she said. 'Anyway, I prefer to choose who I get bedded by… or who I bed.' She sighed and peered up at me from the corner of her eye. 'Have you… come with anyone tonight?'

Even through the loud music I felt my heart skip a couple of beats. Was that a deliberate *double entendre* or my filthy mind?

'No. By myself.' Covering both bases, just in case.

Jane raised an eyebrow to show she hadn't missed it. Then she took my hand. 'Goody. Let me show you around.' She leaned in towards me and her cheek touched mine. 'Stick very close, won't you? I wouldn't want to lose you in this crowd.'

Not a snowball's chance in hell, I refrained from saying, but it was a close call. Instead I allowed her to lead me out of the study and across the hall, her cool fingers entwined in mine. As we eased through the crowd I felt as if I was being observed, but when I looked around they were all too intent on their own thing to pay us any attention.

Was this a smart move? I didn't care.

We walked up two flights of thickly carpeted stairs and entered an attic room where the music was reduced to a muffled thump. It was a guest room of some kind, with an extending armchair, a bookcase, a drawer unit… and a double bed.

'There,' said Jane, closing the door and sliding the catch with a sexy *snick*. She evidently knew her way around, which made me think she was either the hostess or a regular visitor. 'That's better.' From somewhere on the way up she had acquired a fresh bottle of wine, which she placed on the drawer unit.

'It is?'

She moved against me and suddenly my hand was being pressed against a firm breast and moved around in a softly circular motion, the nipple hard and urgent under my palm. Then she lifted one leg and hooked it around my waist, pressing herself against me like a cat going up a tree. That's when I realised that the only thing under the dress was her.

'What's up, Jake?' she whispered with a grin, breathing into my mouth. 'Cat got your tongue?'

THIRTEEN

Whatever my brain was thinking, the rest of my body was doing its own thing and pursuing an entirely different agenda. It was as if someone had taken a surgical knife and cut off any connection between the two, allowing my physical self to react where I would have expected my mental self to have hauled me up short.

Could this really be happening? Had I scored a home run on my first outing in God knows how long? Was this a wonderful dream and I was about to have the bubble burst with a damp pop and wake up in my own bed?

'Who the hell cares', I heard a part of me say, and responded with all the gentlemanly enthusiasm of an elephant on heat. My free hand developed a life of its own, drifting round Jane's waist and sliding down to cup a firm buttock, delving into the warm cleft of her cheeks and bringing a soft groan from somewhere between our bodies that could have been one or both of us.

Then her mouth was reaching up and pressing against mine, her tongue darting across and between my teeth like a thing possessed. She tasted sweet and soft and fragrant, like warm chocolate with a hint of wine. If I had any senses in action at that moment, vision was the least of them. I relied instead on touch and taste and feel as I found myself drawn towards the double bed.

I stumbled after her, the small voice of caution that had served me so faithfully over the years when faced with what my father had called 'sticky moments', silent and unhelpful. I didn't mind; if it had any sense it was sitting on my shoulder watching the action and hollering approval.

After what seemed like hours, but could have only been seconds, my vision cleared sufficiently to show me that the green dress had mysteriously vanished in a whisper of silk, revealing a glorious panorama of pale, smooth skin, a tiny fuzz of soft, gingery hair and a pair of erect nipples pointing at the ceiling. And beyond them was Jane's smile, her arms held out as I flung aside the last of my own clothing.

'Mmm, nice,' she purred, and grasped the only part of my body which was upright. It sent a tremor right through me and anchored me firmly to the bed. 'Very nice.'

Just then there was a noise as someone rattled the door handle.

Jane froze, her hand gripping me like a vice, inadvertently applying a delaying tactic I'd once read about in Dr Comfort's *Joy Of Sex*. I'd always thought it would fail miserably, given the rampant and unstoppable nature of the male member when sensing victory within reach. But right then it worked like a bucket of ice-cold water, and my ardour disappeared as if by magic.

Jane felt it, too, unwanted visitor outside the door or not.

'Oh, no you don't,' she whispered against me, and gently bit my nipple. Fortunately, she didn't take her hand away but began to move it up and down in long, gentle strokes.

We waited as the handle moved again, then heard footsteps retreating downstairs.

'Oops,' Jane murmured with a faint giggle as she looked down. 'I think someone got distracted.'

'Sorry,' I said, and cursed. *Why now?*

But she appeared not to mind and peered up at me with a wicked smile. 'Don't worry. Nurse Jane's coming to the rescue. We have a procedure for this kind of emergency. Don't go away, will you?' Then she slid slowly down, trailing her breasts so deliberately across my stomach I thought I was going to have a heart attack.

It was like being bathed in soft, warm liquid. I felt the background disappear as she moved her head up and down and did things with her tongue which made me want to howl like a wolf.

A long time later she was back up with a triumphant grin.

'There,' she said. 'The operation was successful and the patient has been revived. Now it's my turn.'

Your turn? Oh, right. Backsies. Seconds later, guided by her helping hands, I moved down her slender body, breathing in her perfume and revelling in the smooth skin of her breasts and tummy. Then someone began making noises like a wounded buffalo in mortal agony... or at least, something close to it. It was me.

'Are you all right?' she asked, peering down at me. I felt her tummy tremble with suppressed laughter, which merely added to my sense of abandonment. Who was it that said sex was a serious business?

My mother had impressed on me that I should never speak with my mouth full, so I made do with a vigorous bout of nodding, which, in view of where my tongue was, quickly had her gasping and rolling her head from side to side.

'*OhmyGod!*' she yelped, and flopped back on the mattress as if I'd slugged her with a piece of four-by-two. Her breasts quivered invitingly as she bucked and moved violently beneath me, thrusting upwards with her hips and using her hands to press my head ever more firmly into her groin. Moments later, at her urging, I moved up her body and slipped inside her while she locked her legs around my back and imprisoned me.

'Wow!' I finally managed, grinning like a six-year-old trapped all night in a sweet-shop. '*Wowbloodywowwowwow!*'

FOURTEEN

It was either very late or extremely early when I staggered down the two flights of stairs and out into the fresh night air. The number of guests was now seriously depleted. The music was a shadow of its former self, too, but as I stumbled along the hallway, I could hear the same yah-yah trio banging on in the kitchen, while a jumble of bodies writhed around the front room like a box of worms, unwilling to let go their grasp of the night's fun. The air smelled vaguely of alcohol, cigarettes and a heady mixture of perfume and something sweet. Whatever it was, it all seemed a lot stronger than in my day.

I bagged a cruising taxi two streets away and was halfway back to Marcus's place before I realised that the sinuous Jane had somehow managed to wake me up and get me dressed and out of the door with the minimum of resistance, as if some instinct had been at work telling me it was time to be gone. It was like one of those dreams where you do everything without being able to fight back. I'd complied without a murmur.

It seemed that Marcus hadn't made it home yet, so I crashed on the settee and tried to make sense of the night's activities. All my wrecked brain could manage to work out was that I'd gone to a party thrown by heaven-knows-who, had wandered about with little chance or even expectation of anything happening, and had met a gorgeous woman who had dragged me up two flights of stairs and had her wicked way with me. Or was it the other way round?

Did I have any feelings of remorse? Shame? Disgust? Not for a second. Then I remembered Susan's words at the tapas bar and the unassailable feeling that I was the one expected to feel the guilty party.

Sod it. I was too tired to cope with the semantics of right and wrong. I finally felt myself sliding into blackness and wondering why I hadn't managed to get Jane's phone number.

When I woke up, the electronic twins were playing their virtual reality game dressed in pants, T-shirts and little else. They were oblivious to my presence, wrapped in their helmets which were issuing high-pitched noises like a swarm of angry bees. Beyond the noise I thought I heard Marcus cursing from the kitchen about some idle bastard not doing the bastarding washing-up.

I joined him, rubbing my cheeks to get back some feeling of normality. It felt a little like the aftermath of a visit to the dentist, and I wondered if the drink had been spiked or if I'd been sleeping on my face. Whatever, I felt like death on a plate and managed to point at the coffee jar in his hand and raise two fingers to indicate my need for something spoon-floatingly strong.

'I'll have some of that,' I confirmed, just to check my mouth was still in working order. 'What's up? You sound cross.'

'Cross? I'm bloody furious,' he muttered angrily, and yawned at the ceiling, showing me his teeth and a furred-up tongue. He looked even worse than I felt, with an unhealthy pallor which wouldn't have been out of place in a mortician's.

'Why? Didn't you have a good time last night?'

'No, I bloody didn't. It was a wash out. Tess didn't turn up and Basher was seriously pissed. And I mean seriously. He was looking for a fight when I left, the bloody maniac.'

Tess? Basher? Who they?

Tess, it turned out, was a girl Marcus had been hoping to see at the party. She'd said she would probably drop by, but in the end hadn't. He'd been keen to get to know her for months, he said, but was fast coming round to the idea that she didn't share the feeling.

'You should have taken her in the first place,' I said, suddenly the old experienced hand at this party business. 'No wonder she's a bit cool, you taking your brother instead of her.'

He shook his head and poured our coffee. 'Yeah, well, it's not that simple. She's kind of involved.' He looked quickly at me. 'I don't mean married – but she has a bloke. Nice guy, too.' He looked gutted by his own sense of dubious chivalry.

Great. First Susan, then me – now Marcus. It must run in the family. Condemned by our genes to be unfaithful or to bring it about in others. Like the Borgias, only engaging in secretive sex rather than cruelty.

'So what about this Basher, then?' I said, changing the subject. 'Who is he?'

Marcus instantly forgot about the involved and untouchable Tess and looked up at the ceiling with an expression of despair. 'His name's John Lyons but everyone calls him Basher. Christ, it was seriously uncool,' he said, his voice dropping to a whisper, as if he was in awe of this mysterious person. 'It was his party, see. He was the bloke I was talking to in the front room – the one who looks like a prop forward.'

'The cash-rich investor you mentioned?'

'That's him.'

'I remember.' I did, too. Thick-set, dressed in a rugby shirt with an upturned collar and looking as if he'd run into the goalposts several times too often. Christ, what was wrong with calling each other John or Peter or Christian or whatever? All that palaver at the font was a waste, otherwise.

'Well, when he holds a party it seems he likes throwing himself into the fun with the lads. The party's for business, right, but he's all for leaving that for later. Anyway, the trouble was, while he was getting off his face with the rest of us, he discovered someone had been upstairs shtupping his wife.'

'Shtupping?' That was a new one. My vocabulary was widening by the day. Much more of this kind of exposure and I'd be able to mingle down there with da kids big time.

'Yeah. Sleeping with… as in sex. Can you believe it – in his own house!' Marcus looked truly shocked, as if the mysterious shtupper had transgressed some deeply sacred law of hospitality whereby visitors to one's house simply did not partake of one's hospitality *and* wife all in the same spirit of freedom.

On the other hand, put like that, it did sound pretty low-level. A bit like helping yourself to a slug from someone else's wine glass.

'How did he find out?' I asked, and forced down a mouthful of coffee. It was thick as tar and just as bitter, and personally, I'd already lost interest in the psychotic Basher, and badly wanted to go somewhere to throw up. It had been a long time since I'd drunk enough to make me feel this bad, and I wondered how many glasses of wine I'd knocked back without realising while under the spell of the languorous and incredibly sexy Jane.

'Someone saw his wife dragging some bloke upstairs and disappearing into a bedroom.'

'Bloody cheek,' I said, barely able to stop myself making a snide comment about how it would never have happened in my day. It would have been a lie in any case, because it would and frequently did. 'You just can't believe some people, can you?'

To my surprise, Marcus looked sideways at me, giving the impression of a leer. Now we were all lads together again. 'Right. Not that I blame him, the lucky bastard. You should see Basher's wife; she's seriously hot. Some of the guys said she likes putting it about behind Basher's back, but I thought it was all talk. I mean, Basher's running a serious business and all that, but they say he's not the sort of bloke to mess with. He comes from somewhere out beyond the Mile End Road and knows a lot of people.' He gave me a kind of knowing look and a nod as if that was supposed to mean something.

'Goodness,' I obliged. 'Beyond the sound of Bow bells? He must be a rough customer.'

'Huh? Oh. Right. Anyway, if he catches this bloke, they reckon he'll bury him in pieces somewhere in Hackney Marshes. Some say it wouldn't be the first.'

I sighed and decided Marcus's feverish imagination had got the better of him. Or maybe this Basher character thought being considered a bit of a gangster was good for business. What a moron.

'Mind you,' Marcus continued with an unhealthy snigger, 'between you and me, I'm not sure I'd say no if Jane asked me, you know?'

Jane? Did he say Jane?

Images of a sensuous body in – but mostly out of – a green dress floated across the front of my mind, followed by the not unwelcome memory of her naked shape thrusting energetically and sinuously beneath me on the guest bed. At least it explained how she knew her way around the house.

Oh, Christ on a skateboard. What have I done?

'Would I have seen this lady around the house, do you think?'

'You must have – unless you were already blind drunk. She was wearing a green silk dress. It didn't leave much to the imagination, either. She's a bit of a show-off, I hear.'

'Right,' I murmured as casually as I could muster, my stomach going into a nosedive. 'I think I saw her. Ginger-ish hair? Pretty?'

He pretended to look shocked. 'You noticed? Hey, I hope you weren't the guilty party, were you?' Then he sniggered as if that was beyond believable and waved an apologetic hand. 'Sorry – just kidding.'

Fortunately, before he saw the look of guilt which must have stitched itself across my face, his phone rang and he went off to answer it. It left me time to compose myself and try to come to terms with what I'd gone through in the space of a few hectic days. Separated, locked out, locked up, financially and socially-ostracised and now the unwitting cuckoo in another man's nest. If I'd been reading about it in the *Daily Mirror*, I'd have been shocked and dismayed by my unseemly behaviour. All I could do right now was wonder if the name Basher was an honorary title or whether he was really as violent as Marcus thought. I told myself if he ever did find out who his wife had been dallying with I could simply deny it. After all, Marcus clearly thought I was way past such a thing.

'It's Hugo,' said Marcus, handing me the phone. 'He's got news.'

I took the phone, glad of the distraction. 'Hugo?'

'Ah. Jake, old boy,' he boomed. Juliette must have allowed him back into the marital bedroom with all his tackle in one piece. 'Marcus sounds terrible. Is he all right?'

'He's fine. Hasn't found hair of the dog yet.'

'Ah. What it is to be young, eh? Mind you, you don't sound too chirpy yourself, old sport. Rough night, was it?'

'A quiet night in, actually,' I lied. 'Thinking about my future, that's all.' Or lack of one, I might have added. 'What can I do for you?'

'Want a job?'

'Of course. Where and what?' I grabbed a piece of paper and a pencil off a side table. A job away from there was sounding more attractive by the minute. The further away the better. With large angry men in rugby shirts and venal lawyers driven by Susan's need for a quick kill, my survival chances were beginning to seem equal to those of a blind, three-legged wildebeest on the Serengeti.

He gave me a name, address and phone number and said, 'Give this chap a call soonest. Charles says he's got just the job for a well-travelled man with a clean passport. Cash in hand and you're as free as a bird to select your own timetable. Suit you?'

'More than you know,' I breathed fervently. It sounded like freedom. Freedom I could manage. And something on which to focus other than destitution and dismemberment.

'Good.' He hesitated, then said, 'Don't you want to know what it involves?'

'Not really. As long as there's some travel and I get paid in real money.'

'Oh, there's travel. Lots of it, if I know Red.'

'Red?'

'Charles' nickname at school. Better not let on I told you, though. He gets a bit sensitive about it.' He sounded slightly sombre at that and I wondered briefly what he was getting me into. On the other hand, Hugo was the least adventurous person I knew. Anything out of the ordinary run of commercial practice would have given him kittens. Even travelling on the Circle Line was something he regarded as an extreme sport. Evidently, this wasn't far enough off the wall to prevent him passing it on to me.

'I'll bear it in mind.'

'Good stuff, old chap. By the way, I'd hold on to that severance cheque if I were you. I could get someone to cash it, but you'd lose too much on the trade. Who knows, if Susan comes round, you might get to keep some of it. Behave yourself, won't you?'

'Too late for that,' I told him. 'And Hugo – thank you.'

I skipped breakfast with Marcus, mainly because he kept going on about the mysterious man at Basher's, and how he was sure he'd end up propping up a motorway flyover if he was ever identified. The idea seemed to give him some sort of perverse delight, and I wondered what he would say if he knew it could be me taking a dive into an East London cement mixer.

'You make it sound as if this Jane woman didn't actually have anything to do with it,' I put in, feeling a little peeved. 'It takes two to tango, you know. She must have been a willing party.'

'I know. But that's not going to help the guilty fella.'

'How come?'

'It's what one of Basher's mates said – right before Basher chucked him through the front window.'

FIFTEEN

I took out the piece of paper with the details Hugo had given me. Charles Clayton, it read, and a phone number. The address was in Mayfair.

I rang the number and a voice remarkably similar to Hugo's answered: just as posh and with a definite vein of authority running through it. 'Clayton.'

'Jake Foreman,' I said. 'Hugo said to—'

'Yes,' he interrupted briskly. 'Come and see me. One hour.' The phone went dead so suddenly it left me wondering if the man on the other end had fallen off his chair.

I trailed slowly across town, stopping for coffee on the way to kill time and mull over the events of the last few days. I enjoyed the coffee but the mulling was fruitless; all it got me was a new level of depression. I eventually arrived outside a Georgian townhouse with black, wrought-iron railings lining marble steps up to a glossy, black door. An entry-phone at head height bore the initials 'CJ'. Nothing else.

I pressed the button and heard the door buzz, then click open. I was puzzled until I noticed the cold eye of a camera pointing down at me. Clayton evidently took his security seriously.

Inside was a run of deep-pile carpet leading up to an antique desk, behind which sat a man who, apart from his natty pinstriped suit, would have looked more at home on a building site. His face was broad and craggy, topped by a severe brush-cut, and he was staring at a computer screen on the desk before him with his meat-like hands resting on the keyboard.

'Go right through,' he said without looking up, and gestured towards a door behind him.

As I passed, I saw the computer screen held a frozen image of myself on the doorstep, and alongside, another image in pale greys showing the jumbled silhouettes of keys and coins in my jacket pocket. Curiouser and curiouser.

I knocked on the door and stepped inside a luxurious office decked out with shelves of books, glass display cases full of silver ornaments and a large desk. I got the impression of quiet good taste backed up by solid money.

Behind the desk sat a good-looking man in his mid-forties wearing a dark blue suit and striped shirt. He pressed a button on a console and ordered coffee, and pointed to a button chair in front of the desk. He didn't offer to shake hands.

'Hugo tells me you've run into a spot of bother, job-wise,' he said, tapping a slender brass paperknife on the edge of his desk. His cuffs were brilliant white and starched, and his fingernails looked as though they had been expertly manicured. It made me feel as if I'd spent the night sleeping rough in Hyde Park.

'Redundancy,' I replied. There is something deeply personal about confessing to another man – an evidently successful man like Charles Clayton, especially – that you are no longer employed, that you have no place on a career ladder and see no immediate sign of regaining it.

It was like admitting to your mother that you'd taken up some deviant sexual practice. Not that I'd ever done that.

'Tough shout,' he commented sympathetically. 'Happens all the time, Jake, believe me. Lots of people working for me have been in the same boat. Military people, mostly, like myself. But it's all the same in the end. A job's a job.'

A few seconds ticked by, during which he seemed to have fastened on another point in time altogether. Then the door opened and the large minder from out front appeared with a tray holding two tiny china cups of coffee, with sugar and cream.

I waited until the man had closed the door, then asked Clayton what the nature of the job might be.

'I run a multi-level security consultancy,' he explained, slowly stirring his coffee with a solid silver spoon. 'One of the levels is a courier service. Small packets, envelopes, that sort of thing – always within hand luggage size and usually one item at a time.' He smiled genially. 'It's a high cost-per-item delivered, but our clients demand the best. We provide it.'

It sounded simple enough. Too simple, in fact. It reminded me of the packages I'd delivered for HP&P which had reeked of illegality. A small worm of concern began to move in my gut. But only a small one. However, I had to ask the obvious question.

'Why send them by hand? Why not by post or FedEx?'

He looked as if he'd been expecting it. 'Because they're high-value items. Too much to leave in the hands of normal services. They're often time-sensitive, too, and need to be delivered when the client says so – not before and not after. And certainly not when Federal Express or UPS happen to have one of their little vans in the area. Problem?'

'As long as it's not drugs,' I said, recalling a line from a film. It seemed a sensible if slightly dramatic thing to say. 'I don't carry drugs.'

'I should bloody hope not, otherwise you won't be working for me.' He fixed me with a cool stare. 'I need absolute reliability, punctuality and self-discipline. Ordinarily, the kind of people meeting those criteria come from a military background, but Hugo assures me you can match them. He rates you very highly. What did you do for your previous employers, incidentally?'

I'd been thinking about how much I could tell him on the way over. With Dunckley's warning still fresh in mind, I knew the full truth would be too risky. But at the same time, I guessed this man would soon pick up on anything less than fact. So I met him halfway, giving him a vague rundown of where I'd spent the years travelling to and from, the sort of people I'd been dealing with at both ends of the line, but little in the way of real detail. He raised his eyebrows once or twice, but said little until I wound up.

He nodded a few times, which meant he either believed me or knew more than he was letting on about my previous work. Hugo, no doubt.

'Excellent,' he said finally. 'You've managed to tell me almost nothing about your former employers, which is fine. I do know a little bit about HP&P already, in any case.' He moved a slim manila envelope around on his desk. 'They're not people with whom I would ever do business... they or their new owners. You should consider yourself fortunate to have been let go.'

That was pretty blunt, and the look he gave me made the hairs on my neck move.

'What do you mean?' Whatever it was it sounded unpleasant, and confirmed my worst fears.

'They have a reputation, that's all I'll say. As for your boss Dunckley, as unimpressive as his appearance might be, he's particularly bad news. I'd advise you to give him a very wide berth, no matter how badly you feel about your... circumstances. You wouldn't come out of it well, believe me.'

'I'll bear it in mind,' I said, and wondered if there was some personal history there, maybe a shared background. I tried to picture Dunckley in military uniform, something I'd never considered before, and suddenly it wasn't so hard to imagine. 'Does the fact that I didn't say much go against me?'

'Not at all. The reverse, in fact. I trust you'll be just as discreet about me. Discretion is a commodity I value highly. I couldn't do business otherwise. Now, I need a trial run.' He slid the envelope across the desk. 'That's got to get to Paris by tonight, eight on the dot. If you give it to anyone but the person whose name is on the envelope, don't bother coming back.'

The change from ex-public-school geniality to cold menace was as scary as it was sudden, and I made a mental note to ask Hugo why Charles had been called 'Red' at school. Maybe it was the colour of the mist which came down over his eyes when he was given a questionable 'out' decision in cricket.

'What if anyone asks what's in it?'

'Like who?'

'Customs.'

'Tell them. Papers. If you're pushed you'll have to open it for inspection, although I'd rather you didn't, frankly. If you do, don't read them.'

'Why?'

'Because then I might have to kill you.' The nearly-smile he gave wasn't even remotely warm enough to convince me he was joking.

As I picked up the envelope he handed me a smaller one which crinkled with a familiar feel. 'Your fee. Call it a goodwill gesture. Do this right and I'll have other deliveries for you. Ring me when you get back. Have a safe trip.' He was sounding almost bored, and I guessed he was already focussing on something else. Now I was on board and had taken his money, anything further was a distraction.

I stood up and made my way to the door. When I turned and looked, he was watching me, a sharp glitter in his eyes. I shivered and went out.

I met Hugo at lunchtime in the pub near his place and told him about the meeting with Charles 'Red' Clayton.

'Good,' he nodded. 'Glad he found you something.' He turned to plant himself between me and the landlady who was lurking nearby with a damp cloth, and lowered his voice. 'Just one thing, old boy. You will be careful, won't you? I mean, I suggested Charles because I knew he could give you something to tide you over. But it wasn't meant to be anything long term. He moves in some pretty mysterious channels.'

'Mysterious? You mean like HP&P mysterious?'

'Yes.' He saw the expression on my face and raised a hand. 'Oh, nothing illegal, I promise. Well, as far as I know, anyway.' He grinned weakly, and I felt the little worm of concern I'd first experienced at Clayton's place growing more assertive.

'As far as you know.' I sipped my drink and waited for Hugo to say something else, but he seemed more concerned with catching the landlady's attention. I tapped him on the shoulder until he looked at me. 'Why do they call him "Red"?'

'No idea, old boy,' he murmured. Then, when I stared at him he continued, 'Really, I don't know. Someone once said it was because

114

his father was friendly with the Russians back in the Fifties – made a lot of money in Moscow, apparently: import-export and so on. Not that he was a commie – far from it. He lost it all when Her Majesty's Government took a dim view of consorting with the enemy and made his life a bit difficult with trade barriers and exchange controls. Charles joined the army and he's managed to do all right for himself since.'

'Doing what? He mentioned security.'

'That sort of thing.' Hugo shrugged. 'He probably got into it via the army, being a familiar line of business, only with a whole new line of customers. I understand it pays rather well.'

I sighed. The old school tie: even the whiff of something faintly unpatriotic wasn't enough to break the connections. Still, if it helped me out of my current dilemma and earned me some money along the way, I wasn't about to complain.

'You sounded awful when we spoke this morning,' Hugo observed, partly, I thought, to change the subject. 'Been up to anything you shouldn't have?'

I looked at him and wondered if his antennae had picked up something or whether he was just fishing. Juliette wasn't the only incorrigible old gossip in the Palmerston household, and I could hazard a pretty good guess that Juliette would try and wrangle any information she could out of Hugo to help Susan.

'Just a headache,' I said.

'You, too?'

'Pardon?'

He grinned wolfishly. 'You said Marcus was hungover, too. Were you two out on the razz together, by any chance?' He snapped his fingers. 'Good God – you went to a party! Marcus took pity on his poor old brother and took him out on the town.' He almost smacked his lips, he was so excited, the question of Charles Clayton and his ethics suddenly tossed into the long grass. 'Come on, Jake – lowdown, you old dog. Did you score?'

'No. I didn't,' I snapped, and discovered that, after all these years, I still couldn't prevent a blush from burning my cheeks at a critical moment. Hugo spotted it and pounced like a tiger.

'You did – you took my advice!' he crowed, attracting the landlady's attention and the ear of more than one of the other drinkers present. What sad lives they must lead.

I gave Hugo a very potted version of what had transpired, leaving out the enjoyable details in the upstairs guest room. I also told him of the subsequent revelation by Marcus that someone – no guesses as to who – had been an unwitting party to adultery with the wife of a serial psychopath.

'You ever breathe a word,' I said heavily, staring him in the eye, 'especially to Marcus, or anyone who even remotely knows Susan – and when I'm found off Beachy Head with a hundredweight of scrap iron tied to my ankles, I'll bloody come back and haunt you and your whole brood.'

'Scout's honour,' said Hugo, holding up two fingers. He'd obviously never been in the Scouts. His family would have been more into prep school and summer camp with the Combined Cadet Forces, but I took it as a sign of faith. 'Won't say a word, I promise.' He smirked. 'Now we're even-Stephens, right?'

'We're nothing of the sort,' I muttered. 'You played hide the sausage with Lorraine – what was it… three times? And while you were happily married. My wife has left me and has already slept with another man. There's no comparison.'

'Oh, really?' He snorted. 'For heaven's sake, Jake, don't be so bloody precious. You've done what thousands of other marrieds are doing every day… every minute of every day. In fact, I bet there's someone upstairs in this place bouncing around on the bedsprings even as we speak.'

We both looked at the landlady and tried to imagine it, but there are things the human brain can't cope with, and we sank some more alcohol instead.

'Thanks, Hugo. You make it sound almost mundane. If it's so casual, explain to me why I didn't indulge much earlier.'

'Beats me, old son.' He finished his drink. 'Maybe Susan was right – you could always be counted on to be faithful. Ever thought that could be boring, too?'

I stared down into my glass and wondered how Hugo could have known what Susan had said to me in the tapas bar. I know I hadn't told him; there are only so many things you tell a friend – if you're a bloke, anyway. And being looked on by one's other half as two points above a faithful old Basset hound isn't one of them.

No doubt Susan had been on to Juliette, exchanging the latest gory details of our sunken relationship, and she in turn had told Hugo, probably with some relish.

'Don't you feel… I don't know, depressed about any of this?' asked Hugo.

'I don't have time. I'm too busy dodging the fickle fist of fate which is doing its level best to flatten me. First the job, then the house, then Susan. Now I'm guilty of shtupping another man's wife.'

'Shtupping?' Hugo looked puzzled, proof that I was at least a step ahead of him in current parlance.

'Think about it,' I said, and finished my drink. 'On the other hand, next time you see Dunckley, ask him – he's the bloody expert.'

He opened his mouth as if to say something, then closed it.

'What?' I said.

'Nothing. Just… be careful with him, that's all. Dunckley, I mean.'

'Clayton said the same thing. What is it with Dunckley? I thought it was HP&P or their new owners who'd have me skinned and pinned on an ant hill if I talked out of turn.' It was certainly the impression Dunckley had given me.

Hugo looked puzzled. 'I don't know about that. But I do know Dunckley's not a man to cross.' He held up a hand. 'Don't ask for details because I don't know any for sure. There've been whisperings that he's got interests outside of HP&P – and that's all I'm saying. Oh, and I suggest you try and make some kind of peace with Susan, if only to save me from an ear-bashing every time I go home.'

It was only as I was walking away down the street that I realised with a considerable degree of confusion that during the entire passionate episode with the lovely Jane, I hadn't given Susan a single thought.

SIXTEEN

I grabbed a seat on the Eurostar and arrived in Paris just before six.

It felt odd after all these years to find myself cut adrift from the twin clutches of work and relationship. I was a bit like a long-term prisoner released from some easy-going institution, now at the mercy of whatever fate decided to hurl at him. Even though I'd been fairly independent with HP&P, there had always been deadlines and targets to be met, which meant I was always under some kind of mental hammer, one way or another. Now all I was under was the basilisk stare of Charles 'Red' Clayton and his requirement that his little envelope be delivered on time, unopened and to the correct recipient. Otherwise find a deep hole somewhere and pull it in over my head. On the surface the job should have been laughably easy; get to the destination, take a bus or taxi, knock on a door at the appointed time, and bingo. What could be simpler?

Only I knew from long experience that something which looks simple on the surface is likely to be booby-trapped with nasty surprises for the unwary. The main one being that nothing this simple could be entirely legal. Clayton's dismissal of established courier services was probably reasonable, but plainly not the whole story. Even I knew that for a fee, a reliable courier service could be hired with little or no delay and delivery guaranteed.

Which meant that whatever I was carrying had an element of risk – evidenced by the generous fee Clayton was prepared to hand over for my services. In fact, money for this one trip was very nearly the equivalent of what I had earned each week with HP&P. Two trips a week and I would be laughing all the way to the bank – albeit not the bank which Susan had so casually frozen me out of.

Feeling like a character in a Tarantino movie – hopefully minus the blood and gore – I checked the envelope and took the Métro to Mairie d'Ivry in the south of the city. The address was in a broad, tree-lined street and looked solid, respectable and about as expensive as you'd want to get in Paris. Evidently Charles Clayton didn't do business with shifty men in greasy vests under railway arches. At least not this time.

At five minutes before eight I found the number and pressed a bell push alongside an entry-phone. There was no identifying name but I hoped I would find the name on the envelope. I took it out and checked it: M. P. Philipet.

'Oui?' A man's voice came through the grill, accompanied by a growl from what sounded like a large dog. I stepped back. Small dogs were okay; big ones not so much.

'A delivery for Monsieur Philipet,' I replied.

'Who wants him?'

The response was aggressive enough to curdle milk. I explained that I had a package for M. Philipet and could only leave it with him. The reply to that was a bleep from the entry-phone and the click of the door opening.

Inside was a passageway, running past a cubbyhole containing a man behind a glass screen. A camera hung from the wall, its unblinking eye staring down at me. I heard another growl and stopped moving, but the man beckoned me forward. He looked hard-faced and tanned, with hands like grabs. The giant Alsatian alongside him looked even less friendly and eyed me with interest. I noticed there was a large flap in the door to the cubbyhole which looked disconcertingly Alsatian-sized. One wrong move and I figured the pooch would be out and all over me like a rat on a dung heap.

'Passport?'

I held my passport against the glass and he scrutinised it carefully.

'Give me the package,' he said, once he was satisfied. 'I will pass it on.'

'Sorry. No can do. My instructions are that this has to be handed by me to M. Philipet himself, no exceptions.'

He showed me his teeth, which were yellow with nicotine. '*Tant pis.* This is as far as you go.'

'Fine. Explain it to your boss. Then it'll be *tant pis* for you – and your dog.' I turned back towards the outer gate. When it comes to games of bluff I have some experience born of years of dealing with petty functionaries.

He must have watched me on the camera feed because I was almost out of the door before he shouted, 'Wait.' When I got back to his cubbyhole he pressed a button and motioned me to go down the passageway towards a door at the end. 'He will meet you in the yard.' He smiled as he said it, and I wondered if this had been some kind of test.

I walked through the door and into an open yard and garden. It was cool and quiet and contained a man standing by a doorway into the building behind.

He was tall and elegant, dressed in a plain, blue suit and white shirt. I guessed he was about fifty, but it was difficult to be certain.

He had glossy, white hair and grey eyes behind frameless glasses, which gave him the appearance of an academic.

'My apologies for the precautions,' he said, holding out his hand. 'But we live in uncertain times.'

I wondered what kind of trade he worked in if this kind of precaution was necessary, and decided not to ask.

'Do you have some identification?' I asked politely. 'Only, my instructions were to give this to M. Philipet and nobody else.' It felt pedantic, but I'd done this too many times before to be embarrassed. Losing the envelope to the wrong person would be the end of my new-found career and would make me an enemy in Clayton that I didn't need.

He smiled and produced a wallet, out of which he took a business card. It was printed with his name in embossed script. M.P. Philipet. Nothing else.

I handed him the envelope and he turned and walked back inside the building. Transaction over. 'Please find your own way out,' he said, as he disappeared.

I went back out past the guard and his dog, reflecting that for the money I'd been paid, people could be as abrupt or as cautious as they liked. And if future deliveries went as smoothly, I wasn't going to complain.

It was already too late to go back to London, so I decided to enjoy the delights of Paris and indulge in a spot of relaxez-vous. First, though, I needed to make contact with someone who would be able to show me the ropes.

I checked my address book and dialled the number of an Australian I hadn't seen in a while, but had shared airport lounges with on many occasions. John Crane worked for a Singapore-based engineering conglomerate and had lived in Paris for twenty years. He was loud, opinionated, very often drunk and not the sort of person to take home to meet your mother. Which made him just the sort of company I needed.

'Stone the crows, mate,' John blurted forty minutes later, splashing a jug of red wine into two very large glasses. 'Thank Christ you rang me when you did. I was going stir-crazy.' He gulped down half his glass and slapped his thigh with a meaty hand. 'This bloody thing's really pissing me off. Nicole reckons I should be chained to a bed until it heals, but bugger that for a game.'

Nicole was his French wife, an endlessly tolerant woman with a heart of gold, and the 'thing' in question was a broken leg, encased in plaster from the thigh down. I noticed he had a knitting needle poking out of the top, no doubt for use when itchiness became intolerable.

'Skiing accident,' he explained. 'Took a black run by mistake and hit one of them – what d'ya call em – moguls. Went up in the air like a rocket and landed like a sack of shit. Poles one way, skis the other, head up my arse. They had to bring me down on one of them stretcher things with ropes. Bounced me around like a bastard all the way down. Never felt a thing, though.'

'The shock?'

'Nah. Pissed as a rat. Only way to ski, in my opinion… saves all that keepin' the legs bent thing they always go on about. Drink enough and it comes natural as breathing. So, how ya doin', Jake? I heard you got dumped by the shaggin' badgers.'

I started off by giving John the abridged version, until the wine began doing away with my natural reticence and I told him about Susan as well. They had met once or twice when he was in London, but he was way too blunt for Susan's sensibilities and they'd never really hit it off. I think she'd found him oafish and obscene. Even so, he was genuinely sorry.

'Jeez, mate, that's a shame. So what are you doing over here – making up for lost time?' He grinned dirtily and jiggled his eyebrows.

'Working, as a matter of fact.' I told him about my temporary assignment, which caused his eyebrows to knit together. 'It'll do until I can find something more permanent.'

'Or until you get locked up,' he said bluntly. 'I've heard of outfits like that before, Jake. They transport anything that can't be sent by regular mail only because it's illegal. I'd steer clear of any sniffer dogs if I were you. Talking of which.' He looked across the bar we were sitting in, just off La Concorde, at two unattached ladies who had been hanging around in an obvious manner for the past ten minutes, trying to look as if they'd landed there by accident. The light wasn't that good, but they looked as if they liked to work out two or three times a week on heavy weights. I figured they were either serious health nuts or aerobics queens on a night off.

'What d'you reckon?' he asked.

'I don't,' I said. They looked a bit over-seasoned to me, and I wondered why on earth he was showing interest in women on his own patch when Nicole, a beautiful French blonde, was only a few streets away. Tolerant she might be, but if she caught even a hint of him fooling around, a busted leg would be the least of his problems.

'You'd be right. They're Romanian army deserters – and I don't mean from the women's section. Take a walk with them and you'd end up with your equipment spread out on the banks of the Seine and whistling *adieu* to your credit cards.'

I took another look and got a wink from one of them which sent a shiver down my back. Jesus, things had got really bad if I was getting a come-on from a Romanian transvestite.

I ducked my face into my drink and said, 'What's the alternative?'

'Hitting a couple of drinking dives I know. I need to dull the ache from this leg and you need to do likewise for your wounded pride. There's only one way I know of to do that.'

'Right behind you, brother,' I told him, feeling myself being dragged down and unable to do a thing about it.

SEVENTEEN

I arrived back in London next morning with most of my fee intact and my head stuffed with cotton wool. John had been as good as his word and led me into a world of basement drinking clubs where people went to forget for a short while whatever was plaguing them. Then he'd poured me into a hotel and allowed me to get some sleep while he went back to fight best-of-three with Nicole, whom he belatedly told me he'd forgotten to inform about our evening together. Fortunately, I wear a reasonably distinctive aftershave, so she wouldn't think he'd been consorting with undesirable women.

I remembered to call Clayton from the airport, and when I got to his office he handed me another envelope with another payment. He raised an eyebrow at my pallid appearance, but made no comment.

'This needs to be in Frankfurt by six this evening,' he said. 'The person you're to give it to will meet you at the airport – the details are in the envelope with the money. If you make it quick you can probably get back on the return flight. Do you have a phone?'

'Sure. Why?'

Clayton opened a cupboard and tossed me a small Nokia. 'Use that. In case I need to contact you. It's cleared internationally. I'll pick up any personal calls as long as they're not too unreasonable.' He nodded and drifted back into his office, leaving me to be escorted out by his tame bouncer.

I flew to Frankfurt airport and was met by a heavily-moustachioed gent who introduced himself as Willi. He had the impressive gut and flushed cheeks of a seasoned beer drinker, and steered me through a crowd of excited meeters and greeters into a corner where we exchanged identification and I handed him the envelope. Then I returned to London and found a cheap hotel in Bayswater to wait for Clayton to call me again. I debated going home to join the hippy commune, but decided I could do with some peace and quiet for a while; after two trips and a mammoth drinking session, I was beginning to feel my age.

I rang Hugo the following day and he agreed to meet for lunch – my treat – just off Piccadilly. He turned out to be in an odd mood.

'So,' he greeted me, sinking a rapid gin and tonic and calling for another. 'How goes the world of secret parcels in shady places?'

'I can't talk about it,' I told him seriously. 'If I do, I'll have to kill you. How do you know what I'm doing, anyway?'

He shrugged evasively, which made me wonder how much he and Clayton might be talking together. I'd never have put Hugo in the same area of operations, old school tie or not, but one never knew.

'Susan came round the other night,' he said, changing the subject. 'Wanting to know where you'd disappeared to.'

'Which you, being my one and only true friend and confidant, didn't tell her, of course.'

'I couldn't, could I? Juliette got a bit sniffy about it; she thought I was hiding you somewhere.' He looked hurt at the implication.

'Was that all Susan wanted? No heavy lawyer type following her with writs and so forth?' If I knew Susan like I knew Susan, she wasn't going to let sleeping dogs lie. She'd rather they were well and truly woken up and baying at the moon.

'Well, if there was anything else, she wasn't about to tell me. I'm contaminated by association. I left her and Juliette plotting and went for a drink.'

'And?'

He looked at me. 'What?'

'Unless you're on pillow talk rations, you usually know everything Juliette knows a few minutes after she knows it.'

Hugo sighed heavily. 'Well, the thing is, old boy, I think Susan's really got her dander up. She was pretty upset after your chat the other day and your unwillingness to meet her halfway. She says you've basically given up on the relationship and forced her hand. I know, I know.' He held up a conciliatory hand. 'I'm only telling you what I hear. It sounds as if Susan intends to nail you – fair or unfair. I mean, what can you do?'

'Plenty,' I muttered. 'Present a moving bloody target for one thing. Better than waiting round for the axe to fall.'

'Is that wise?'

I didn't know was the short answer. Probably not. But since the chances of me coming out of a fight with anything but a small part of the house and proceeds and a severe bruising in the process was infinitely small, I might as well fight for pride if nothing else.

Hugo, as it turned out, had other things on his mind.

'I'm beginning to wish I'd never got you involved with Charles Clayton, if the truth be known.'

'Why?' I said. 'I'm big enough and old enough to know what I'm doing. Anyway, I'm quite enjoying it.'

Hugo looked amazed. 'How can you be enjoying it? It's not a career, for God's sake. It's delivering iffy packets to iffy people you've never met before in obscure corners of the world. It's so...' He struggled to find words for something to which he'd originally given the all clear on the basis of his old school tie. And therein, I figured, lay the problem.

'Dodgy?' I finished for him.

'Yes, quite. Dodgy.'

'Well, of course it is, Hugo,' I said. 'I didn't spend years coming up against slush funds and backhanders without gaining some insights. But maybe that's what I enjoy about it – the faint whiff of danger after all these years of being so bloody strait-laced.' Or deluding myself that I had been, I thought. Maybe boring and strait-laced were stable mates, bestie pals on the road to nowhere exciting, and I'd never noticed.

'But you had danger with HP&P, didn't you? I'd never go near some of the banana republics you used to visit. Your bloody insurance premiums must have been appalling. Did you know Matheson in Accounts went across to Latin America last week and got himself kidnapped? One of the government departments they had a contract with decided they didn't want to pay, so he went to browbeat them on orders from Dunckley. Poor bugger was lucky to come out with his balls intact, I gather.'

I pictured Matheson and recalled how he'd once been responsible for losing a project, when he'd called into question the financial status of a certain oil-rich African state on the grounds that he had never heard of it. 'Unlikely,' I said. 'Matheson never had any to begin with.'

Hugo smiled grimly. 'You're probably right. He said he'd talked his way out of it, but it didn't sound quite gen. Anyway, what's this sudden taste for danger you've developed?'

'I don't know,' I confessed. 'Second childhood, mid-life crisis. Haven't you ever had a yen for doing something risky?'

'Risqué, certainly. I wasn't born into a family of risk-takers, Jake. My forbears believed in taking the long-term view, like the Chinese. All to do with the family line, you see. Lines can be broken by thoughtless acts of bravado, according to my grandfather. Very selfish when you've got responsibilities.'

'What did he do for a living?' I asked, and refrained from pointing out that several illustrious British families were littered with risk-takers, most of whom had helped build the Empire.

'He was a lawyer. Made a mint and bought land.'

Hugo made it all sound so simple and accessible. If anyone was to research my family line, they wouldn't get too far back before it broke up into dots and wandered off the page. The Foremans had made a habit of moving around a lot – probably to keep a step or two ahead of people like Hugo's grandfather, the legal land-grabber. Just as I was considering doing right now. It almost made me proud to be continuing a fine family tradition.

'So what are you going to do with your new-found wealth? I bet Charles is pretty generous with the loot, isn't he?' Hugo's question was casually put, but I thought I detected more than a grain of real interest.

'I haven't thought about it. Anyway, I haven't got that much. I bet you make more in one day's share transactions.'

He flipped a card across the table at me. It was for a hotel in the Lake District, on the edge of Derwent Water near Keswick. It read 'Social Weekends. Relax in comfortable surroundings with people of like minds and interests. Special rates available.'

'What's this – are you adding pimping to the family interests?'

He looked hurt. 'I say, old boy, steady on. That's a bloody fine hotel, I'll have you know. Owned by friends of mine. It was merely a suggestion… in case you needed to get away for a bit.'

'How thoughtful of you,' I said coolly. 'But if I want a bit, I'd rather choose my own place to get away to and find it, thank you very much.'

After leaving Hugo to get back to work, I pottered around a bit, kicking my heels, until I found myself down in the wilds of Richmond. I tried telling myself it was by accident, but at the back of my mind was a small, insistent voice which had been asking me a question ever since the night of the party: had it all been for real? If so, was that it? Nothing else to look forward to but baked beans on toast and memories?

Well, I couldn't very well ask Marcus; he'd have a fit. So there was only one way to find out.

After years spent in taxis travelling to out-of-the-way places, I'd developed a habit of subconsciously memorising routes. It was part of the survival gear I'd found necessary to ensure I always came back in one piece. It took me just a few minutes to find the street and wander past the house where the party had been.

I debated a frontal assault by knocking on the door and hoping Jane was the one who opened it. But when I saw a large, gleaming BMW parked on the drive alongside a sleek little sports saloon, I had an attack of the cautions and recalled the appearance of her husband, Basher, and Marcus's description of his volatility.

Instead, I hung around in the area until I saw Jane emerge and walk along the street towards where I knew were some local shops. I set off in pursuit, feeling like a stalker and hoping a local

Neighbourhood Watch person wasn't already dialling the police and reporting a furtive character in the area.

Jane was in jeans and a sweater, dressed for comfort rather than elegance, yet still managing to out-do several other young women in designer wear. She had that air of casual gloss which some women never lose, and I followed her to a small supermarket, a baker and a delicatessen, and enjoyed watching her move those long, elegant legs. I also experienced an unsettling surge of memories of her guest room, and forced myself to clear my mind before I ended up walking with a limp. Somehow I didn't think Richmond would welcome a middle-aged man lurking in the area with an obvious sign of excitement for all to see. Just as I was preparing myself to tap her on the shoulder, she turned in the middle of the pavement and gave me a quizzical look.

'Jake, isn't it?' she said, making my chest pound. God, she was lovely – and she remembered me.

'Hi,' I said, pretending surprise, and failing. 'Jane. How are you?' What I wanted to say was 'Any chance of a re-match?', but I figured that would be a bit crass.

'I'm fine. I didn't realise you were local.'

'I'm not. I happened to be in the area,' I lied. 'Would you like coffee?'

She considered it for a moment, then nodded cautiously. 'All right.'

We eased into a coffee bar where there wasn't a person under seventy, and I placed our order while Jane found a table away from the entrance. Was this how people did it? How easy it was to slip into the role and subterfuge of an adulterer! Stolen moments in mundane locations, with one eye on the door in case Mrs Jones from number thirty walked in.

I looked at Jane across the table and saw her eyes were actually hazel, rather than green. But she was still beautiful, with a magnetism even daylight couldn't hide. For a swift second, remembering the other evening, I wondered indelicately how many other men had faced her across a table and had the same thoughts.

'So, did you get lucky?' she asked, unwrapping a sugar cube and nibbling away at the edges with perfect white teeth.

'I thought I did,' I said with a grin, thinking of her on the bed in the guest room.

She half smiled in a gently reproachful way, suggestion that I was a naughty boy for bringing it up. 'I meant your job. That's why you're down here, isn't it? Looking for a job?'

It brought me back to earth with a jolt. She wasn't supposed to bring reality into the conversation; reality was cold and unwelcome and boring. I was still somewhere above ground level, my subconscious basking in an attack of self-satisfied smugness after getting a home run on my first foray into the field. We had shared something special, I was thinking, and I'd rather continue with that than consider the ordinary and everyday.

'Not really,' I confessed. 'I came down hoping to see you.'

'Really. Why?'

The coolness of her tone had me flustered. This wasn't how it was supposed to go. I wasn't expecting her to fling herself into my arms, exactly – although it would have helped. But surely she didn't mean to be so aloof?

She pushed away her coffee untouched and glanced towards the door, and I realised she was still holding her purchases in one hand, as if she'd merely paused for a few seconds amid the pressing tasks of a busy day. Her stance reminded me of the look of a small, delicate animal about to take flight, and I felt a sudden surge of mortification at the idea that I'd overstepped the mark and was actually frightening her. Then it hit me with all the force of a sledgehammer: she wasn't scared of me – she was embarrassed by my presence! I was a factor in her day that she could have done without. Like an leak in the bathroom.

'It was fun,' she said calmly, further killing off any wild ideas I might have had about taking our intimate interlude any further. 'But that's all it was, Jake. We met, we had fun. There's nothing else.'

It was surprising how so few words could do such an efficient hatchet job on any dreams I might have harboured, and I instantly wanted to be away from that place, preferably in a deep, dark hole where nobody could see my face. Was this what people referred to as a man's mid-life foolishness? Fooled into chasing after a young, attractive woman and failing to recognise that there was nothing to be gained by it save huge, mind-numbing embarrassment?

She stood up and stepped away from the table. 'Sorry, Jake – I can't stop. Good luck with the job.'

Then she was gone, leaving me like a deflated balloon, lost in the humiliation of my own making and just a whiff of her perfume hanging in the air to remind me she'd ever been there.

Smart? I'll say it did.

EIGHTEEN

As if by some sort of celestial interference, jobs from Clayton began coming thick and fast after that, and whatever cringing self-pity I might have dragged back from Richmond after Jane's rebuff soon died on the altar of flight timetables, plastic meals and the near comic-book, furtive exchanges of ID and documents.

After a few trips it even became mundane, and the round of cities faded into a blur of half-remembered faces, names and strange impressions. I met Willi in Frankfurt twice more, the last time, at his insistence, in the rear of a sex shop in the Arrivals hall – a dubious national advert, I'd always thought. I'd noticed the place several times over the years, located by the official meeting point, but had never seen anyone entering. Not once. Yet when Willi ushered me through the door, it was packed with men browsing, their travel bags and briefcases at their feet and one eye cocked – if that's the right word – on the departures screen on one wall next to a life-sized inflatable doll. I wondered how they had got in there, and if there was a special entrance accessed, like the First Class lounge, on production of one's boarding pass, only with copies of *Hustler* available instead of *Fortune 500*.

'This is bloody good shop,' Willi informed me knowingly, proudly surveying the shelves of blue videos, magazines and sex aids. He nodded with obvious familiarity to the bearded giant behind the counter, who steered us through a plastic curtain into a back office. 'You have same in England, ja?'

'Ya,' I agreed, stepping carefully over a broken box of inflatable strap-on breasts. 'Not quite so out in the open, though.' The thought of a sex shop opening right opposite the Arrivals door at Heathrow was a bit of a stretch. But it was nothing like the surprise I got when I handed him his envelope, and he reached into a box behind him and slapped a giant rubber penis into my hand. It was a lurid pink and purple and covered in veins, and looked like something I'd once seen hanging underneath a shire horse when I was a kid. My brother and a couple of his friends had spent ages flicking small stones at it until the horse had tired of the game and trotted away, its lengthy appendage swinging back and forth.

I gave Willi his toy willy back, and he looked crestfallen. 'You don't like?'

'If it was my own, I'd be delighted,' I said. As I left the shop a trio of nuns went by. The looks they gave me should have scorched my socks.

Some days you can't do anything right.

I returned on three more occasions to see M. Philipet, during which I managed to hand over the envelopes without having to fight off the huge dog. In fact we became quite good friends. A Señor Fuentes lurked in morose and sinister fashion in Madrid on four occasions, reeking of strong tobacco and accompanied by a large helper who insisted on patting me down and checking my bag every time. A small, neat Frenchman named Gustav darted up to me on two occasions in Nice, identified himself and took the envelope I had for him, all without saying a word. And a Belgian named Ruyncke, with two assistants hovering in close attendance, waited for me in the multi-storey car park at Brussels airport and made no attempt to look anything other than furtive. With the collar of his black leather coat turned up and a cigar hanging from his lower lip, he looked like a character from an old Jean Gabin movie.

It was a pale reminder of my old job visiting hospitals, sewage plants and bridge projects in out-of-the-way places, and I wondered how many other similar jobs there were out there, being done by individuals like me, all trotting around the globe with mysterious and apparently innocent little packages for strange and secretive clients.

The packages themselves, in sealed envelopes, felt like A4 papers, with the occasional memory stick in a jiffy bag. Whatever they were, I was neither curious nor desperate enough to pry under the flaps. Having seen at close quarters some of the people I was handing them to, I needed no warning to keep my fingers to myself.

It was after my second delivery to Gustav on the Promenade des Anglais in Nice that I discovered I was being followed.

Nice being the kind of place it was, it seemed criminal to go there and not take a stroll along the famous seafront now I was in no particular rush. Having spent years going to places where doing the tourist bit was neither encouraged nor safe, I handed the silent Gustav his packet, watched him dart away like a minnow in a stream and decided to walk in the direction of Monaco to take in the sights and some sea air before heading for the airport.

As I turned, a man coming the other way did an abrupt about-turn and slammed into a Lycra-clad jogger running diagonally across the promenade. Amid the yells of pain and flailing arms and legs, I couldn't help but note the man who'd caused the accident. He was of medium build, wearing a business suit, and had a florid face and a thin moustache, with a slight kink in one side which could have been caused by an accidental slash of a hasty razor. He picked himself up, muttered to the stunned jogger, who'd now got a severe case of promenade rash on the kneecaps, and bustled away towards the centre of town. He seemed unaware that he had a strip of fabric hanging from the side of his trouser leg where the concrete had torn it.

'*Espèce de con, va! Idiot!*' yelled the jogger in true subtle Gallic fashion, with a pumping clenched-fist gesture in case anyone was in doubt about his feelings. He looked round for support, but when he saw none was forthcoming he clambered to his feet and limped away at a half-jog.

Thirty minutes later, as I wandered through the narrow backstreets back towards the town centre, I noticed a familiar figure in the reflection of a silver-backed window display. He was lurking about fifty yards behind me in the doorway of a pizza restaurant. The strip of fabric hanging from his leg was too much of a coincidence for it to be anyone else.

At first I dismissed it. He probably had business in the area. Like me, perhaps he'd fancied a stroll along the front until his unfortunate collision with the jogger. But when I saw him a third time, loitering on the other side of the street when I came out of a shopping mall, internal alarm bells began to shrill.

I'd harboured no illusions about what I was involved in. Delivering small packages with strict instructions about whom they should be handed to, the proviso being that I shouldn't return at all if I made a mistake, was evidently not normal business. I'd argued with myself on several occasions about how illegal they might be, and managed to convince myself each time that they were innocent. It wasn't as if I was transporting little plastic bags of white powder or diamonds; nor was I hefting a Russian AK47 down my trouser leg. But who was I kidding?

Were they technical plans? Commercial blueprints? Design specifications? Product information? Anything was possible.

True, I'd heard of papers being soaked in a drug solution for extraction later, but since these envelopes seemed perfectly ordinary and not airtight or protected against airport sniffer dogs, it seemed unlikely.

I made my way back to the airport and, within minutes, spotted my follower lurking near the check-in desk after I'd gone through. He evidently didn't want to risk getting too close to me in such a restricted area. I lost track of him on the plane, then saw the damaged trouser leg sticking out from a seat several rows ahead of me. Whoever he was, he wasn't being overly subtle. Maybe he was just lousy at his job.

As soon as we landed and cleared immigration I found a quiet corner and rang Clayton.

'Are you sure?' No denials, no incredulous laughter; just a calm, steady request for confirmation.

I told him about the incident on the promenade and spotting the man again in the town centre and on the plane.

'It does seem more than coincidence,' he said blandly, as if discussing the authenticity of a piece of fine antique furniture. 'Can you see him now?'

'No. He hasn't shown up yet.' Unless he'd handed over to somebody else, I thought.

'Okay. Leave it with me. Well spotted. You'd better keep your head down for a couple of days. I'll call you as soon as I have anything else.'

'Is there a problem?' I asked.

'Like what?'

'Could he be official?'

'I doubt it. He's probably working for one of Gustav's competitors. He may have picked you because you were a new face. Don't worry – it happens.'

Not to me, it didn't, which was why I was worrying. Being followed by strange little men isn't part of my normal routine. It made me wonder if he was nothing to do with Clayton or Gustav at all. Perhaps he'd been employed by Susan's solicitors to find out if I had gainful employment and therefore some income they could latch on to.

I rang Hugo and asked him, in case pillow talk had been exchanged.

'No idea, old boy,' he said unhelpfully. 'Juliette hasn't said anything. Why – has someone in a dirty mac been taking compromising piccies of you?' He chuckled as if being watched was his idea of a boyish prank.

'Not exactly.' I told him about the incident on the promenade at Nice.

If I was expecting support from him, I was disappointed.

'Told you, old son,' he muttered quickly, his voice dropping to a conspiratorial whisper. 'You should stop doing that delivery stuff – it's not safe. This fellow watching you might have been Inland Revenue… Customs and Excise or whatever they call themselves nowadays. Christ, Jake – they could even be the anti-terrorist squad! They could lock you up and chuck away the key!'

'Thanks a lot for that, Hugo,' I told him. 'But I got this job through you, remember? One of your old school pals? The old alma mater? Not what you know but who you know?' It was a little ungrateful, turning it back on him, but I was beginning to feel isolated, like someone pronounced stricken with a disgusting and extremely contagious fever and not to be approached unless wearing rubber gloves and carrying a very long stick.

I rang Marcus, who at least was friendly and interested in where I'd been. We met up in a burger bar off the Strand and faced each other over weak coffee and greasy food. I watched him squeeze ketchup over a giant burger and take a bite. He chewed for a few seconds, then looked at me.

'Are you OK?' he asked.

'No, I'm not,' I sighed. I didn't like bringing him into this but there seemed to be no other option. 'Is Susan having me followed?'

NINETEEN

'Really? You mean by a detective?' I could have sworn he looked almost excited at the idea.

'Christ, I don't know – I didn't think to ask him for his card!'

He shook his head, shedding pieces of lettuce and bun-crumbs on the table. 'But why should she do that?'

'Money,' I said bluntly. 'Someone's been dogging me, that's all I know. I thought it might have been Susan's idea.'

'She's definitely pissed off with you, I can tell you that. After your chat the other day she said as far as she was concerned you'd burned your bridges.' He shrugged. 'But she also said there couldn't be another woman because you haven't got–' He stopped and looked down at his burger, stopping short of a faux pas. I felt sorry for him. Being caught in the middle and watching two people galloping away in opposite directions couldn't have been fun.

'Haven't got it in me?' I finished. 'Haven't got the balls?' I tried not to sound bitter but it wouldn't come out any other way. Some things just set you off, especially having your manhood called into question.

He nodded. 'Something like that.'

'Well, don't you believe it,' I said defiantly. 'I may not be in the Action Man class, but I'm working on it.' I gave him a sanitised version of what I was doing for Clayton and some of the odd characters I'd met, although I didn't mention where I'd been or my suspicions about what I might be carrying. 'But that stays between you and me, okay?'

He looked at me as if he was seeing a different person. 'Bit of a change of pace, isn't it?'

'Well, it's not a long-term career, but it has its moments.'

'But why? I mean, why not go back to your old work? There must be other firms out there you could approach, people who know you.'

'I've thought about it. But right now there's nothing I'd like less. Maybe Dunckley was right; we're a dying breed and computers are taking over.' Big mistake; thoughts of Dunckley reminded me that Susan was now sharing his bed, and I felt a burning indignation rise up at the thought that the devious toe-rag, even while he was giving me the elbow, was probably thinking about her. Oddly enough, though, the idea of them together no longer rankled the way I'd expected.

'I saw him the other day.' Marcus looked gloomy. Clearly he wasn't in favour and I felt a rush of gratitude. It would have been unbearable if he'd found even a grain of interest in the slithery little bastard. 'He was at the house.'

'Our house? What were you doing there?'

'I dunno... just happened to be in the area and went for a look.' He picked at a piece of limp lettuce and dropped it on his plate. 'I saw them – him and Susan. She was trying to get those squatters evicted. They'd called the police to get them out on the grounds they'd caused damage and forced their way in. But the police weren't having

143

much luck. Some big Aussie was standing in the upstairs window laughing at them. It was a real carry-on. Dunckley was making threats and trying to come over all manly and in charge, but it didn't seem to have any effect. Mrs Tree was shouting about refugees taking over the country.'

'They're Kiwis,' I corrected him absently. 'From New Zealand. The big bloke's name is Dash. He has a girlfriend called Dot. They're just passing through. I doubt they'll be around long.'

'You know them? I wouldn't have thought they were your sort.'

I smiled, suddenly pleased at being able to spring another surprise and shake his perception of me. 'Well, that was then. This is now. Seen 'em, met 'em, liked 'em. I even said they could stay a while. It'll keep the house aired, at least. They made me my very own coffee mug for when I come calling. And I can contact them on the internet. They're nice people; you'd probably get on well with them.' I made a mental note to warn Dash off tangling with Dunckley; as big as he was, if Clayton's comment about Dunckley was true, the young Kiwi could find himself in trouble.

Marcus had a vague smile beginning to dawn on his face. I wasn't sure what it conveyed, but at least he wasn't scowling any more. 'You're enjoying this, aren't you?' he said eventually, with a tone of wonderment. 'I mean, I've been waiting for you to be all depressed and wanting to go out and get off your face. But you're not. I thought breaking up was supposed to be hell… and that I'd have to be talking you out of wanting to chuck yourself off a bridge somewhere.'

'What's the point? Susan made her choice, and on reflection I can't say I blame her. Anyway, what good would it do for me to wear sackcloth and ashes or to top myself? Besides, I can't stand heights. And if you mean I'm enjoying my change of direction, well, I suppose

I am in a way. Not what brought it about, though – that's not fun.' I wondered if he'd feel the same admiration if he found out I was the phantom intruder into Jane and Basher's relationship, however brief and unintentional it had been. That thought prompted another.

'How's things with your friend Basher? Has he found out who was with his wife yet?'

Marcus shrugged, uninterested. 'I don't know. It all got a bit boring and dramatic in the end. He even went and hired a private detective. I think he's nuts.'

'Detective?' I felt my bowels contract as a cold shiver went through me, and wished I hadn't mentioned being followed earlier. If Marcus put two and two together, I was done.

'Yes. Some bloke from Acton who specialises in surveillance work. Basher says he's had the man watching Jane for a while now.' He finished his coffee with a frown. 'Which is really odd, because I spotted her in Piccadilly this morning.'

'What was odd about it?'

'Well, I spoke to Basher at lunchtime, and he said this private snoop was following up a lead he'd picked up. But he can't be following Jane at the moment because he said he'd just flown to France. Somewhere down south, I think Basher said. Was it Marseille or Nice? Nice – that was it.' He smiled dreamily. 'Always wanted to go there. Casinos, the Promenade des Anglais, sun, sea and beautiful women – what more could a bloke want?'

A deep hole to hide in would be good, I thought.

TWENTY

As soon as I could get away I rang Clayton and asked him if he had any jobs lined up. It seemed suddenly prudent to be off and doing somewhere rather than hanging around waiting for Basher's private stooge to catch up and put the finger on me. I didn't think I'd look very good propping up a motorway, and adding to the methane in Hackney Marshes would play havoc with more than just my sinuses.

'I've got plenty,' he said. 'Are you free and clear?'

'Sure, why not?'

'Okay.' He paused and I heard the keys of his computer clicking in the background. 'I've got a delivery for a place on the Dutch coast, near The Hague. Scheveningen. Do you know it?'

Oddly enough, I did. I'd been to a conference there once, on land reclamation. It was a small seaside resort much favoured by the Dutch, and was virtually a suburb of The Hague. Ideal if you liked brisk winds fresh off the North Sea, it boasted sweeping sands and a smattering of good restaurants for the clean-living burgers of Den Haag, or the not so clean-living conference delegates who weren't allowed anywhere near the fleshpots of Rotterdam.

'Good,' said Clayton. 'Come round tomorrow morning and the

package will be ready for you.' He hung up in his customary fashion, and I took it as a good sign that he hadn't raised the question of stalkers in torn trousers. Far be it from me to confess that it may have been Basher's man following me in France; I had a feeling Clayton may not have taken kindly to a divorce snoop elbowing in on one of his transactions by mistake.

After a night in a local hotel, I collected my car from the garage, then drove to Clayton's place and picked up the package, along with brief instructions about what to do. I flew to Rotterdam, where I picked up a taxi for the short drive to Scheveningen. The roads were busy but flowed smoothly, and if anyone was following me, I didn't spot the same car more than once.

I examined the envelope on the way, which felt as if it contained either A4 sheets of pasteboard or even acetates – the sort used for overhead projector presentations. Written on the envelope was the name of the conference centre – the Kursaal – where I was to meet someone who would identify himself as Rik Heysens.

The resort of Scheveningen was quiet and upmarket, with an air of calm that was at odds with the city of Rotterdam not far away.

The atmosphere inside the Kursaal was steady, well-heeled, with small knots of people enjoying sophisticated coffee or an early lunch. A snooty-looking man in a penguin suit was playing a piano in the bar as if the whole thing was beneath his capabilities, and if there was a single suit among the patrons which came off a peg or a dress which wasn't handmade, I didn't spot it. Whoever these people were, they wore their wealth comfortably.

I ordered a drink and waited, wondering how furtiveness would go down in this plush joint. On the other hand, maybe some of the world's most sensitive deals were hammered out in places just like this, where they were least expected. In between sips I scanned the people already there to see if anyone was watching me. Clayton had told me to wait until Heysens made the approach, which meant the man must have a good description of me. Then I recalled the camera above Clayton's front door. He'd probably been sent a photo. It put me at an uncomfortable disadvantage, but at the rate I was being paid and as a way of getting out of London for a while, I was happy to go along with it.

Ten minutes after I arrived, a tall, slim young woman breezed up the stairs and walked in my direction. She was dressed in tight, black leather trousers which squeaked rather fetchingly with each stride, and a leather jacket which set off her long blonde hair. The way she sashayed over on high-heeled boots raised the temperature in the place by several degrees, and more than one male diner was brought abruptly back to earth by a sharp comment from a female companion. Even the pianist managed to hit a bum note as she passed by, which warmed me to him no end.

'Are you Jake Foreman?' she asked me. Her accent came as a surprise: Newcastle through and through.

'That's me,' I said, and stood up. She still topped me by at least an inch,

'Rik says you're to meet him at this place in thirty minutes.' She handed me a slip of paper with the name of a hotel on it.

'Why the change, pet?' I asked amicably and felt a twinge of apprehension. So far I had never been asked to go anywhere other than the locations stipulated by Clayton. This was a change of plan, albeit small.

The girl shrugged elegant shoulders. Up close I could see she had brown eyes and that blonde wasn't her original hair colour. 'No idea – sorry. It's a ten-minute walk down the other end of the promenade.

You can't miss it. Room one-eight-two.' She glanced at her watch, which looked as if it might have set her back a few hundred euros or sterling. 'I make that eleven on the dot, so don't be late… pet.' Then she turned and squeaked away, leaving a faint aroma of perfume hanging in the air.

I sat down and finished my drink. I was now the focus of attention for everyone in sight, and wondered whether Rik Heysens had intended to draw attention to me in this way or whether he was simply careless. Or innocent. I went outside and down onto the sand, and strolled towards the far end of the resort, turning occasionally to see if I was being watched from the promenade. If there was anyone there, however, they kept themselves well out of sight.

There were a few people taking the air and stretching their legs with earnest vigour, and I wondered what it was about the Dutch that made them so different. If this had been Scarborough or Margate the place would have been infested with screaming kids and stressed-out mothers smoking their lungs into a state of wrinkled leather, while the dads would have been propping up a bar or chucking their money across the counter of the nearest bookies.

The hotel the girl had indicated was sitting high over the promenade with a prominent view of the beach, and just beyond the busy area which included the seafront boutiques and cafes. I walked up a concrete ramp and found the reception area busy with several men in suits all chuntering quietly to each other and getting in everyone's way. Since none of the reception staff seemed available, I decided to go up to the room unannounced. I skirted the crowd of business types and took the back stairs. It might not be good protocol or whatever Clayton and his types might call it, but it was better than being late.

I was just coming up to the third floor and breathing heavily when I heard shouting from above, followed by the slamming of a door and the clatter of footsteps coming down the stairwell. Whoever it was seemed to be in a hurry.

I flattened myself against the wall as a large, red-faced individual flung himself round the bend in the stairs, using his hand on the rail to slingshot his body in a 180-degree turn, his feet barely touching the treads. When he looked up and saw me there, his eyes nearly popped from his head and he ran past shaking his head and mumbling, 'No. No. No!'

Then all hell broke loose as more footsteps sounded behind him, and a man's voice bellowed down the stairs in Dutch. Something told me it wasn't his personal fitness coach telling him to keep his knees up and not to forget to breathe.

I turned and followed the runner, betting on my instincts and hoping they were right. By the look on the man's face he had recognised me, which put him down as Heysens or someone closely connected to him. Quite what the fearful shaking of the head was all about was a puzzle, bearing in mind we were supposed to meet any time now. Maybe if I kept on his tail I'd find out.

He hit the bottom door like a torpedo and burst into the reception area, scattering visitors like ninepins. Two of the men standing in a huddle near the check-in desk promptly turned and jumped on him, waving badges and proving that the Dutch police force encourages its officers to watch too many American cop shows.

Fortunately, they were so busy with their prisoner they failed to notice me following him stealthily out of the stairwell, and I was able to sidle up to the check-in desk and buttonhole one of the staff, who was staring transfixed at this slice of life going on under his nose.

'What's going on?' I asked. 'I thought this was a quiet hotel.'

He nodded, staring between me and the wrestling match, now augmented by the pursuer from the stairs, a short, stocky man in a suit who pitched in with flailing handcuffs and helped subdue their prisoner.

'It is, sir,' the receptionist said eagerly, switching into PR mode. 'This is most unusual, I promise you. We are not having this kind of thing going on here. Not at all.'

'So what's he done – stolen some towels?'

He didn't answer for a moment, cocking an ear to something the stocky cop was saying to the prisoner. Then he shrugged and looked back at me, a fatalistic expression on his face. 'He has been arrested, sir. For forgery. You know – making bank notes? That is a very grave crime here in the Netherlands. This man's name is Heysens. He is being asked where is the–' He searched for the correct word, then clicked his fingers. '–Where is the film of the templates he was waiting for to be delivered here at the hotel.' He listened some more and looked shocked. 'But the man is not telling them, sir. No, he is not a happy man, I think. He is saying they should all fuck off to bloody hell!' He looked pleased with himself at being able to give me such a literal translation, then remembered he was supposed to be shocked as any good citizen would be. 'Now, sir, what can I do for you?'

I shook my head. 'Thanks. If it's all the same to you, I'll find somewhere less exciting.'

As I stepped out of the front entrance, Heysens was being loaded into a cop car, with a surprising number of 'customers' clapping each other on the back in a 'Nice one, mate', sort of way. It reminded me that I had in my possession, if the receptionist was correct, film copies of some banknotes which would be enough to have me join Heysens in the back of the police car if he said anything.

Discretion being the better part of valour, and not wishing to give Susan the pleasure of hearing I'd added international financial crime to my list of offences against womankind, I beat a quick retreat and headed for the nearest taxi rank.

Clayton had some explaining to do.

TWENTY-ONE

By the time I made it back to London my nerves were fried. I was constantly looking over my shoulder expecting to feel the heavy hand of Interpol, Europol, HMRC, MI5 or the Salvation Army. If not them, it would be someone brandishing Basher's credentials and a return invitation to his house for another party which I knew wouldn't be as much fun as the last time. I had a sense of what it was like to be a double agent, used by both sides, trusted by neither and eventually buggered by both.

I drove round to Clayton's place and handed him back the package, and described what had happened. He seemed fairly nonplussed and merely tossed the envelope into a drawer.

'Occupational hazard,' he said casually. 'It's the kind of business Heysens is in.'

'Which is?'

Clayton gave me a look which said 'do me a favour'.

'It's up to the client what they want us to do next. As long as you weren't implicated you have nothing to worry about. Leave it with me and I'll sort it out.' He flicked through a small book, then gave me a keen look. 'I know what you're probably thinking: that we transport stolen, illegal or otherwise prohibited goods between certain individuals. Well, we certainly transport goods in the way of papers or

153

electronic data, but there's nothing illegal about what we do, you can take my word on that. Now, you've been to the States, I believe?' The speech was over and it was back to business. Oddly enough, I felt relieved. Whether I believed him or not was another thing altogether.

'Several times. Have you got a trip there?'

He nodded. 'Coming up any time. But you've got to be clean. No past misdemeanours on American soil, I take it? No unpaid bills or charges for possession of toxic substances?'

I confirmed I had never misbehaved on US soil, which promptly set me thinking about whether it would have made any difference to Susan's view of me if I had. Probably not.

'Good. Their immigration people only need a whiff of something and they'll have you listed and be waiting for the next time you hop back over there.'

The queues for ordinary, innocent visitors waiting to go through immigration in the States were legendary. Their officials were so rigorous in their form filling it seriously made you wonder if they really wanted anyone to go back there. Polite, though, I had to give them that. When they wished you to have a nice stay, they actually sounded like they meant it.

'Can you hang loose for a couple of days?' said Clayton. 'I'll call as soon as I have the package and details.'

'I think so,' I said, and decided I needed to go to ground somewhere. Preferably somewhere quiet and remote from London. I looked at his desk and had an idea. 'Do you mind if I use your PC for a second?'

'No. Go ahead. I'll be back in five.' He strode out, leaving me to slide behind his desk and pull up the keyboard to his computer.

Half an hour later I pulled up outside my house and sat there for a while, watching my rear mirror. Immediately after leaving Clayton's place, I'd got a distinct feeling of being watched and, after a few tentative Bond-like turns down back-doubles, I realised I was being followed by a small, dark anonymous car of Japanese design which had now nosed into the kerb at the end of the road. I sighed, recognising a familiar silhouette. It looked like the man from Nice had come back. I wondered if he'd had his trouser leg repaired.

I looked at the house. It felt an age had passed since I'd last been there. The community bus had gone, leaving a deep imprint in my border, and the front door still needed repairing properly, but otherwise it was pretty much as I'd left it. There was no sign of Mrs Tree and her aged posse, although I didn't doubt she had me in her sights and was logging my arrival.

In the end I walked up the drive and knocked on the door. The only way of avoiding her was to skulk along a footpath at the back and hop over the rear fence like a thief in the night, but I was damned if I was going to let her inhibit my movements. If the old biddy decided to come out, so be it.

A wan girl of about fifteen opened the door in answer to my knock. She was dressed in baggy trousers and jump boots, and her upper body was wrapped in what looked like half a sari of the most vivid orange. She stared at me with big eyes for a moment before holding the door open in invitation.

'You must be Jake,' she said simply, her accent the same as Dot's. I wondered if her father was a lawyer, too.

'That's me,' I said. 'How do you know?'

She shrugged. 'I just know things.' Then she walked ahead of me into the kitchen and picked up my mug from the sideboard. It was full of hot coffee. Freshly-made, too, by the smell of it.

'Did Dot tell you about me?' I was trying to recall what I'd said last time I was there, and wondered whether this girl was on something. She certainly seemed a little odd. Maybe she was psychic.

She shook her head. 'No.' Then she reached into her sari top and fished out a key on a silver chain. 'You'll be needing this to get your things. Oh, and there's this.' She opened a drawer next to the sink and handed me a pile of mail bundled together in a rubber band.

I must have looked at the key with dumb blankness, because she rolled her eyes. 'You sent an email to Dot saying you wanted to get some clothes? She had to go out, so she asked me to look after you.' She giggled and disappeared, so I went upstairs to the bedroom, where I found a large padlock and chain on the wardrobe, guarding my possessions.

I grabbed more socks, pants and a couple of shirts, then checked through the pile of mail. There was one thick, expensive-looking, cream job which instinct told me was the result of Mr Sweaty's threat at the tapas bar. I could do without reading that right now. The rest were bills and reminders, junk mail and flyers. I noticed there were none for Susan, and concluded she must have put an intercept on them, leaving me with all the brown stuff. Surprise, surprise.

I stuffed everything in the wardrobe and went back downstairs, where I found Dot sitting on her perch in the kitchen, grinning her wide open smile. She was wearing a long, shapeless smock with Batik flower motifs, and the customary big boots.

'Hi, you!' she said, and jumped down to give me a big kiss. It was as if I were her long-lost brother come back from the wars, instead of someone of very recent acquaintance and decidedly differing background.

'Hi, yourself,' I said, and felt pleased at being on the receiving end of such open affection. 'Thanks for looking after my stuff.'

'No sweat.' She looked at my coffee mug. 'I see Miz looked after you all right, then?'

'Miz? Oh, you mean... yes, she did, thanks. Even down to the coffee being just the way I like it. You've got a good memory.' I handed her the key and chain Miz had given me.

'Memory?' Dot looked puzzled. 'I didn't tell her. She has this thing... you know. She knows things without anyone saying. Didn't she mention it?'

'I thought she was pulling my leg.'

'No way. She's serious. But, hey – a pity she wasn't here the other day when your wife came round. Jeez, what a snooty bitch! Can that lady yell up a strop, or what?' She looked sheepish and touched my arm in apology. 'Heck, I'm sorry, Jake – that wasn't nice of me. I guess you still love her, and here's me badmouthing her.'

I thought about it for a few seconds, like I'd been thinking about it on and off for a while, ever since Susan had stormed out of the tapas bar. 'I do a bit. But there's no need to apologise. And if it's any consolation, you're right – she can yell up a storm when she gets her temper up.'

A shadow loomed into the room, thankfully ending that particular topic. It was Dash.

'Hiya, mate,' he said cheerfully, and slapped me on the back, re-arranging one or two vertebrae. 'How's it hangin'? Did Dot tell you about your wife comin' round and slaggin' us off? Boy, is she a screamer? I tell you–'

He grunted as Dot elbowed him in the ribs, then looked crestfallen as he caught the warning look on her face. 'Oh, mate, I'm sorry. Christ, I've got a mouth. No offence, huh?'

I shook my head and smiled, wondering how it was I'd managed to get through life without having forged some friends like these. Whatever their lifestyles, I couldn't fault their honesty and good intentions, and it struck me that I'd become closer to them in just a couple of meetings than I was to many people I'd known for years.

'No problem.' I told him. 'But there's a way you can help me.'

'Name it,' he said fervently. 'Anything.'

I took him to the front of the house and pointed towards the car at the end of the road. 'See that car? He's been following me around all day. When I leave here I'd rather he didn't.'

Dash gave me an excited grin, as if I'd just proposed setting fire to the Houses of Parliament and introducing a new World Order. 'Sheesh, mate – what've you been up to? Sorry – my big mouth again. I didn't ask that.' He clapped his big hands together and thought for a second, then nodded and produced a mobile phone. 'It'll take me five minutes. Can you wait that long?'

'No worries. But no violence, understand? I just need you to get in his way until I'm gone.'

'Easy-peasy. He won't even know it's happening.'

I left him to it and went to say goodbye to Dot and Miz and finish my coffee. Then I went out to the car and waited for Dash to give me the thumbs up.

A few minutes later the familiar shape of the community bus ground round the corner and chugged along the road, laying down a curtain of exhaust fumes that would have choked a cow. As it drew level with the waiting car carrying my follower, there was a loud bang and the front wheels suddenly veered sharply to one side. It skewed across the road and wheezed to a halt, completely blocking the car from our sight... and more importantly, us from his. It was neatly done and looked nothing like the deliberate act it obviously was.

Dash appeared at the side of my car with Dot in tow. 'All clear, Jake,' he grinned, evidently enjoying the conspiracy. 'We'll hold him for a couple of minutes, okay? Better put your foot down.'

'You're a wizard, Dash,' I told him. 'You can stay here as long as you like.'

'Cheers, mate – that's real sweet.' He looked at Dot, who looked faintly wistful. 'But some of the guys are talking about moving on. Maybe to France for a while, or Spain. We don't want to overstay our welcome.'

'I'm sorry to hear that.' I was, too. They were a breath of fresh air. 'But best of luck to you.'

'It's time we moved,' Dot agreed. 'It's been great here, but we can't stay for ever. But you keep in touch, Jake, right?' She looked at Dash for support, and he nodded vigorously and pounded my arm in a surprising if clumsy show of affection. It was like being thumped by a friendly gorilla.

'Too right, or we'll bloody come find out why!' He grinned and stepped back. 'You'd better scarper before your friend figures out what's going on.'

'I'll do that,' I said. 'And keep my coffee mug safe. I might catch up with you one day and want to use it.'

TWENTY-TWO

Clayton called and told me to come round. The US trip had come up earlier than expected and he needed me. Now. I dropped what I was doing, which was staring at four walls, and headed to his office. Being on the move was a relief and promised some action that might stop me sinking into depression.

'This one's important, Jake,' Clayton told me as soon as I arrived. He ushered me into his office and poured coffee from a silver vacuum jug. On the desk alongside the cups lay a brown envelope, like so many of the others I'd delivered for him. The address was written in a careful hand: Gus Mekashnik, 184 Cedar Point Road, Lake Lure, N. Carolina. It was followed by a flight number and time. 'Your ticket's waiting at the airport.'

'Fair enough.' I picked up the envelope. I'd never been to Carolina, north or south; to me it was simply a spot on the map somewhere in the middle of the US.

'Mekashnik lives near a small town called Lake Lure. Quiet, splendid scenery, so I'm told, about eighty miles west of Charlotte, North Carolina. Not exactly on a major highway, if you get my meaning, but don't let the backwoods location fool you. Mekashnik's as sharp as a tack and didn't get where he is by sitting on a porch all day whittling sticks and chewing tobacco. Don't hang about: get in, drop the package and be on your way.'

A worm of anxiety squirmed in my gut. I'd felt it before more than once and was fast becoming accustomed to it. But this was the first time Clayton had given me what was, in effect, a warning. It was also his longest speech yet, prompting me to break an unwritten rule and ask a question.

'What does he do for a living?'

Clayton looked surprised, but I managed to stare back without flinching. If he was sending me into a situation where he felt I ought to be careful, he at least owed me some honesty. He put down his coffee and paced over to the window, as if deep in thought. Then he turned and looked at me as if it was decision time.

'That's a fair question,' he said quietly. 'I should have mentioned it, sorry.' He walked back to his chair and sat down again. 'Gus Mekashnik sells guns and other... materiel.'

I must have looked surprised, caused by hearing the inflection he placed on the second 'e' in materiel. I knew enough to know that meant military equipment. Clayton gave the ghost of a smile and explained. 'To use the correct term he's a federally-licensed firearms dealer, and he's been at it for a long time. I think he's somewhere close to the top ten in dealers in the US, if it helps. Does that make you feel better?'

'So he's legit?' It at least made me feel a little safer. Not the fact that he dealt in weapons of death, but that he was regulated by the US Government. I figured there was a chance there had to be some kind of controlling influence there. You take what comfort you can in these situations.

'Well, he doesn't deal out of the back of a truck in alleys, if that's what worries you. I've never met him, but our paths have crossed on occasion. He's a businessman like any other. The only difference is, you want it, he'll get it – for a price.'

'Like Harrods.'

He didn't even blink. 'I wouldn't know.'

'So who does he sell to?' For some reason I got a picture in my mind of the crazy doomsday militia groups and survivalist gun nuts who camp out in the hills, pick up their automatic weapons as they get out of bed and drive armoured half-tracks for fun.

'I didn't ask. Everyone has the right to bear arms – it's in their constitution and selling guns is a legitimate profession. I did hear he recently began trading overseas because there's been a drop in sales since Trump came in, although how long that will last is debatable. He's also rumoured to have personally disposed of at least four men who crossed him.'

'*What?*' My Adam's apple did a double bounce, a result of speaking and swallowing simultaneously. What the hell?

'Apparently he buried them in more than four locations.' He waited blank-faced for a couple of beats while I worked out the maths, then smiled. 'I'm pulling your leg.'

I opened and closed my mouth, relieved and confused at the same time. So Clayton had a sense of humour? Good to know, but there's a time and place. I looked at the delivery envelope and wondered what was inside it. Papers, by the look and feel of it. But what kind of papers could Clayton be delivering to an arms dealer? And what did it say about Clayton himself?

'Before you ask,' he said, 'I have no idea what the documents in the envelope might be. This is a delivery on behalf of a client and we're simply the intermediaries. As I said, if you don't want this one, please say so. I've never believed in sending a man out to do something he's not happy with.'

I believed him, and with all that information, such as it was, I already knew I would still go through with the delivery. What the hell else was I going to do – sit there in London and wait for Basher to catch up with me? Even so, a tiny voice in my head told me I'd finally lost whatever limited grey matter I might have possessed. I wasn't sure if I was driven by pride, obstinacy – or plain stupidity – but whatever it was, I was in. A part of me wondered what Marcus would say if he knew. I was concerned about that. I already knew what Susan would say – and found I didn't give a damn. Wow. Look at me – a new man.

'Right,' I said, and stood up. 'I'll do it.'

He nodded, and I got the feeling he wasn't surprised. In his business he must have got very good at reading people. 'Good man. To be honest, I'm not sure who else I could have asked if you'd decided not to go. My other people are all tied up.'

I'd wondered about that. In a business relying on people, I figured he must have other couriers like me, roaming the globe with parcels for faceless persons in faraway places. You don't get to sit behind a smart desk and pull strings without having some kind of regular income.

'Even Francis?' His assistant seemed perfectly capable and looked as if he could chew the wheel nuts off a moving truck without blinking. And he made great coffee.

He shook his head. 'Francis is an amazing man. He's intelligent, resourceful and doesn't know the meaning of fear. I've seen him in action in Afghanistan, among other locations, and there's no better man to rely on in a fight. But when Francis walks into a room everyone knows what he is and what he does and reacts accordingly. That can be useful in certain situations but not this one. People like Mekashnik like to feel top dog at all times, and Francis has a way of causing their hackles to rise. It's not his fault, it's the way he is.'

He didn't add anything, and I figured out the rest for myself. Francis could intimidate people or fight his way out of trouble if he had to. The Gus Mekashnik delivery required a less obvious approach: a talker rather than a fighter. Right up my alley.

'I can live with that.'

He smiled and reached into his desk drawer and handed me two white envelopes. 'Good man. There's a bonus payment up front.'

'Danger money?'

'There's no such thing. Call it an inconvenience allowance – for the extra time and distance travelled.'

I pushed the second envelope back across the desk to him. I figured I could trust him, which was a long way from where I'd first come in. Right now I didn't have time to arrange a new bank account and didn't want to carry around more cash than was clever. It would be handy to have something waiting for me when I got back.

'Hold it for me, would you? Hugo will know where to send it.' I winced as I said it. It sounded absurdly dramatic, as if I was going over the top of some far-distant trench into the jaws of death.

But Clayton didn't seem to notice, or if he did he kept his thoughts to himself. He slipped the envelope into a drawer and gave me a half smile with a hint of genuine warmth. 'That's not a problem. Have a good trip and keep your head down.'

TWENTY-THREE

One-eight-four, Cedar Point Road turned out to be a large colonial-style house covered in white clapboard, and surrounded by about two acres of rough lawn dotted with a few bushes to break up the view. It lay on a side-road leading up into the Chimney Rock State Park near Lake Lure, a spit from the Pisgah National Forest in North Carolina's southern Appalachians. It must have taken a lot of hard work to hack it out of the dense woodland, which spread across the undulating slopes like a thick coat of fur as far as the eye could see.

After touching down at Charlotte airport and weathering the steely questions from US immigration, I'd hired a 4WD Blazer and taken a relaxed drive west past Gastonia and Forest City and out on Route 74 towards Asheville. Two hours after leaving the airport, I discovered the satnav had lost all trace of the address. I stopped three times and discovered that the locals didn't know where my destination was and plainly couldn't care a whole heck of a lot either. I drove slowly along a winding lakeside road until I came across a small bunch of dusty shops and one restaurant-cum-fast-food joint. The name over the door read 'Cappy's Diner', and promised home cooking just like Momma used to bake, as well as the lure of a free trail map with every purchase over two dollars.

Since Mekashnik wouldn't know what time I was arriving, I figured I had time to smell the coffee and see if Momma knew how to bake a cake or whether she was lying through her cotton-picking teeth.

I waited while a couple of tourists from somewhere further north finished ordering enough food to feed a small army, and gave my order to a grizzled character standing behind the counter arranging some flapjacks. I guessed this must be Cappy. He was surrounded by plastic containers of scones, biscuits, cakes and other assorted goodies, proving that even if Momma couldn't really cook like they did at home, she certainly had some kind of production line going. He nodded sleepily and said, 'Sure. Take a seat.'

By the time he came over with my coffee and jumbo maple-syrup flapjack, two locals had drifted in, wearing plaid work-shirts and baseball caps, and both on the high side of sixty. They had the same grizzled air of the great outdoors about them as Cappy, with hands like shovels and eyes squinting into the distance like Marlboro Man. They nodded silently to Cappy and gave the rest of us doubtful looks, then parked themselves on high stools at the counter. The way they eased themselves into position made it look like they'd been using the stools since they were old enough to jump.

'Mekashnik,' I said to Cappy, as he placed my order on the table. 'Do you know where I can find his place?'

He squinted at me and cocked his head slightly. 'Say what?'

'Mekashnik,' I repeated. 'Cedar Point Road. It's around here somewhere, I think, but the satnav doesn't know where.'

There was a squeak as both the men at the counter turned on their stools and stared at me. My question had carried in the quiet room, and they were watching Cappy to see what he was going to say. Maybe this was what amounted to excitement in these parts. Ooh, a lost tourist!

Cappy shook his head and wiped away an imaginary crumb. 'Nope. Can't say I do.' Then he turned and walked away, flicking his cloth as he went. I had the feeling that if there had been a spittoon in the corner, he would have filled it. He was lying, of course.

The two locals continued staring at me as if I'd passed wind, then turned lazily on their stools and muttered between themselves. In old westerns, this would have been the point where the honest townsfolk would have had a meeting and demanded to know what the mysterious stranger wanted. Then the local Black Hat would have strode in and gone for his hog leg.

I bit into my jumbo flapjack and thought kind thoughts about Momma. She knew how to bake all right. A pity she hadn't taken a hickory stick to Cappy's butt when he was knee-high to a grasshopper, and taught him some manners at the same time.

I saw a local map on the next table and scoured it for Cedar Point Road. If it existed at all it had to be right in this area, but I couldn't see any sign. If Cappy's clipped response was anything to go by, Gus Mekashnik must have upset the locals so much they'd excommunicated his address, if that was possible. It made me wonder why a man dealing in weapons at Mekashnik's supposed level would want to live out there in the middle of nowhere. Did the locals – who were probably fairly keen on Sunday prayer meetings – know what his business was?

I finished my coffee and left the diner under the steady gaze of the three men, and wandered along the street to a small wooden building with a 'U.S. Post Office' sign outside. This should be the best place to get the information I needed. I walked inside and found it wasn't anything like post offices in England, merely a room full of mail boxes and a large bulletin board covered in local notices, with no staff in evidence anywhere.

When I stepped back outside I found one of the grizzled workmen from the diner waiting for me.

'You're lookin' for Mekashnik's place, I hear.' he said. He had a large lump of something in one cheek and looked about ready to spit whatever it was out on the road. I got ready to duck in case his aim was off.

'That's right. Do you know where it is?'

He nodded and jerked with his chin back along the road in the direction of Charlotte. 'I figure you came from the airport. Go back the way you came towards Forest City for about a mile, then turn left up a side-road. There's a sign pointin' to a Forestry depot… that's if it ain't fallen down again. That'll lead to Cedar Point. Mekashnik lives about two miles along on the right. Fancy big place – you can't miss it.'

How many times have I been told that before and driven right past a place? I thanked him for the information. 'How come Cappy didn't know?'

He frowned. 'Who?'

'The man in the restaurant.'

The light dawned, and he almost cracked a smile. 'That's ain't Cappy… that's his son, Norm. He and Mekashnik don't get on so well. That map you were lookin' at? He prints those for customers. He deliberately missed out Cedar Point just to piss him off.'

'Why don't they get on?'

But he'd obviously gone far enough in helping me. 'You'd have to ask him that,' he said, and turned and walked away along the street.

I climbed back into my rental car and drove back along the main road until I came to the turning into Cedar Point. It wasn't so much a road as a narrow, metal track, and by the twin trails of bark, mud and twig debris on the surface, the Forestry workers were the main users. I only saw two vehicles on the way – both pumped-up Toyota pickups covered in bumper stickers and driven by young men wearing high-crowned baseball caps and vague, *hi, y'all* smiles.

I passed one property with locked gates and a melancholy air of desertion about it, and continued on for a good quarter mile until I spotted a wire fence which led me to a large pair of wrought iron gates on rollers. It all looked very old and weather beaten, but I guessed the construction was probably no more than five years old – it had that carefully-designed look about it.

Out front was a standard mailbox on a pole, the kind with a little plastic or metal flag so you could see if anything had been delivered. The body of the mailbox had been drilled with an ominous-looking hole, like the sort you see in westerns or on war reports about Kabul.

I thumbed the button on the entry-phone built into one of the stone pillars and waited while the insects and heat and silence settled around me like an itchy blanket. If this was humidity, I'd seen worse, but I couldn't recall when it had affected me more. Maybe it was all the trees hemming me in or the flight from London finally catching up with me. Somewhere in the distance I was sure I could detect the sound of running water, which made me feel even hotter.

'Yeah?' A reedy voice came from the entry-phone, sounding bored.

'Jake Foreman to see Mr Mekashnik,' I announced, and wondered if they would allow me to take a shower or point me towards the nearest lake where I could throw myself in for a week or two.

'Who?'

'Jake Foreman–'

'No. Who're you lookin' for?' Now the voice sounded testy, as if I'd spoiled an afternoon nap with some damn-fool question about a house owner who was most likely down at the next property, anyway.

'Mr Mekashnik. Gus Mekashnik.'

'Oh. Gus. Hell, why didn't you say so? Are you the guy from England?'

'Yes.'

'Good. C'mon in.' There was a buzz and the gates began to trundle slowly back on their tracks. From somewhere nearby came the hum of an electric motor.

I drove slowly up the curving drive, admiring the lawns the way I was supposed to and wondering where the owner had buried the bodies Clayton had mentioned. After two minutes the drive opened out into a turning circle, and I stopped in front of an impressive plantation-style house with rows of windows and a clapboard front. Twin pillars stood guard either side of marble steps leading to a gleaming black door mounted with a huge scroll-shaped knocker made of brass. Or was it burnished gold? Whatever – it was bigger than any postman back in London would have cared to lift.

As I stepped out of the car a man appeared at the side of the house and waved a tired hand. He was carrying a pair of shears and wore canvas gardening gloves. Under the weathered baseball cap clamped on his head he was burned a deep tan and looked about ninety, but by the way he moved I guessed he was in his sixties.

'Hey-up, young fella,' he greeted me, and beckoned me to follow him round the back. 'Gus said you was comin' and to see you wuz settled 'til he gets back.' His voice was as reedy in the flesh as it had been over the entry-phone. 'He's out seein' some people 'n said for you to wait. I'm Frank, by the way.'

I told him that was fine, and on the way round the side of the house asked him about the mailbox with a hole in it.

'That's from a point-two-two long rifle,' he replied shortly. 'A squirrel gun. Some dumb kids have been goin' round drillin' mailboxes. Less brains than a squirrel, most of 'em.' He gave me a knowing look. 'I guess that don't happen much where you come from, huh?'

'Not so much,' I told him.

The windows of the house were all blanked off by curtains pulled across to cut out the light. It gave the effect of a house deserted by the occupants, although plainly that wasn't the case. Obviously Mr Mekashnik liked his privacy – although who was going to spy on him out in this wilderness was beyond me.

We arrived on a vast patio bordering a fifty-foot swimming-pool, overlooked by a double set of French windows and, above them, a balcony with an identical set of doors, all with drawn curtains. I was reminded of the house and pool in *High Society* – the one where Grace Kelly fenced around with Frank Sinatra before opting for Bing Crosby. If all this opulence was a guide, Gus Mekashnik's business was doing very well.

Upholstered loungers were scattered around the patio, while in the pool itself an inflatable version with sunflower motifs drifted lazily in the faint movement of air across the surface. Off to one side was a barbecue bay big enough to roast a small elephant.

In the background, beyond a ghastly faux-summerhouse, more lawns and the odd flower border, the garden extended into a thick belt of trees which rose up a slope for about half a mile before meeting the sky. I couldn't see any signs of a fence, so guessed Mekashnik owned all of it.

'There's drink 'n stuff on the table,' said Frank, pointing with the shears towards a patio table standing in the shade of the house. 'You fancy a swim, go right ahead – there's towels there, too. Won't cost you nuthin'.' He laughed at some private joke, his face creasing up like old, soft leather. 'I gotta go fetch the boss, so you'll have to pour drinks yourself. Don't go in the house, though, y'hear?'

This last sounded like he meant it, so I nodded. He pottered away, swinging the shears and humming. Moments later I heard a car start up and speed away down the drive, and I was left with the sound of the pool pump clicking away and the trickle of a small fountain at the far end of the patio.

I dropped my travel bag by the table and poured myself some orange juice, allowing a few ice cubes to drop in as well. Then I slugged it back, feeling the coldness begin to seep outwards as it went down. It felt so good I topped it up and went for a stroll round the pool.

Out in the open the sun was fierce and heavy, and I squinted against the glare off the water's surface. It seemed a waste just to stand there looking at it, but I realised I hadn't brought a swimming costume. Somehow, being invited to take a dip in a client's pool hadn't been on the itinerary.

I took another stroll round the property and listened carefully, but if there was anybody about they were keeping a low profile. To hell with it, it was too hot and too good a chance to miss. Anyway, a quick dip was all I needed.

I was stripped off and in the water inside ten seconds, leaving a pile of clothes on the patio and a ripple where I plunged through the still, blue surface. It was cool, but embracing and so pleasant I wanted to gurgle with delight. Anyone who has been skinny-dipping as an adult will know the difference of not being encumbered by a swimming costume; it's a whole new experience which has more than just a little to do with losing one's inhibitions and kicking off all traces of convention. And maybe I just got a secret kick out of being bare-arse naked in someone else's pool. For some reason it made me think about Jane... which also made me think about Basher.

Bad idea.

I kicked my way down to the far end under water, lazily counting tiles on the bottom, and surfaced with a gasp into bright sunlight and the heat of the great American outdoors. It had been a while since I'd done any swimming, so I did two lazy lengths of the pool, letting my muscles find their way into the rhythm of a crawl while I struggled with adjusting my breathing to coincide with having my face out of the water rather than in it. At least, that was the idea, but since nobody was watching I didn't bother too much about ingesting the occasional mouthful and having to stop to cough it up again.

After that I swam over to the lounger and pulled myself aboard, gasping like a fish and settling back to soak up some rays while I drifted across the pool. It felt good to have my belly open to the skies, even if I was exposed to anyone flying overhead. But frankly, my dear, I didn't give a hoot.

A few minutes later the lounger spun gently in the water and the position of the sun told me I was turning to face the house. I opened my eyes and squinted against the glare, a sudden surge of natural caution making me check I didn't have an audience of several dozen old ladies from the local church harmony-singing circle.

I didn't see an audience, but I did notice my clothes had disappeared.

TWENTY-FOUR

Trying to get some emergency traction on a floating sunbed is not easy. I had a moment of wild panic, feeling the air-chambers move beneath me, providing a platform like wet lasagne. I was desperately trying to get a glimpse of my travel bag which I'd dropped by the table when I poured myself some juice. Inside was the envelope from Clayton, my sole reason for being there and without which I might as well have consigned myself to a lifelong exile somewhere so remote even God couldn't find me.

I finally managed to flop to the side of the pool and haul myself onto solid ground, spitting a lungful of chlorinated water across the patio. When I rubbed the water from my eyes, I looked up and saw my travel bag was where I'd left it by the table. Thank God.

'For a moment, there, I thought I was going to have to come right in and rescue you.'

The voice was low and languid and tinged with amusement, and came from the shadows near the refreshment table. I squinted, my eyes still blind after the glare of the sun off the pool, but all I could see was a long, bare leg swinging to and fro, with a stylish sandal hanging from five elegantly painted toes.

Then the owner of the voice stood up and stepped out from the shadow towards me, shaking my shirt gently in one hand as if to dislodge any dust that might have landed on it. A faint jangling sound came from a clutch of bracelets on her wrist.

It was only when I saw the amusement wasn't confined to her voice, and that her eyes were looking down at a point below my navel, that I remembered I was naked.

Caught between the urge to flip backwards into the pool and to suck my stomach in and try to look good, I was saved the decision when she handed me my shirt and turned away.

'I picked up your things to save them getting creased in the sun,' she said by way of explanation, and went back to the table and poured two glasses of orange juice. Her voice was a slow drawl, the vowels stretched and drawn out as if the effort to release them for public hearing was almost too much bother. The effect was not a million miles away from Lauren Bacall. To my London-tutored ear it sounded alien and affected… and, either in spite of or because of the circumstances, unbelievably sensual. But that may have been because I was naked and my imagination was instinctively getting ahead of itself. 'Down here everything wilts in the humidity, y'know?' She glanced back with a raised eyebrow as I covered my embarrassment with my shirt. 'And I mean everything.'

I sighed and wondered how long she'd been watching me. Humidity, my eye. Hadn't she noticed that thing about men and cool water before?

'I'm sorry,' I said, retrieving my trousers and the rest of my things and grabbing a large, fluffy towel. 'The gardener – Frank? He said it was okay to take a dip. But I didn't have a costume.'

'Costume?' She handed me a glass of juice. 'Oh, you mean swim shorts. Say, are you from New York or Canada or what?'

'England, actually,' I said, and remembered that many Americans wouldn't recognise a British accent and often confused it with one from north of the border. 'England, UK,' I added helpfully.

'Oh, I know where England is,' the woman said, and sat back down by the table. 'I may live in the boonies, but I have travelled, y'know.'

While she obligingly turned her gaze away, I towelled myself dry and got dressed. It gave me a chance to study her profile. She was tall and slim, with auburn-tinted, glossy hair cut to her shoulders, and clear, dark eyes that still had an air of amusement. Her mouth was wide and curled at the edges, and one eyebrow was slightly cocked as though she found the world permanently puzzling. She was wearing a thin cotton sundress with brown polka dots on a cream background which set off her evenly-tanned skin to perfection. She wore no jewellery apart from the bracelets on her wrist. I put her age at somewhere in the late thirties.

'I'm Jake Foreman, by the way.' I may have been presentable at last, but it didn't stop me feeling ridiculous for having to introduce myself in such circumstances. After all, in one sense she was now better acquainted with me than people I'd known for years.

'Well, hello, Jake.' She nodded formally and sipped her drink, then looked at me. 'And I'm Lilly-Mae Breadon. Gus said someone would be dropping by, but he didn't say who.' She glanced at my bag on the floor by the table. 'You've got a little something for him, right?'

'That's right. Is he going to be long?'

She waved a hand. 'Well, you ask me, the only person knows that for sure is Gus. He takes just as long as he likes about most everything.' The tone sounded mildly vexed, as if she was talking about a child beyond her control, but who was okay, all said and done. She used a fingertip to wipe a trace of orange juice off her top lip. 'It all depends on what it is you've got for him, I guess… and how bad he wants it.' She looked at me with those wide open eyes and the trace of a smile which made the hairs rise on the back of my neck. It was like being zapped by a laser, and I felt my breathing drag to a stop. Somewhere in the trees something screeched, a high-pitched sound which made me jump. Lilly-Mae seemed unaffected by it.

'So, are you gonna tell me what it is, Jake?'

The question threw me – almost as much as the use of my name. I was surprised she was interested, and for a moment wondered if this was another test. I also wondered what her relationship with Mekashnik might be.

'I can't,' I said truthfully. 'Boring papers, as far as I know. Are you related to Mr Mekashnik?'

Lilly-Mae gave me a sideways look and ignored my question. 'Oh, I doubt they're boring, Jake. I doubt that very much. Still.' She stood up, the matter closed. It brought her nearer to me, and I could see she was nearly my own height, and carried with her a delicate perfume with traces of lemons. She eyed me directly and nodded towards my glass.

'Bring that with you, Jake. How 'bout we go for a walk? I'm sure Gus will be along soon. On the way you can tell me all about yourself.' She walked away and skirted the end of the pool, her long stride taking her out across the grass towards the trees. I stopped to pick up my travel bag with the all-important envelope and hurried after her. As I caught up, I couldn't help but admire the movement of muscle down the back of her thighs under the sundress, or the fact that the dress had no back above the waist and showed a bare expanse of smooth, well-toned and tanned skin.

'To save you asking,' she said conversationally, 'I'm, shall we say, a visiting friend.' She turned her head to fix me with her eyes, and I

177

realised that she had dropped the country-girl drawl. 'No more, no less. Gus likes to think of me as a trophy as far as his brain-dead, gun-carrying buddies are concerned, but since they don't matter anyhow, who cares? How about you, Jake? Have you really come all this way to deliver papers?'

Brain-dead gun-carrying buddies? That didn't sound much like a leading arms dealer. I'd been expecting a smart, modern office full of suited employees armed with nothing more lethal than the latest iPad, with maybe a warehouse nearby full of things that only went bang in someone else's war far, far away. Before I could reply, a car engine sounded from round the side of the house, followed by doors slamming and footsteps echoing across the patio. Lilly-Mae stopped and turned, rolling her eyes in what looked like vexation, and muttered, 'Shoot. Just as we were getting acquainted.' Her face took on a welcoming smile and she waved a hand in greeting. 'Hi, Gus, darlin'. Guess who I've got here?' The drawl, I noticed, was back in place.

'I know very well who you've got there, Lil,' a deep voice replied sourly. 'Just where'n hell were you planning on taking him is what I want to know.'

The muscles in my back flinched at the man's aggressive tone and I turned round to see a big bear of a figure standing by the pool, dressed in work jeans and a check shirt, with two other men behind him, both dressed similarly and with lookalike faces. Their bunch-shouldered stance gave them the look of a wrestling tag team, but in comparison to the first man, they looked fairly harmless.

In his hand was a rifle with a telescopic sight, pointing right at me.

TWENTY-FIVE

Gus Mekashnik had the aura of a bad-tempered construction foreman, a breed I'd come across frequently in my former work. He was large, meaty and looked permanently irascible, as if the entire world was there solely to get under his skin and cause him acute disappointment. He also seemed to like shouting. His sandy hair was cut in a military-style crew-cut and his eyebrows ran in a thick and unbroken line. It gave him a fierce appearance which went well with the gun he was clutching like a child's toy in one big, muscular fist. I guessed his age at fifty-plus, but it was hard to tell.

He merely nodded when I finally managed to untangle my bowels at the sight of the rifle and say hi. I guessed his lack of warmth implied that as I was merely a hired help I shouldn't get any ideas of us becoming friends. It was reinforced by the beady look he switched between Lilly-Mae and me as we approached across the lawn, as if we'd been caught getting up to something naughty in the woodshed. I should be so lucky.

As I made to follow him inside the house he stared down at my feet. In the confusion of meeting Lilly-Mae, I'd forgotten to put my shoes back on.

'You some kinda nature freak?' he muttered, then turned and went inside before I could answer. In the background the wrestler twins stared at me as if I'd passed wind at a funeral, their dull expressions making me wonder if they were the results of local in-breeding. I scrabbled for my shoes and socks and followed their boss inside.

The house was cool and dark, every trace of sunshine kept out by the drawn drapes. Mekashnik jerked his head at Lilly-Mae, who went round opening them, flooding the room with light. It revealed a large, modern rectangle with a scattering of armchairs, ditto coffee tables, a couple of settees and, in one corner, a huge desk bearing a leather blotter, a telephone, a small lamp and a laptop. The floor was deeply-polished hardwood block on which sat three Persian rugs. The overall effect was relaxed, expensive and stylish, but more like a hotel foyer than a home. It certainly wasn't the corporate office environment I'd been expecting.

Mekashnik looked at Lilly-Mae and jerked his head towards the door. 'You got some things you gotta be doing, Lilly-Mae?'

It wasn't a question. But Lilly-Mae didn't seem to mind. She shrugged off the less than courteous dismissal and drifted towards the door, pausing only to look back at me. 'Say, Mr Foreman,' she drawled in that low, husky voice. 'You have a nice trip back, y'hear?' Then she winked at me in a meaningful manner and said, 'It was real nice seein' ya.'

'Thank you,' I said, and felt my face burn. I eyed Mekashnik to see his reaction, but he'd already turned away and appeared not to have heard. As the door closed behind her, he put the rifle down by the desk, then switched on the laptop. As it started up, he held out his hand. Taking it as my signal to leave, I handed him the envelope and made for the door.

'Where the hell are you going?' His voice brought me up short.

'Package delivered,' I said. 'I'm booked on a flight from Charlotte.'

'Take a seat.' He pointed at a chair across from the desk, the finger brooking no argument. Plainly he was a man accustomed to being obeyed, and I remembered Clayton's joke about what had happened to people who upset him. Joke or not, I'd met quite a few people who gave off the same kind of vibe as Mekashnik was right now, and they were people I'd always been very careful not to upset. Something told me that Clayton had either been telling fibs about this man or he didn't know Mekashnik as well as he thought he did.

'Pardon?' I felt the hairs stir on the back of my neck, and wondered what he wanted. Suppose the contents of the package didn't match his expectations? Was this my chance to find out what was meant by the words 'don't shoot the messenger'?

'Relax,' he growled, and sat down himself. 'I may have a job for you – a delivery. It's what you do, isn't it?'

'Yes. But I'm working for Mr Clayton.' And Clayton had told me quite clearly to get in, drop the package and leave.

'Yeah, I know who you're working for. I already checked with him, and he said it was okay to ask you. Now, you want to earn some extra money or just go back to London with what you've got?'

It was an interesting question. I was in no tearing hurry to get back, since it would mean simply sitting around until Clayton called, then picking up another package and jetting off somewhere else. That or facing more flak from Susan or her solicitors. On the other hand, I had no idea what Mekashnik would be asking me to transport for him. Why didn't he use his own people, of which there were at least three kicking their heels around the house? Maybe they couldn't read road signs.

'All right,' I said. 'But no drugs.'

He gave me a hard look not unlike the one Clayton had given me. 'What is it with you Brits? You think every American's a dealer in crack cocaine?' He reached into one of the desk drawers and pulled out a slim envelope which he tossed across the desk at me. 'There's your fee. It's for an envelope to go to Palm Springs. It'll be ready for you to collect in the morning, which should give you time to arrange a flight from Charlotte. It'll likely be a connection with a stop-over so don't expect it to be quick. This is a big country. Any questions?'

'Only one. Is there a hotel near here?'

He nodded. 'Ask Frank on the way out. Be back here in the morning so I know you're ready to take the envelope when it gets here. And next time try keeping your shoes on.'

I stepped out through the French windows on to the patio, then walked round the side of the house and found Frank waiting for me, idly clipping dead heads off a shrub. He gave me directions to the only local hotel before I'd even asked him, which made me wonder if he'd been listening. Then he stood and watched as I reversed the car and drove back down the drive.

As I looked back, I noticed a movement on the front balcony above the entrance. Lilly-Mae was standing with her hand on the wooden railing, watching me go.

For some reason it was a disturbing image to leave with.

By ten the following morning I was back at the Mekashnik mansion, after a good night's sleep, waiting for someone to answer the gate. The hotel had been a few miles away, nestling on the tip of a lake, along a winding road which hugged the water. Set in breathtaking scenery which demanded to be admired, it was surrounded by trees marching across the hills like a conquering army. It probably looked a riot in autumn, or fall, as the locals called it, and I wondered if I'd ever be back this way to see it. The day was threatening warm and I could have done with staying a little longer and letting go of all the tension, but it didn't look like that was going to happen.

The inside of the hotel had been like stepping back to the Thirties, with heavy, brooding décor, dark corridors and staff outnumbering guests. If there was any entertainment on offer they were keeping it hidden, but it was clean, cool and spacious and, after a meal in a local fish restaurant recommended by the receptionist, I'd hit the hay to reverse the effects of jet lag. Before sleeping I'd tried calling Clayton, just to let him know I had reservations about Mekashnik, the allegedly normal businessman, but the call went to voicemail. I didn't bother leaving a message.

I thumbed the entry-phone button again, leaning a little harder, as if it would make a difference. Maybe Frank was too busy killing off a few more flowers to attend to his door-keeping duties.

While I waited, I stepped over to the gun-shot mailbox for a closer look. The flap was hanging open like a drunk's mouth and the box was empty. I poked my forefinger through the hole and felt the sharp edges on the inside. On the other side of the box the thin metal was curved outward in the same manner, where the bullet had passed straight through. I didn't know much about shell calibres but it seemed pretty big for chasing squirrels. Maybe they bred them big around there to match the trees.

I went back and pressed the button again. Still nothing. Then I noticed the iron gates were slightly open, as if they hadn't quite caught the latch.

I eased them back far enough to get the car through and drove up the access road, wondering how Gus Mekashnik could be doing the kind of work he did while retaining such a laid-back lifestyle – if a palatial house and property could be called laid-back. Presumably he paid people to do all the running around for him.

I dropped the scroll door-knocker and heard the echoes inside. Maybe they'd had a late-night barbecue after I left and were having trouble surfacing. I guessed if I lived there, I'd have the same problem.

The thought prompted ideas about the pool out back, so I walked around the side of the house towards the sound of running water, expecting to find Frank killing off a few more plants before their time.

I found Frank all right. But he wasn't doing any gardening.

He was floating in the shallow end of the pool, head down as if he was searching for something on the bottom. Trailing away from him was a widening ribbon of blood leaking from a hole in the middle of his back.

TWENTY-SIX

I stared at him for a few seconds, willing myself to do something. But my mind and body were in suspension, as if expecting Frank to turn over and ask me if I wanted some juice and, by the way, why not take a swim while you're waiting but don't take off your shoes?

Then common sense kicked in. I ran to the end of the pool where there was a long-poled skimmer for collecting dead leaves and debris off the surface of the water. I slid it under his body and hooked it on his clothing, then dragged him carefully to the side, taking pains not to let him sink; the last thing I wanted to do was go back in that pool and fish him off the bottom. As his shoulder bumped against the side, he finally turned over with a slow-motion roll and stared up at me with a look of surprise etched on his weathered face as if I'd caught him doing something nasty in the water.

Have you seen those films where the hero finds a dead floater in the pool and drags it out to give mouth-to-mouth resuscitation? They always make it look so easy, don't they? Well, I took a tug at Frank's body and knew there was no way I could lift him out, even if his life had depended on it, much less give him a kiss. Dry and alive, he wasn't that big or heavy; dead and wet, he weighed as much as a small family car. And he was leaking.

I decided to leave him where he was.

Using the buoyancy of the water to flip him over again, I looked at the hole in his back. I'm no expert, but he'd either been shot with a large calibre bullet or stabbed with a big spear. Then I noticed the blackened edges of his shirt around the wound and realised he'd been shot at close range. No wonder he looked surprised.

I let him drift away on the basis that he couldn't go far and turned to study the house, hoping it would yield a clue as to what had happened. The curtains were all drawn just as they had been the previous day, shutting out the sun and prying eyes. The only difference now was that there seemed to be a truly deserted air about the place, with none of the faint echoes of life held in abeyance until someone came home.

I tried the French windows but they were locked. Obviously. After that I hoofed round the side of the house and checked the windows, in case someone had been careless. Eventually I arrived back at the front door. After a second I tried the handle.

It's the one thing cinema audiences always expect the hero to do, but he rarely does, have you noticed that? And when he does, the door is always locked and he has to take out his gun and either shoot the lock off without giving a thought to the consequences of a ricochet, or use the butt to smash a window. All very useful if you have a large gun to hand somewhere, which I didn't.

As I touched it, the door obligingly swung open.

A wave of cool air washed over me as I stepped inside, and I could hear the hum of the air-conditioning. Was this a good or bad sign? Was the house vacated temporarily or deserted?

'Hello?' I called out politely, feeling desperately English, like a character in a Noël Coward play. I should have been holding a tennis racket and wearing flannels and pumps. On the other hand, it was my first time coming to a house and finding a dead body in the pool and, if there were any rules laid down about these things, my dear old mother had never bothered mentioning them. What should I shout next? That in case the inhabitants didn't know it, they had a dead gardener floating in the pool and might want to help get him out? That the good news was, they could save having to pay Frank this month's wages but the bad news meant they couldn't go swimming until they'd changed the water? I hoped for their sakes that replacement help was easy to get round there.

I walked across into the living-room where I'd had my chat with Mekashnik the previous day. It looked the same, even down to the envelope I'd brought him all the way from London. Only now it was ripped open and empty on his desk. There was no sign of the rifle. Otherwise the room looked undisturbed. The laptop was hibernating, with its green power light winking rhythmically.

I found the kitchen. It didn't look as if it was much used for anything other than opening bottles, if the box of empty beer stubbies in one corner was any guide. No notes, no open drawers, no ransacking. I was halfway up the stairs when that little voice of caution which is supposed to sit on your shoulder and kick you in the ear at times of danger finally decided to wake up. What the hell are you doing? Frank didn't commit suicide – there could be a killer up there waiting to blow your fucking head off!

Since running upstairs is not a silent activity for a man of my years and fitness, and shock at Frank's demise was making me breathe like a carthorse, I figured it was already too late for backing down, and shook off the warning voice. But I did move a bit faster.

I found, in rapid succession, two bathrooms, a dressing room and four bedrooms, all of them deserted, opulent, if slightly garish, and with no signs of a potential assailant, armed or otherwise. And no signs of a forced entry. One of the bedrooms held a familiar aroma and an array of dresses thrown carelessly across the queen-sized bed and a jumble of shoes in disarray on the floor near a dressing table. I checked the en-suite bathroom, but there were no bodies there, either, just the usual debris of bathrooms the world over. That Lilly-Mae was a messy liver.

So, whoever had shot Frank evidently hadn't come inside and gunned down the rest of the household. But that left the aching question of where they were. Then another thought occurred: what if Frank's assailant had come from the house rather than to it? Had Gus finally got fed up with Frank's attempts at horticulture, taken his gun in a fit of rage and shot him? Had Lilly-Mae?

Ridiculous. That kind of thing doesn't happen. Police. I should call the police. What was the number people dialled in the movies? 911? On the other hand, what would I tell them? That I'd come to pick up a package to take to Palm Springs – and no, officer, I had no idea what was in it, nor who it was for – and found Frank the gardener trying to drink the pool dry? The thought of trying to explain what I'd found to a suspicious, hard-nosed, gun-chewing American cop made the friendly station sergeant back in London seem like a long-lost brother. I'd seen those programmes about how some US law dealt with miscreants – even innocent ones. They beat the crap out of them. Or worse.

It was time to go.

As I scurried down the stairs and skidded across the foyer, a shadow moved in the open doorway. I found myself face to face with a gawky youth in jeans and a T-shirt bearing a company logo. Behind him was a bright red transit van with the name of a pool-maintenance service and the same logo emblazoned across the side.

'Hi, sir,' he greeted me with a cheery wave. 'Should I go on round back?'

Hell, no! The inner voice screamed at me, and I managed to unscramble my brain just enough to shake my head. Somehow I didn't think bodies were what pool cleaners usually found among all the leaves and other debris they were accustomed to dealing with.

He looked at me. 'You don't want the pool cleaned?'

'Yes,' I said. 'No. I mean.' I tried a smile and rubbed my eyes, desperately trying to think of a way of stopping him going round to the pool. Then I realised I must have looked a sight, and capitalised on it. 'Sorry – heavy night last night. Can you come back later?'

He grinned in understanding. There's nothing another man can relate to more than a night on the tiles and the need for absolute silence from the entire world the following morning. It comes with the genes… unless the other man is a priest or an accountant.

'Hey, sure thing,' he chuckled, giving me that 'boy, do I know how you feel, 'cos we're all guys together' look. 'Do it all the time, myself. Say, I can leave it longer if you want. Come back tomorrow, maybe the day after? I got plenty of other pools to take care of. It ain't as though I came here special.'

I nodded and waved a hand, using the hangover act to avoid the need to talk further. He probably recognised my accent as anything but local, and I didn't want to take the risk of saying more. Knowing my luck, he'd probably turn out to have studied at Oxford for three years and able to spot a UK regional twang at a hundred paces.

'Okay. No problem,' he said pleasantly. 'I'll call back tomorrow. Have a nice day.'

I closed the door and leaned against it, breathing slowly to lower my blood pressure. That was as close as I ever wanted to come to true disaster. I waited as he drove off and gave it another couple of minutes, then stepped outside and closed the door after me.

The gates were still open the way I'd left them. I paused at the road, and was about to drive on when something caught my eye. It was the mailbox; it was still open, but balanced carefully on top was a small, brown envelope.

It hadn't been there earlier.

Out of curiosity I jumped out of the car. The envelope had a padded interior, like many I'd carried before for Clayton. It was light and through the padding I could feel the hard outline of a memory stick. On the front of the envelope was a neat line of writing.

D. Selecca – Hyatt Regency Palm Springs.

It had to be the package Gus had wanted me to deliver. But why wasn't he there to give it to me himself, along with the handover instructions? Where were his two goons, the Inbred Twins? And where was Lilly-Mae? And who had delivered it already marked for the recipient without coming up to the house?

There was no date or time written on the envelope, but maybe that hadn't been settled yet. Or maybe now, with Frank floating in the pool and the house deserted, there was no delivery to make. In which case why leave it there in the mailbox? Had Gus hoped I would find it?

Three minutes later I was driving past Cappy's Diner and heading back east towards Charlotte, praying I didn't meet a police car coming the other way filled with a testosterone-charged SWAT team. Somehow 'English tourist dies in police shoot-out on lonely mountain road' wasn't quite the ending I'd been hoping for.

I headed for the airport, praying there was a quick shuttle connection out. Where to, I wasn't really fussed. Palm Springs beckoned, but for no other reason than that it was an excuse to be as far away from the house as possible before anyone else showed up and started screaming for the cops. In any case, I'd been paid, so I had a job to do.

TWENTY-SEVEN

As Mekashnik had suggested, getting to Palm Springs wasn't as simple as taking a direct flight. The first one out meant dog-legging via Phoenix. It would get me to Palm Springs hours later than I'd hoped, but I had time to spare and nothing else to fill it. I spent the waiting time watching out for men in uniform who looked like they might be looking for a British guy to throw in the slammer.

As soon as I cleared arrivals in Palm Springs I used a payphone to call the Mekashnik house. I wasn't sure if using my Nokia would tie my presence to the area, but decided not to risk it. The ring tone burbled away without being picked up. By now if anyone such as a cleaner had pitched up, they would have found the unfortunate Frank taking his final swim, and the house would be teeming with murder-squad detectives firing off questions and bawling at each other to get results from the lab and did anyone think to bring coffee and bagels. It's what they do on re-runs of *Columbo*, anyway.

I replaced the phone with mixed feelings and took a cab into town. It was only a couple of miles and didn't take long, and luckily the driver was the non-talkative type. The city looked nice; the lawns were lush and green, the streets tidy and the buildings low-rise and stylish – a kid's model toytown set down completed in the middle of scenery which looked like something from *Blazing Saddles*. I was surprised by how small it was. I'd imagined Palm Springs to be a busy, bustling and even brash glare of colour, reflecting its popularity among the Hollywood elite. But it sprawled gracefully in the sun like a dozing lizard, its boulevards and golf dunes, shopping malls and ranch-style villas set behind tile-topped walls never quite managing to lose the air of a slightly off-planet experience created for the tired, city-burned movie slaves down in Los Angeles.

The Hyatt Regency was a neat, restrained building along North Palm Canyon Drive in the centre of the downtown area. I paid off the cab and walked past a patio dining area fronting the street and into the cool interior, to be greeted by a smiling receptionist who bore a striking resemblance to a Hollywood starlet I couldn't quite put a name to. Several, in fact. Or maybe it was just the perfect, white teeth.

'May I help you, sir?' she twinkled. The way her dentistry lit up the foyer, she must have been very useful in a blackout.

'I've come to see Mr Selecca,' I said, going for the assumptive angle and hoping she didn't ask me for his room number. I was taking a gamble on Selecca being a man, since all the recipients of Clayton's envelopes had been male so far. But since this one was Mekashnik's contact, it might well have been breaking the mould. Somehow, though, I couldn't see Mekashnik doing business with a woman.

'I'm so sorry,' the receptionist sparkled with deep sincerity, 'but Mr Selecca has just stepped out for a while. Would you care to wait? I'm sure he won't be long. Perhaps I can take a note of your name?'

It was like being served by a pretty speak-your-weight machine, and just as unnerving. I gave her my name which she committed to memory before going on to suggest several nearby restaurants and bars where I could either eat or get smashed while waiting. I opted for the patio out front where I could indulge my favourite occupation and watch the world go by.

I hadn't eaten since I'd snatched breakfast, so I ordered a club sandwich and sank back in my chair with a cold beer, letting a cooling breeze fan my skin and the stress drain out through my feet. Since leaving Mekashnik's place I'd had the unsettling feeling of having someone behind me, watching my every move. It had brought back memories of the follower in Nice. But Charlotte airport had proved small enough and sufficiently open to make spotting a tail easy, even for my amateur talents, and Palm Springs even more so. I told myself repeatedly that my imagination was simply working overtime after seeing the unfortunate Frank, but it didn't help as much as I thought.

I was just finishing my sandwich and reading a brochure extolling the wonders of the local Indian Canyons, when a shadow fell across my table. I looked up to see the receptionist smiling down at me as if I was her favoured client in all the world.

Mr Selecca, she announced, was back and would see me now.

After the arid heat outside, the interior was a welcome relief. I hoped my deodorant was doing its job; I didn't want my credibility taking a nosedive because of a small hitch in bodily care. I followed the receptionist's directions to Selecca's suite on the first floor and knocked on the door.

The man who opened it looked like Clark Kent. He had neat hair, heavy glasses and a conservative suit sitting on a muscular frame. He nodded and gestured me inside, somehow managing to pat me down as I passed without being in any way offensive. On the other hand, with a build like his, what was I going to do – object?

Sitting by the window was a compact man in golf slacks and a sports shirt, who looked as if he liked the sun, although the temperature in the room was icy cold. Behind him was an impressive view of what I'd read were the San Jacinto Mountains, shrouded in a blue haze. Even from across the room I was immediately aware that the man was wearing an obscenely bad hairpiece, and wondered how I was going keep my face straight. How could someone staying in this place – and evidently well-known by the staff – let himself be topped by something that looked as if it had been scraped off the road that morning?

'Mr Selecca?' I asked, and came to a stop in front of him. The man at the door stayed in the background, hands folded across his front.

'Who are you?' Selecca stared up at me and licked his lips with a quick, darting flick of his tongue, like a lizard on a rock. His eyes were coal-black and small, giving away nothing of the man behind them.

'People call me Jake,' I said. Always a good idea to open on a genial note; it disarms the latently hostile.

'Yeah, I got the name,' he grated. 'I meant who are you and what do you want? I'm a busy man.'

'I have a delivery from Gus Mekashnik.' As I spoke I reached into my flight bag for the package. Time to get this over and done with and hightail it back to the airport.

'Don't.' Selecca held up a finger to stop me, and I froze.

They say that in the presence of danger you can feel a sudden charge of energy, as if the spirits themselves are warning of something dramatic about to happen. I got a momentary fizz, but it may have been my imagination after mentioning Gus's name and all that it implied. What was much clearer in the quietness after Selecca spoke was a snick of metal from behind me. I turned my head very slowly and found the Clark Kent lookalike holding a large automatic pistol pointing vaguely in my direction, like he wanted to use it but was reluctant in case he made a mess of the carpet.

I shivered, not merely from the cold, and hoped I wasn't about to make a different kind of mess.

'I know Mekashnik,' said Selecca, and flapped a restraining hand at the gunman. 'Sorry about Paulie – he watches too many bad films where some guy comes in and says he has a delivery then pulls out a gun and starts shooting people. You want something to drink, Jake?' He nodded towards a tray of drinks in one corner.

Actually, after seeing Paulie's cannon, I badly needed a pee, followed by a very large brandy. I decided to give the drink a miss and go for a hasty withdrawal before I ended up joining Frank in his celestial garden.

'No, thanks,' I said politely. 'If I can see some ID, though, I'll be on my way.'

'Oh. Okay, sure. Why not?' He looked mildly surprised, but reached into his back pocket and produced some credit cards all in the name of D. Selecca. One of them was an Amex Platinum. 'That do you?'

'That will do nicely,' I said. I gestured at the flight bag. 'Can I do this?'

He nodded, so I delved very carefully into the bag and handed over the envelope.

He ripped it open before I could move and slid the memory stick into his palm, turning it over a couple of times like he'd never seen one before. Then he peered into the envelope as if expecting to find something else. Somewhere in the distance I heard the whoop-whoop of a police car. The atmosphere in the room went very still and quiet. I swear even the air-conditioning took a break.

'What's this?' he asked, and looked up at me with those cold, dark eyes. He was holding up the memory stick.

'It's what I was given to bring here,' I said, and pointed to the envelope with his name on it. 'The envelope was sealed. That's all I know.' After all the deliveries I've done for Clayton, I thought bitterly, I have to go and make one for a third party which turns out to be not to the liking of the recipient. And he just happens to have a companion wielding a very large gun.

Bugger.

The police siren was getting closer, the noise seeping into the silence of the room which, until then, had been disturbed only by Selecca's breathing and the rustle of the envelope he was scrunching up in his hand.

'And he said bring it here? To me? Just that and nothing else?' Selecca was looking annoyed. 'When was this?'

'Yesterday. I was on my way back to the airport and he asked me if I would make this drop-off.' I wondered how friendly Selecca and Mekashnik were, and whether this man's next question might be where I came from. It suddenly occurred to me that if he was seriously cross, I was a long way from home and help.

The phone gave a harsh jangle, making us all jump. I tensed, hoping Paulie's finger wasn't curled too closely around the trigger of his gun. Even I was aware that the statistical evidence for accidental discharges of firearms in the US was horribly high.

'Yeah?' Selecca had snatched up the phone. He listened a moment, then looked at me. 'Sure – he's here. Who is this?' Then he shook his head and handed me the phone with an irate snarl. 'What's this, a family business? You got your sister keepin' tabs on you? We ain't finished, you and me, by the way, so don't think we are.' He tossed the balled-up envelope away from him with a flick of his wrist and waited for me to react.

I took the phone with a sense of unreality, wondering if I was actually having a dream and any minute now I'd wake up in my bed at home, with Mrs Tree next door complaining about the increase in traffic and demanding the installation of speed bumps.

I also remembered that I didn't have a sister.

'Hello?'

'*Jake – get out of there!*' It was a woman's voice, speaking low. In the background was a clatter of noise and a man's voice issuing orders. 'You've got two, maybe three minutes at most, you hear?'

'Wha– who…?' The phone went dead, leaving me with the feeling I'd heard that voice before. But where? It was a British accent… well, sort of. Like somebody trying to sound British. I forced myself to put down the receiver and smile, aware that something momentous was about to happen, although God alone knew what. All I knew was that whatever I did next had to involve leaving this room and these two very odd individuals as quickly as humanly possible. Preferably without getting shot.

'My sister – Emma,' I explained, snatching for a name. 'She came with me for the ride. She's a worrier, says I have to catch a flight out in the next hour. I'd better go.'

I started towards the door and found Paulie standing in my way, his gun at waist height. Then a police siren gave a whoop right below the window, before being shut off in mid-stream. Instantly Paulie turned, the light flashing off his spectacles, jumped to the window and looked down. He cursed and looked at Selecca in a panic, the gun held down by his side.

'The place is crawling with cops!' he hissed, like someone out of a bad movie.

I caught an expression of dawning realisation cross Selecca's face, grabbed my bag, and was across to the door and through it before he could stop me. As I slammed the door behind me he shouted something that sounded like 'That *bastard* Mekashnik!'

Out in the corridor I followed my instincts by turning away from the reception area and heading for the emergency stairs. I had no idea what the police activity was about but, after the mystery woman's warning on the phone, it didn't need too much imagination to tell me that Mr Selecca and his gun-toting pal were about to get a visit from the boys in blue.

Halfway down the corridor was an ice machine and a sweet dispenser set in a small recess. I slung my bag over my shoulder and grabbed a plastic ice bucket someone had left on the side. I filled it with cubes, then continued on my way just as the door at the end squeaked open and two men in suits appeared. Behind them was a uniformed cop. They looked like they meant business.

I stepped aside, holding the ice bucket in front of me. They didn't even spare me a glance, but hurried by, the uniform even holding the door for me to go through. Whoever their attention was focussed on, it evidently didn't include guests bearing ice.

Downstairs, another cop was standing like a statue at the rear door of the building. The no-nonsense look on his face was enough to tell me this one wasn't going to let me go by so easy. I might be carrying an ice bucket, but he'd soon find out I wasn't checked in. And as soon as the receptionist saw me, I'd be nailed as a visitor to Selecca's room.

I had no option but to go for broke and hope for the best. I turned towards the reception area where some uniforms were mingling with men in suits and a few obvious holiday guests who were looking bemused. I wandered through as casually as possible, keeping as far away from the receptionist's megawatt smile as I could.

Then someone grabbed me by the arm.

TWENTY-EIGHT

It was Lilly-Mae.

'Keep walking, Jake,' she muttered through gritted teeth, grinning at me as if we hadn't seen each other in months. She guided me towards the front door, chatting away excitedly about what a wonderful time we'd have on the aerial tramway and how tomorrow we could take a hot-air balloon out over the desert or maybe drive out to see the Indian Canyons. In between she batted her eyelashes until I almost believed we were actually the newly-wed couple she was pretending we were.

Her wonderful performance took us clear of two uniforms standing in the front entrance. I wished my part could have been half as good, but I was still reeling from having Paulie pull a gun on me and trying to work out how the hell Lilly-Mae came to be there. And why.

I placed the ice bucket on one of the outside tables as we passed, and breathed a sigh of relief when I felt the sun on my face. This was getting way too exciting. Sorting out site problems on half-built reservoirs in snake-infested jungle was a doddle compared to this.

Five minutes later, at Lilly-Mae's urging, we were in a Tex-Mex restaurant a few blocks down, facing each other over margaritas and a plate of nachos. Our table was conveniently placed behind a tall palm tree where she said we could keep one eye on the entrance.

'Shouldn't we be heading for the airport?' I suggested. It seemed a wise move to me, to avoid being caught in a neighbourhood search. First rule of not being caught: run away as fast as possible.

'Uh-uh.' Lilly-Mae shook her head and sank a healthy draught of margarita. She looked wonderful, as if she'd been relaxing on a beach all day instead of rescuing intrepid Englishmen from the clutches of Mafia-type gunmen. 'We're safe enough here, Jake.'

'We are?'

'Sure. Selecca won't set the police on you. He'll be too busy trying to worm his way out of trouble. With his record, he'll have his work cut out.'

'Having a man with a gun in his room won't help,' I said.

She nodded. 'Paulie, you mean? That numbnuts. Gus said he should have got rid of that moron years ago.'

I looked at her, reminding myself that she was obviously well in with Mekashnik, and therefore would know a lot about him and people like Selecca and Paulie. I felt suddenly depressed. Why couldn't I meet someone normal?

'So how come you turned up in the nick of time?' I asked her. 'Thanks, by the way. You saved me from either being shot or arrested – although I'm not sure the arrest would have come in time. Not a bad British accent, either.'

She looked modest and preened herself with a genuinely pleased smile, as if it was something she didn't get to do too often. 'My pleasure, Jake. Us lil' girls have our uses, y'know.' Then her face went sombre. 'Gus mentioned you'd agreed to make a delivery for him here

201

in Palm Springs, although he didn't say where. The only person he knows here is Selecca, so I guessed that's where you'd be headed. How come you went through with it? Didn't you find Frank?'

'You know about him?' I felt a chill go down my back. I'd been hoping she wasn't involved in the gardener's demise. Was I sitting there with a ruthless killer?

She nodded, then shook her head, confused. 'Yes, I knew something had happened to him, but not what, exactly. It was all a blur, y'know.' She shivered and finished her drink, and I ordered refills. By the pallor which had invaded her face, I could tell that events of the last day or so had suddenly caught up with her.

'So what happened?' I asked, Uncle Jake the psychologist at work; a problem shared is a problem pushed onto someone else, according to my dear old mum.

'A few hours after you went to the hotel – it must have been about two in the morning – Gus came in saying there were intruders in the trees behind the house. He saw their flashlights or something. Anyway, he went ape-shit and got his rifle, and went downstairs to get Frank. I stayed in my room. There was a lot of shouting, then a shot followed by a splash from out back. I figured someone took a fall in the pool, but I couldn't see because my room's at the front. Next thing, Gus comes back upstairs and tells me Frank got shot and to grab my things and get ready to bail out.'

'What about his two goons?'

'Jesse and Dino? They don't stay in the house. They live a few miles away. Gus said there wasn't time to call them, but I don't think they'd have been any help, anyway. Gus has known them for years. They're more like buddies than employees.'

'And where is Gus now?'

She looked back at me for a moment, then shrugged. 'I don't know. He took me to another house he owns outside Charlotte, then blew town. He said he had something to attend to and I was to wait there for him to get back. But I figured if whoever it was who was mad at him had tracked him down and killed Frank, they could soon find out where I was, too. Better I should leave town until things calmed down. Then I remembered you, so better than waiting there, I came to Palm Springs.'

'To do what?'

'I don't know. I hadn't figured that part out. To stop you getting caught up in it any further, I guess.' She stared back at me with a faint frown. 'You seemed to me like a nice guy who didn't deserve it. And besides, it gave me something to do which was a whole lot better than sitting on my tush waiting to hear from Gus.'

It was all a million miles from anything I was accustomed to, and I wondered what Clayton would make of it. It reminded me that maybe I should call him and let him know that his legitimate businessman had slipped over to the dark side. 'Do you know who the intruders were?'

'Gus said they were sent by some people he'd had some dealings with. A dispute of some kind – over money, I figured. I asked him what kind of dispute ends in shooting, but he wouldn't say.' She shook her head and took a sip of her fresh drink when it arrived. 'Gus can be such an asshole.'

She was right; ordinary commercial disputes don't end in people being shot.

'What kind of business is he in?' I asked. I knew, of course, since Clayton had told me, but I wondered how involved Lilly-Mae was. There was a large part of me hoping she hadn't a clue, but since she lived in the same house and didn't appear to be mentally retarded or deaf, she had to know something.

She gave me an odd look, as if I was kidding her along. 'You don't know? You must know.'

'I don't. Why should I?'

'Well, the fact you delivered the package is one thing. Usually the kind of guys bring things to Gus, they conform to a type, you know? They don't walk with their knuckles on the ground or anything, but they don't exactly swim too high in the human gene pool, either.' She smiled. 'I'm not saying you're like that, of course. That's what surprised me.'

'That still doesn't tell me what Gus does.'

She sighed and pulled a face. 'He's into what he calls "supply and demand". I heard him boast once that if you want something that doesn't come from Walmart, he can find it.'

'Forgive my ignorance, but what sort of things? Illegal things? Stolen goods?' I don't know why I didn't just tell her I knew, except that out of a perverse sense of need, I wanted to hear her say it; to confirm that Charles Clayton hadn't been kidding me along. Which, in the end, she did.

'Guns,' she said quietly. 'He deals in weapons.'

So she knew. And why wouldn't she, I told myself. Over there selling and buying guns was a recognised business. 'I may regret this, but what kind of weapons are we talking about? Pistols? Hunting rifles? Shotguns?'

She winced at the tone in my voice. 'I guess. Bigger, too.'

'How much bigger? Machine guns? Mortars? Mortars are big. No, it wouldn't be mort–'

'Mortars!' Lilly-Mae said, pointing a finger in the air. 'I heard him talk mortars one time, when he didn't know I was listening. I don't know all the terminology, but that's one I recognise. I guessed, because of the way he was acting, that it was all a big secret. He didn't even like having Frank around lately, not when he was talking business.'

I wasn't surprised. Frank had evidently disapproved. So Clayton had been telling the truth. But this wasn't just supplying a few friends with the means to shoot squirrels for a bit of mindless amusement up in the hills. Mortars could only be used in theatres of war.

'Oh – and arpeegees,' she said, sending my spirits diving even further. 'I heard him mention them. I don't know what they are, though.' She frowned. 'Arpeegees, is that right?'

Oh, great. RPGs or rocket-propelled grenades, were not on anyone's list of personal protection handguns. They were used for lobbing serious amounts of ordnance at armoured vehicles. And I'd just performed a delivery on his behalf. The memory stick wouldn't harm anyone, not unless they cut themselves opening the envelope, but what was on it might be explosive in a different kind of way. And that put me squarely in the same frame as Mekashnik and therefore legally questionable, no matter what Clayton had told me.

That confirmed it: I had to call Clayton. This was getting out of hand. So much for an easy drop-off.

'What about Selecca?' I asked, to change the subject. No doubt she would tell me he was into aircraft carriers and intergalactic starships, with a few battle tanks to keep business ticking over on the side.

'He's in the same line of business, I think,' confirmed Lilly-Mae. She shivered as if someone had walked over her grave. 'I met him once. He gave me the creeps, like something that crawled out from under a rock. He calls himself Dwight, but Gus said his real name is Diego – he pretends he's American but he comes from somewhere in Latin America. Colombia, I think.'

Colombia. Other than its other main export of coffee, Colombia equated with something far worse than arms, which was drugs. So what did that make Mekashnik?

'I was told Gus was a legitimate businessman.'

'He is,' she replied. Then hesitated before saying, 'Or was, anyway.'

'How do you mean?'

'He's been… I don't know, different for a while. Like he's got things going on in the business that he can't control.' She shook her head. 'He doesn't let me in on that kind of stuff and I don't ask questions, but I hear stuff and I get some bad vibes, you know? He's had some cash flow problems, I know that.'

'Things he can't control – like Selecca, you mean?'

'I guess. There have been others, too. He's had some phone calls late at night which he got mad about. And I know he's been using WhatsApp because it's encrypted. He's kind of developed a thing about being hacked lately, but that's all I know.'

'Could the intruders at the house have been sent by Selecca?'

She considered it for a moment. 'Maybe. Or the others. I heard Gus cussing him out a few days ago, called him a cheating, lying fuck.' She flushed. 'Sorry. The thing is, why would Gus send a packet to Selecca if they'd had a bust-up? Did you see what was in it?'

'A memory stick. I got the impression Selecca wasn't too pleased about it – as if it was all a big surprise. He was just quizzing me about it when you rang. Then the sirens started and spooked the pair of them.' I paused and looked at her as a broad smile spread across her face. 'Did I say thank you for that?'

She nodded and crinkled her nose. 'Yes, you did.'

'Was it you who called the police?'

Lilly-Mae looked shocked at the thought. 'No! Are you kidding?

They were already on their way in when I got there. As soon as I saw the lights and uniforms I kind of guessed where they might be headed and realised if you were still there, you'd get swept up along with Selecca. I just called on the off-chance you were with him.'

'Quick thinking.'

'Thank you. After I spoke to you, I thought maybe I should start a diversion, like they do in the movies. Only I didn't have time to start a fire or nothing. Then I saw this police cruiser standing out back with nobody in it, so I leaned through the window and let it whoop a little. Gosh, it was loud, right?' She rolled her eyes and patted herself on the chest. 'Man, that was a buzz.'

'Thank you,' I said again, and meant it. I decided I didn't want to ask how she happened to know where to find the siren button in a police car. 'But being arrested was the least of my problems. I think Paulie was about to shoot me when the siren went off. You saved my life.'

She grinned and made a face, dropping into the cornball drawl again. 'Aw shucks, really? Down where I come from, that means I now own you. Gee, I ain't never owned nobody before.'

I couldn't not laugh, in spite of the seriousness of the situation. There was something about Lilly-Mae which verged erratically from the sophisticated and elegant to the plain screwball, all interwoven with a sense of fun I hadn't seen in anyone since I was a teenager. Which was real and which was put on I couldn't tell, but right now I didn't see that it mattered.

'So where do you come from?' I asked her.

She looked coy. 'Me? Oh, nowhere and everywhere. My dad was an army sergeant and we sort of moved all over. Home is where they are, I guess – although I haven't caught up with them in a while.'

'Don't you miss them?'

'Sure. Some of the time. But they live their life and I live mine. I told my dad about Gus once. He didn't approve. Said any man outside the government who traded in arms was a revolutionary commie scumbag. My dad's a bit conservative, y'might say.'

We fenced back and forth for a while, with me trying to draw her out and find out more about her, and Lilly-Mae resisting neatly. I got the impression it was less to do with her not trusting me enough, more simply not trusting anyone in general.

But reality soon intruded again. There was something bothering me about the delivery; something Lilly-Mae had said which was tied in with the events at the house. It kept slipping away, then suddenly came back.

'I'm confused,' I said, looking Lilly-Mae straight in the eye. 'If you both left in such a hurry after Frank got shot, who left the envelope on the mailbox? Surely Gus wasn't intending to leave it there in the hope that I'd find it? What would have happened if I'd found Frank and headed straight for the hills without stopping? I mean, anyone could have picked it up after that.'

'Anyone?' Her big eyes looked back at me with what I was convinced was total and utter innocence. Or maybe she was another resting actress. If so, she was better than most.

At that point I looked out of the window just as two police vehicles with flashing lights went by. In the first were three men in plain clothes, with a uniform driving. In the second were two plain clothes sitting in the front... and in the back, looking aggrieved and angry, sat Paulie and Dwight/Diego Selecca.

'Anyone,' I said, and nodded towards the cavalcade going by outside. 'Like the police.'

TWENTY-NINE

Lilly-Mae looked as puzzled as I felt, but if she was genuinely innocent in all this, it still didn't explain what she was doing there. If she had come to Palm Springs hoping I would get all manly and protect her from the baddies, she was in for a surprise. I might have my moments when faced with unhelpful officials or indolent shop assistants, but fists of fury in the face of guns was not part of my make-up.

'That's it,' she said suddenly.

'It is?' She had a faint smile on her face, like someone who'd suddenly grasped the solution to a knotty problem.

'You said the package you delivered was a memory stick?'

'That's right. Why?'

'Well, that's kinda weird. After you left, Gus was prowling around with a bunch of papers in his hand. He was mad because he'd run out of big envelopes. I said I'd go out first thing in the morning to get some, but he said not to bother as he'd get one of the boys to bring some up before you got there.' She looked at me. 'That sounds like whatever he'd intended you to bring to Palm Springs was papers, not a memory stick, right?'

'Maybe. These papers – did you see what he did with them?'

She shook her head. 'No. I just guessed he was going to hold on to them until morning. After that I never gave it another thought. Gus trusted me fine up to a point, but he didn't like me asking questions.'

I thought about it. 'He might have decided to transfer whatever was on the papers to a memory stick instead. Easier to find an envelope for something that small... easier to carry, too.' I explained about the other items I'd hauled around the world with me. In fact I was surprised at how much people still relied on paper.

Lilly-Mae shook her head. 'Uh-uh. Gus was strictly a papers man. He had a laptop, but he hated using it. He said computers could be accessed by the Feds without him even knowing and they'd know all his business.'

I remembered the laptop on Mekashnik's desk, the power light blinking. 'Yet it was on when I got to the house this morning.' Perhaps my arrival had interrupted someone.

The same thought evidently occurred to Lilly-Mae. 'You think Gus was there when you arrived?'

'Maybe,' I agreed. 'And if Selecca knew Gus didn't trust computers, it explains why he looked so surprised to see a memory stick.' The only problem left to consider was how the envelope containing the stick got on top of the mailbox. I told her how I'd examined the box when I first arrived, and if it had been there then I would have seen it.

'So someone put it there while you were inside the house?' Lilly-Mae chewed her lip over that one. 'But that could have been–'

'Gus.' I nodded. 'He might have counted on me not seeing Frank's body in the pool, and was hoping I'd spot the envelope and bring it to Palm Springs.' It wouldn't have taken him long to scoot out of the house and make his way down to the main gate. If I was right it immediately set me wondering if it had been Gus who'd set the police on Selecca, all part of some plan to deal with his opponent. It made the contents of the memory stick suddenly more than interesting.

'Would it help if we got to see the computer?' said Lilly-Mae. 'I mean, if that's where the information came from, it had to be Gus who put it there, right? Maybe we could see a list of the last documents opened or copied.'

I gave her an old-fashioned look. Suddenly she was one of Charlie's Angels and wanted to go round taking a peek into Gus Mekashnik's dealings. Didn't she know of his reputation for dismantling people's body parts? 'Are you suggesting we go back to Lake Lure and take a look?'

'Sure. Why not? At least we might find out what this is all about, right?' She checked her phone. 'There's a flight out tonight through New York which gets to Charlotte tomorrow morning. We should take that.'

'Not me,' I said truthfully. If I went anywhere near New York it would be to catch a flight to London. 'I couldn't give a toss what was on it. This is where I step out and go back to my humble delivery job.' I'd already had the narrow escape at Scheveningen when Rik Heysens had been arrested. Now this. Why push my luck further? Anyway, I wasn't cut out for James Bond stuff. It had been exciting at first, but the gloss was wearing off as quickly as the coating on a cheap Singaporean watch.

'But I have a key,' Lilly-Mae insisted. 'And I know computers. And,' she grinned mischievously, 'I know a secret way in through the woods. Even if they're still around, the cops will never see us.'

Great. This is what comes of raising girls on Nancy Drew mysteries all those years ago. They become uncontrollable and want to conquer the world. Then it occurred to me that we were planning on sneaking into a house where Lilly-Mae had every right to be. 'Why can't you just walk in the front door? You could say you'd been away on a trip – which is true.'

She shook her head with an expression of alarm. 'Are you kidding? Those local cops would have me locked up in some freaky women's jail in two seconds. Jake, I know those guys. They think with their butts, not their brains. I mean, why pass up on someone who lives there just to waste time looking for the real killer?'

'There's still Gus,' I pointed out. 'He's out there somewhere.'

'Right. But do you know where? 'Cos I don't.'

I sighed and tried one last tack. 'Okay. But I still think going back is a bad idea. Do you really want to hang around to see how many other enemies Gus has? Better to let sleeping dogs lie, don't you think?'

'And do what?' she countered, eyes flashing. 'Forget all about it? Jake, I have stuff back at the house – personal stuff I don't want to lose. Besides, I can't simply walk away without knowing what's happened to him. I know he's not whiter than white, but if he's in trouble I'd like to help. And if he's behind all this, well – I'd like to find out what he's done.'

I argued for another five minutes. It was like talking to a beautiful but obstinate statue with an answer to everything. In the end Lilly-Mae fought dirty by throwing up her hands and suggesting I get back on a plane to London and she would sort it out herself. It was the kind of thing I couldn't agree to, which I suspect she was counting on.

'All right,' I said finally, knowing when to give in. 'I'll come with you. But at the first sign of nasty men with guns or badges, we hit the road. Agreed?'

She smiled again and squeezed my hand. 'I knew you'd help, Jake.

Thank you. Anyway, are you saying you could really go all the way back to England and forget about everything you've seen here?'

I was, actually. Well, I thought I was. But put like that there was no chance. Added to the coy expression on her face, which set my pulse racing, she was still holding my hand and I found myself breathing like an asthmatic sixteen-year-old on his first date. It was no contest; given the choice between being there with this attractive and alluring woman, and London with… well, not a lot. I decided going back was a poor option.

'First thing,' I croaked, when my voice began working again, 'is we find out if the police are around. If they are we stay well away.'

We finished our drinks and went in search of a phone, and I dialled the number at Gus's house again. It rang fifteen times, during which Lilly-Mae crowded in on me and pressed her ear against the outside of the receiver. She smelled fresh and soapy, and for a moment I forgot where I was, recalling what she had looked like on the patio in that backless sundress.

Then someone ruined the perfect moment by picking up the phone.

I waited for them to speak, but all I could hear was some wheezy breathing and what sounded like stubble rasping against the mouthpiece. Definitely not a cleaning lady, unless she had some serious facial hair problems. Lilly-Mae pressed ever more comfortably against me, her eyes like dark liquid pools and her arm round my waist. Oh, Lord forgive me my trespasses but right then all I wanted to do was say to hell with Gus, throw down the phone and grab hold of her with both hands.

Instead I said, 'Gus?'

'Who is this?' It was an older man's voice and sounded polite but gruff with authority. In the background a burst of radio static was followed by voices, and I felt the hairs move on the back of my neck. Cops.

I put the phone down. I could see by the expression on her face that Lilly-Mae had come to the same conclusion. 'They must have found Frank.'

'And now they've got Selecca – and the memory stick.' Lilly-Mae looked at me and chewed her lip. She was still up close and smelled wonderful. Her hair was clean and glossy and her skin like a peach, and I had to work really hard to stop myself leaning in and licking the side of her face. 'We go back to the house and take a look.'

I could think of so many other things I'd rather be doing, mostly involving Lilly-Mae, but now was probably not the time to say it.

'At night, preferably. That should give them time to get fed up waiting and clear out. Do you really know a sneaky way in?'

'Of course. A gal has to have some secrets, y'know. And I didn't have a couple of years' convent education without picking up some field craft. Those Sisters ran a tight ship; we had to learn to move like Marines if we wanted to have a naughty night out.'

I tried to picture an adolescent Lilly-Mae creeping about in the dark, commando-fashion, outwitting the combined forces of the Sisters of Mercy. Somehow I wasn't so much surprised by that as by the fact that she'd been to a convent. I'd assumed she'd had a normal high school education like most American girls, but it seemed there were more things about this woman that I had yet to find out.

Like what was the precise relationship between her and Gus.

'Okay. Where first? Any suggestions?' I had a sudden flash of a hotel room, clean sheets and a nice warm shower, and felt a flush creeping up my face.

'Charlotte,' said Lilly-Mae without hesitation, killing the moment stone dead. 'The house I stayed in before coming here. Gus owns it, but nobody knows about it – not even his accountant. He picked it up recently through a business deal. He was planning on selling it to a guy he knows for cash down and no questions.'

I wondered what sort of deal lands someone with a house rather than hard cash, but bit my tongue. No doubt the arms business traded in commodities other than money when the need arose, and what better than property? No doubt Gus also had access to a team of lawyers to help with the tricky issue of title deeds.

An hour later we were at the airport, keeping a low profile and waiting for a flight out . We had time to spare but it was better there than hanging around Palm Springs waiting to be picked up by the cops if Selecca had spilled the beans. As we sat in a remote corner of the lounge watching planes landing and taking off, Lilly-Mae turned and looked at me with a speculative expression.

'Jake, are you married?'

The question came right out of the blue, as unconnected with what we'd been talking about as it was possible to get. There we were, still only a fingernail's width away from being implicated in someone's death, and she wanted to know about my domestic arrangements.

'Yes,' I said. 'Well… separated. I'm resting, as actors say. Why do you ask?'

She shrugged and gave a half smile. 'No reason. Just making conversation.' She waved a hand as if it really wasn't important, but her next words blew that right out of the water. 'Actually, that's not true… I was just wondering if there was a Mrs Jake waiting in the background for you to come home. You hadn't said.'

'No,' I said truthfully. 'There is a Mrs Jake, legally speaking. But she's moved on and I'm between assignments. The only other family I've got is a younger brother.' I told her about Susan's departure and about Marcus. It didn't take long. 'How about you?'

'Me? I was married once, a few years ago. He was in the navy. We ended up finding out we were too different to stay together. It didn't work out.' End of subject, in other words.

'So how did you come to be with Gus?'

'Living in his house, you mean?' She stared absently across the lounge and slowly shook her head. 'Gus and I are just friends – I told you. I fetched up in San Diego after my husband and I split up. I needed a job and someone who knew Gus told me he was looking for help. He had a place on the coast back then. I think he had contacts in the naval base and could get ex-military equipment before it came up for public auction. I applied for the job and he took me on.' I didn't say anything, which she took for some kind of unasked question, because she looked at me with a hint of fire in her eye. 'We also kind of went out for a while, but it didn't work out. I never knew what, exactly, but Gus has some… problems in that area. He doesn't relate much to women.'

'You mean he's gay?' Well, why not?

'No. Nothing like that – at least, I'm pretty sure not.' Her voice was quiet. It was evidently a touchy subject. I certainly didn't want to know what Gus's problems were, although the news did make me feel unaccountably better, for some deep, doubtless Freudian, reason.

After a while she gave me a nudge with her elbow. 'Jake Foreman, you look like you're thinking too much. If you must know, I lived at Gus's place and did administrative work for him. Nothing to do with the core business, though… he did all that himself. Like I said, he's been good to me. And before you ask, I had my own bedroom.'

216

'I know,' I said. 'I've seen it.' I told her about my lightning search after finding Frank, but decided not to comment on the state of her room. Women can be a little sensitive about that kind of thing.

THIRTY

We had left Charlotte airport along with the late afternoon commuter traffic and headed out into the countryside to the east of the city along Interstate 85. The built-up area had gradually fallen behind, and when we left the interstate we were soon drifting into a region of scattered housing, white clapboard churches every couple of miles, a few farms, the odd country lodge and golf course and two or three groups of commercial buildings.

It was standard scenery, with the familiar signs for Budweiser, Pepsi, Comfort Inns and Toyota pick-ups. Small-town America, with nothing to disturb the peace and quiet of the trees and pastures. Yet being even this close to the house at Cedar Point Road – and we were nearly a hundred miles away – made me feel twitchy, and I wondered why I'd agreed to come back. Anywhere in the same country as Gus Mekashnik was too close for me.

I'd hired a Toyota 4WD at the airport, using the cash Mekashnik had paid me, backed up by my driver's licence and passport. The rental clerk had given me a funny look when I'd handed over the sheaf of notes, but on hearing my accent had shrugged me off as being foreign and therefore apt to do strange things like using real money instead of plastic.

Lilly-Mae elected to drive, which she did in what I thought of as a spirited manner. That involved speed and determination and a finger vaguely stuck up to most of the rules of the road.

The house Gus had acquired in a business deal lay at the end of a lane which twisted through a stretch of trees and small, fenced fields. An overgrown track bisected it not far from the house, where a rusted mailbox stood off to one side and a weather beaten pole blocked the way to an adjacent property. If there were any closer neighbours, they would still have needed a car to make a visit.

While not as big as the house where Frank had met his maker, it was still bigger than anything I'd ever lived in. It was ranch-style, with a stone chimney poking out of a slate roof running down almost to ground level on one side, and big picture windows looking out over a couple of acres of wild grass and trees on the other. By the look of it the previous owner hadn't much liked gardening, leaving everything for nature to do what it did best. It had an oddly ordered wilderness appearance which went well with the house and the surrounding trees and countryside. The only concessions to modern American living were a brick-built barbecue bay to one side and an indoor swimming-pool housed in a long, narrow wood-and-glass extension at the back. It looked deserted, with the same abandoned air I'd felt about the house at Cedar Point Road. On the other hand, I reminded myself, look what I'd found there.

I hoped this was going to be different.

Lilly-Mae unlocked the door and a wave of chilled air swept out to greet us. If there was anyone waiting for us, they were keeping nice and cool while they were at it. While Lilly-Mae saw to the lights and curtains, I took a leisurely look around, peering into four large bedrooms, a den, three bathrooms and a huge kitchen. The whole place was expensively-fitted out and colour co-ordinated – and about as personal as a phone booth. The previous occupant evidently had a leaning towards leather chairs, chunky coffee tables and thick rugs, but they were merely objects in the same room, lacking any kind of harmony.

Close by the kitchen I found a pine door with a strong smell of chlorine coming through. It was unlocked and I gently eased it open with a certain amount of trepidation; the last pool I'd seen had a dead gardener floating in it.

This one was empty, the surface undisturbed, calm and inviting. The air was warm and clammy, and a thin haze of mist hovered just above the surface. It was long and narrow, the kind of pool built by people who want to indulge in some serious swimming every day rather than a lazy splash clutching a can of coke and a burger. A solid pine wall ran down one side, while the other was glassed in, with a view of the trees and the wild garden area. A couple of loungers stood along one edge of the water, while down at the end was an inflated plastic chair with a glass holder in each rounded arm. Maybe the previous owner had had a sense of humour.

I went back to the kitchen where Lilly-Mae was checking the enormous fridge-freezer. It had enough food in it to feed a small regiment for a few days, and meant we wouldn't have to go out shopping and risk running into someone we didn't want to meet.

I told Lilly-Mae I had to call Clayton and let him know what had happened. Apart from telling him I was still alive, I was hoping he might have some ideas about how I could get out from all this. With luck it might involve him sending someone large and scare-proof to give Gus a slapping.

The Nokia battery was dead. Lilly-Mae pointed at the phone on the kitchen wall. 'Use that phone. Just dial out.'

It rang three times before being switched to another line, and I realised I'd called at an unreasonable time. Even Clayton couldn't spend all his time in the office.

'Yes?' His voice sounded guarded.

'It's Jake.'

He breathed heavily with what sounded like relief. 'Thank the Lord for that. You had me worried. Where are you?'

I brought him up to date, without giving him any details about where I was now. Actually, given the tortuous route Lilly-Mae had followed from the airport, I wasn't sure I could have told him anyway. I was guarded about mentioning finding a dead Frank in the pool, on the grounds that I didn't know if anyone else might be listening in, but I think he caught on.

'And Mekashnik told you he checked with me first about you doing the drop to Palm Springs?'

'Yes. Are you saying he didn't?'

'Absolutely he didn't. I would have advised you against it.'

'Why? You said he was kosher.'

There was a lengthy pause before he said, 'That situation appears to have changed. I'm sorry, Jake, but I've only just heard some worrying rumours about Mekashnik. That's why I'm relieved you called. I tried contacting you a short while ago.'

'My fault,' I said. 'I switched off the phone while I was in the air. What kind of rumours?'

'He's recently made some unfortunate investments outside the normal parameters of his business after some of his deliveries failed to go according to plan. That means he's got some bad press and heavy debts, and in his business that's not good. I'm told he's had to sell off a large part of his property portfolio, including his office, stock and main warehouse, to recoup his losses and get people off his back.'

'Would these people be in Colombia?'

If he was surprised that I knew he didn't show it. 'Yes, like that. But it gets worse. He's reported to have been selling black market arms on the dark web, and the Federal authorities are on to him. I'm sorry, Jake, if I'd known beforehand I wouldn't have allowed you anywhere near him. All I can say is, I'm not the only one taken by surprise. It's a bad business.'

The hairs on the back of my neck bristled. Federal authorities? Had they been watching the house while I was there? I mentioned it to Clayton but he said probably not.

'My information is less than twelve hours old,' he said. 'They probably haven't been given the green light yet. Still, that's by the by. Are you in the clear or do you need help?'

While I'd been talking, Lilly-Mae had come up and slid her arm round my waist, leaning into me to listen. Her closeness suddenly made talking all the more difficult. 'Actually,' I lied, 'I'm fine. I should be back soon.'

'Good. So why are you in Charlotte with this… Lilly-Mae Breadon person?'

The Lilly-Mae Breadon person in question heard that and gave the phone a sharp look. I placed a hand on her shoulder in case she decided to tell Clayton what she thought. She responded by looking into my face and smiling, then edging closer.

This was the difficult bit. I really wasn't trying to be heroic in coming back to have a look in the Mekashnik house; I truly did want to help Lilly-Mae. If all it took was a bit of skulking around, that would be it. After that I'd be on the first flight back to England. I explained it to him in brief detail, hinting at the need for a few days' rest and relaxation to round it off. At that, Lilly-Mae peered at me and fluttered her eyebrows. Up close, I could see a faint pattern of laughter lines at the corner of her eyes, and a trace of wrinkles in the soft skin of her throat. The smell of her was intoxicating.

'Good idea,' said Clayton, bringing me back to planet Earth. 'In fact, coming back here might not be the wisest thing to do right at the moment.'

My stomach hit bottom and bounced. 'Why? What's happened?'

'I had a visit yesterday. A man wanting to know where you were. He said his employer, name of John Lyons, needed to contact you urgently. I told him I really couldn't divulge that information.'

'Thank you,' I said gratefully. It had to have been Basher's man. 'I'm sorry, I–'

'Unfortunately Lyons wasn't satisfied with that and came round to see me with a friend of his. A large friend.'

Oh, buggeration. 'Are you all right?'

'Absolutely. Francis was able to convince them to go away. He likes to keep his hand in whenever he can. He can be very persuasive.'

Francis. The man in the front lobby. He looked capable of persuading a tank to change direction.

'I'd better come back and sort it out,' I said shortly. With my face, if Basher had his way. It immediately set me wondering if Marcus was in any danger. I'd better call him and explain.

'I wouldn't advise coming back just yet. Let me do some digging and I'll let you know what to do.'

'What sort of digging?'

'Everyone has their secrets. I'm sure this... gentleman has more than a few. If so, Francis will find something to put him off course. Something to make him get over being a cuckold.'

Cuckold. Now there's a word you don't hear every day. It didn't sound odd, though, coming with a plummy accent like Clayton's, and made Lilly-Mae stifle a giggle with her hand. She also looked at me with what I read as a new appreciation.

'That's very kind,' I said, 'but it's not your problem.' I felt embarrassed. Clayton knowing what I'd got up to with Jane was something I could live with; getting me out of a sticky situation all of my own doing was humiliating. And now Lilly-Mae knew, too.

'Why not?' he countered reasonably. 'You work for me; I need you free of encumbrances. Besides,' There was the ghost of a chuckle, 'you're not the first man to have come unstuck in your situation. It happens all the time.'

'My situation?'

'We checked you out when you first came to me. Standard operating procedure. I probably know you better than your wife does. I'll be in touch.'

I replaced the phone and turned to face Lilly-Mae. She was looking at me with a quizzical expression, her arm still against my waist, and I breathed in her perfume and wondered why she was smiling.

'So,' she asked softly. 'Who's been a naughty Jake, then?'

'I can explain,' I said. But she stopped me by leaning closer and kissing me, her tongue flicking against my lips. My mouth fizzed with static electricity and I felt my knees buckle at the warmth of her breath.

'Explain later,' she whispered, and pulled back, patting me on the chest before kissing me briefly again. 'Come on. We'll eat first. It'll be dark by the time we get there.'

'We're still going?' All I could think about was Federal authorities. Surely they'd have the place in lockdown by now.

'You bet,' she replied firmly. 'I need to get my stuff.'

Damn.

THIRTY-ONE

The road towards Lake Lure was deserted save for the occasional vehicle, and I was happy to sit back and leave it to Lilly-Mae to get us to our destination in one piece. Apart from flicking through the radio channels in search of music she said little, which suited me fine.

My brain was reeling with thoughts about what I was going to do once I got back to England. Whatever Clayton's man came up with on Basher Lyons it was going to have to be a real belter to keep him from getting his hands round my throat. What with the added excitement of having a divorce case lining up against me, which was probably going to put me in penury for the rest of my days, and the shadow of Dunckley possibly having a change of heart about my wellbeing, the prospects for a quiet life didn't look too rosy. But that was jumping the gun considering what might happen if Lilly-Mae and I got caught breaking into Gus Mekashnik's house.

We ghosted past the turning to Cedar Point without slowing; I wanted to see if there was any sign of police activity in the area in case we needed to make a quick departure and couldn't make it back towards Charlotte. The shops and buildings which were neighbours to Cappy's Diner showed no signs of a living soul, and I told Lilly-Mae to turn round and go up Cedar Point Road.

She drove us past the entrance to 184 without stopping, but it was clear in the headlights that that the gates were sealed with a strip of chequered crime scene tape. If there was a police presence at the house they'd taped themselves in and were keeping a low profile.

We followed the road in a gradual winding curl up the hillside, every bend bringing yet another increased incline. On one side was a jagged line of rock, while on the other was a dense black nothingness composed mainly of trees and who-knew-what open space. Our lights occasionally caught flashes of white water where a fast-flowing stream came near the road, and the rounded bulk of heavy boulders covered in dark lichen.

'Where are we going?' I asked as we ground round another bend and growled up yet another incline. If we continued climbing at this rate we'd soon be in open air somewhere above the Milky Way.

'Back entrance,' said Lilly-Mae. 'I told you, I know a secret way in.' She looked ready for skulking around, too. She had tied her hair back in a ponytail and swapped her dress and shoes for jeans, shirt and hiking boots. I wondered how many other surprises she had in store. While the air of made-up and manicured elegance had gone, concealed by the finest products Levi and Timberland had to offer, she still possessed an aura of sexiness which I doubted she could lose if she dressed in an old hessian sack. But there was now something steely about her which I guessed came from far back in her past. Whatever it was, I found it intriguing. Or maybe I'd just discovered I have a thing for sexy women in jeans and big boots.

The lights picked out a sudden shadow in the rock face, and Lilly-Mae swung the wheel and took the Toyota through a gap and up a pot-holed track which burrowed like a tunnel through the trees. We bumped and lurched for about a mile before we reached a clearing and she pulled up and switched off the lights and engine.

'From here on, we walk,' she announced.

I climbed out and stood in the dark, listening to the engine ticking and the noise thousands of trees make as they're growing. Overhead a few stars were visible through the canopy of leaves, and somewhere in the distance something barked. The feeling of our fragility and lack of importance in the sheer immensity of it all was awesome.

'Just one thing,' I said softly, when Lilly-Mae joined me. 'Are there any creatures in these woods I should be aware of?'

'Creatures?'

'You know… the kind that bite lumps out of people who are dumb enough to go walking in the woods in the middle of the night.'

She gave a ghost of a chuckle. 'Oh. You mean bears and things?'

'I wish you hadn't said bears.'

'Well, we've got them, sure. Probably not right here, but further over towards the Smokey Mountains.' Her voice trailed off and I resisted the urge to dive back into the Toyota. Coming from a country where the only thing to avoid is a bad-tempered rabbit, anything larger or fiercer was, in my book, worth worrying about. Especially if it was liable to be sitting in a tree waiting for me to pass by underneath.

'How about snakes? Don't you have rattlers around here?'

She leaned across and brushed my face with her lips. 'You're my hero, you know that?'

'Hey, don't mock. I should warn you I left my Swiss army knife back at the house.'

'Don't worry, you won't need it. The last man injured by a bear around these parts was a tourist over near Ashville.'

'Seriously?'

'Yes. It was a stuffed black bear outside a souvenir store. It fell on him. And as for snakes, well, try not to think about them. The terrain's all downhill from here.' She sounded amazingly calm, as if she was planning a casual afternoon's hike through a grassy meadow. She reached into her bag and took out a small flashlight. 'I'll go first – I know roughly where the path is, but we can't use this too often. Stick close to me and you'll be fine.'

Stick close to you, I thought, and I'll be more than fine. 'Okay, kemosabe,' I agreed, and took out my own slim travel light which I never went anywhere without. It had been a godsend on many occasions when electricity in some backwater had proved unreliable. 'You lead, I'll follow.'

It was easier said than done. Even using the flashlight in brief bursts, the vegetation was so thick I lost track of where Lilly-Mae was within minutes, and only re-established contact when I bumped into her from behind. That bit was quite pleasant, I have to admit. Which was more than could be said for the branches waiting to slap me in the face every few steps, and the wicked lengths of thorn waiting to catch me below waist level and tug at my clothing, or the muddy wallows which Lilly-Mae seemed to avoid as if by instinct, but which I trod in every time. I don't know what it was about them, but the smell was appalling, as if something had fallen in and died at the bottom. The path bore no resemblance to any kind of footpath I had ever known. All in all it made for slow and painful progress.

Eventually Lilly-Mae came to a stop and flicked on her flashlight to warn me. I stopped and hunkered down next to her, and wiped a film of sweat from my face. I felt like the rawest kind of recruit at boot camp: hot, bothered and wishing I'd never joined up. The atmosphere among the trees was oppressive and devoid of fresh air, and I was beginning to feel the exertion in my legs. Walking through airports is no preparation for any kind of romp in the woods.

'We're about a hundred yards from the house,' whispered Lilly-Mae. 'The backyard's right ahead and over a fence. If we keep walking in a straight line after that, we'll hit the pool.' I felt rather than saw her face turn to me in the dark. 'What should we do next, Jake?'

'Do?' I looked at her in amazement. 'What do you mean, do next? You were the one with the gung-ho plan. You said you knew a back way in. I thought you had it all worked out.' I couldn't believe it. There we were having tracked halfway across the southern Appalachians in pitch darkness, surrounded by hunger-crazed bears, snakes and wild cats and suddenly I was voted jungle leader.

I heard a faint chuckle in the dark and her hand brushed against my face. 'That's okay. I didn't want to deny you the opportunity of going all macho on me if you wanted to and demanding to take the lead.'

'Perish the thought. After you, Penelope Pitstop.'

She stood up and crept away, and I stuck to her like a shadow, wishing I could switch on my torch and see her shapely bottom twitching in front of me. At least it would have given me something to occupy my mind.

We found the fence a few minutes later. Beyond it lay the swimming-pool, a faint patch reflecting remnants of ambient light. Further on I could just make out the regular oblong of the roof tiles. The smell of chlorine made me wonder whether the pool man had come back to clean the pool, and whether his description of me had been clear enough to do a number on me when I tried to leave the country.

We took it in turns to slide through the wire strands of the fence, and sat watching the house for a couple of minutes. If the police were waiting, I was hoping they would betray their presence before we moved off. A cough would do, or the jangle of handcuffs or the creak of leather. I kept getting horrible visions of being caught halfway across the open grass by the sudden ping of a security light and the shouted command to freeze and hit the dirt – or whatever the locals called out when they caught a suspect.

'Come on,' I said finally. 'Let's get this over with.'

We scuttled across the grass and approached the house from one side, where Lilly-Mae had said there were fewer windows. Our footsteps sounded much too loud in the darkness, and I was half expecting the glare of floodlights. But we were soon up against a wall, breathing heavily and listening hard.

Two careful circuits of the house revealed everything was locked and sealed, with more police tape across the doors and windows, and around the pool. I couldn't help throwing a quick glance towards the water, but Frank had evidently been taken away.

Lilly-Mae stopped at the front door on the second circuit, ducked beneath the tape and fiddled with the lock. Seconds later we were inside and closing the door behind us. Lilly-Mae switched on her flashlight and shone it around the foyer.

'A back window,' I said. 'We should leave one open just in case.' If anyone did come up the drive our quickest and most unobtrusive way out would be through the back and across the grass into the trees.

Lilly-Mae gave me a quirky look. 'Good thinking, Jake. Are you sure you've never done this before?'

'Positive. Didn't I tell you, I've led a blameless life?'

I followed her into the room where Gus had his desk and waited until she had unlocked the French window and left it barely open. Then I looked around, flicking on my own flashlight. I would have preferred the main lights but there was no guarantee the house wasn't under surveillance from somewhere close by.

The laptop still lay on the desk, but now the power light was off. A thin dusting of white powder covered the casing and the desk where the police had checked for fingerprints, and elsewhere were signs of disturbance where they had conducted their search.

I turned the laptop on. I was wondering why the police had left it behind. If it had been me, I'd have taken it in for inspection by IT specialists, in the hope it might yield some useful information. Gus wouldn't have been the first villain to have left incriminating evidence in the most obvious of places, and I was betting the local police were sufficiently well-informed about his business to be drooling at the mouth at the prospect of taking a peek inside his private files.

'I need to go upstairs,' said Lilly-Mae. 'Can you manage there for a few minutes?'

I nodded. 'Sure. But don't be long. There may be file names you recognise. I'll just trawl through in the meantime and check for the last documents opened.'

She skipped out and I waited for the machine to show some sign of life. Nothing. Dead as a piece of roadkill. Probably the battery, used up by the police taking a sneaky peek at Gus's data.

I checked the desk drawers. They were all unlocked and mostly bare of anything other than standard office equipment such as pens, letterhead, envelopes and the like. And a power lead. I plugged it in and switched on at the wall, and watched the power light glow in the dark.

But that was all it did. The laptop itself remained solidly unhelpful and completely blank, other than a faint ghosting of tiny flecks. No programs. No files. Nothing.

It had been wiped clean.

Just then I felt a ghost of movement across the back of my neck, and remembered the French window. Instinct was telling me it was time to go. I switched off the laptop and took a quick look round for signs of other drawers or a filing cabinet, but Gus evidently believed in keeping his paperwork somewhere else.

Lilly-Mae came clattering down the stairs lugging a large rucksack. She stared at the laptop, then at me. 'What's wrong?'

'It's been wiped. There's nothing on it.'

She looked puzzled and tried switching the machine on again. 'I don't understand,' she muttered, tapping the keys. 'There was stuff on there, I know it. Gus used it for some basic things. Why would he wipe it?'

I recalled Gus switching on the laptop when I'd first arrived, and the whirr of programs firing up. There had definitely been something on there then; something he had felt necessary to check up on the moment he returned. But not now.

'Maybe we can take it with us,' I suggested. 'An expert might be able to salvage something from the hard drive.'

'Just what I was thinking,' said a deep voice from over near the door. Then the room lights clicked on. Lilly-Mae and I spun round like marionettes.

It was Gus Mekashnik, and he was holding a rifle again, this time pointing somewhere between us.

THIRTY-TWO

'Gus?' Lilly-Mae was the first to recover. She was staring at the rifle as if seeing it for the first time, which seemed weird to me; living in this house, in this neck of the woods, she must have seen Gus and his buddies with guns more than just a few times. 'Gus, where have you been?'

'Seeing to business, hon,' Gus replied. 'Seeing to business.' He looked at me with a faint frown on his granite face. 'What are you doing?' He sounded perfectly calm but his tone sent a shiver through me. I noticed the rifle was still midway between Lilly-Mae and me, but it wouldn't take more than a twitch of his finger to direct it, so I kept very still.

'Gus, we were trying to find out what was going on… why Frank was killed.' Lilly-Mae was speaking quickly, and I realised she wasn't as comfortable with the situation as I'd imagined she would be. Maybe seeing Gus at the other end of a rifle put a new slant on their relationship. 'Did you know Selecca got arrested? The police nearly got Jake as well. We got out just in time.'

'Sure, I knew that.' Gus smiled and nodded towards the laptop on the desk. 'You know how to get the hard drive out of there, Lilly-Mae? There's a release catch in the base. Be a doll and take it out for me, would you?'

We waited while Lilly-Mae reached over and found the catch. The hard drive clicked out and slid into her hand. She handed it to Gus, who sidled over to the French window and pushed aside the curtain. The rifle barrel remained solidly on us all the way.

'The trouble with this technology,' he said casually, as if we were friends gathered round a log fire, 'is you just can't trust it. Hell, it's like I've said all along: it's likely to turn and bite you in the ass the moment your back's turned. Ain't that what I'm always saying, Lilly-Mae?'

Lilly-Mae said nothing. The expression on her face told me she was as puzzled by Gus's actions as I was and didn't trust herself to speak. However long she'd known him, this must have seemed a real key-change in his demeanour.

'Which is what Dwight Selecca's now finding out,' he continued with a grin. Then he gave an almost casual flick of his wrist and the hard drive spun through the open door and into the night. There was a faint splash as it entered the pool.

'Problem solved.' He returned to his position by the door. 'As I was saying, all this technology–' He broke off and looked at Lilly-Mae with a pretend look of concern. 'What's up, girl? You look like a bear got her paw stuck in a grinder. You figured old Gus was a big dumb-ass who couldn't figure one end of a computer from another, right? Well, you figured wrong. Just because I play dumb, don't mean I am.'

'What do you mean?' Lilly-Mae's voice was as taut as a violin string.

Gus smiled like the cat who'd got the cream and was only marginally sorry for the kitty who lost out. 'Gee, sorry, girl. I gotta tell you things have changed around here. I ran into a little local difficulty, y'might say and had to sell off a lot of holdings. Got drained, finance-wise… Lost some money in a deal which Selecca recommended to me a while back, had a couple of deliveries go sour. I should never have trusted that greasy little snake. He pulled me in and let me take a beating on some equipment turned out to be substandard. By the time it was noticed it was too late. There's no way back from that in this business. You get a bad rep, it stays with you.'

'What sort of equipment?' I couldn't help it. Maybe if we kept him talking he might not do anything rash, like pulling the trigger.

'Military hardware. Surplus to requirements down in Georgia. Only what Selecca forgot to mention was, it was basically trash, heading for the dump to be crushed and melted down. Selecca had the contacts and I put up the money. When the customers found the hardware wouldn't do nothing he turned round and told 'em I must've done a switch. They wasn't best pleased.'

'They?'

'Yeah. Some folks down south.' Gus looked pale, as if he'd been reminded of something nasty that was eating at him.

South. That was an awful lot of territory, but after what Clayton had told me, I didn't have to ask where. Unfortunately, Lilly-Mae did.

'You mean Latin America?' It came like an accusation, and from her tone I got the impression she was more surprised by the location than the fact that Gus had done something he really shouldn't have.

He nodded and looked even sicker. I didn't blame him. I'd made several trips down that way, to areas where development was much needed but not always welcome without a hefty slush fund and local government assistance. Then there were the non-governmental groups you had to deal with on the side; the ones amounting to private armies with a willingness to leave behind a lot of dead bodies in the name of *la revolucion* or *la libertad* or whatever the current local cause might be. If they saw an opportunity to hone in on a development deal by mounting obstacles which could be 'removed' by an exchange of hard cash, they would do it. If Gus had been supplying arms south of the border, he'd no doubt broken several dozen US Federal and possibly international laws in the process, as well as mixing it with people who had a reputation for being very poor losers.

'What happened to Frank?' Lilly-Mae's eyes were burning into Gus like lasers. No doubt she was only just realising that whatever Gus had got himself into could have repercussions for her, too. Like it had for Frank.

Gus didn't want to answer that one. He pulled a face and looked at me, then motioned impatiently at the French window. 'You. Outside.'

'What for?' There are moments to be argumentative, and this probably wasn't one of them. But right then the last thing I wanted to do was walk out of the door into the night with Gus Mekashnik standing behind me with a big gun. Something told me it wasn't likely to end well. And there was Lilly-Mae to worry about, too, because she knew him better than anyone and was looking as if she wanted to throw up.

I walked towards the open door, my legs beginning to lose their feeling. Was this how people felt before facing a firing squad? Unable to run away even if they wanted to?

Gus stepped back and allowed me to stand in the doorway, with the curtains just touching me, fanned by a faint breeze coming off the garden.

'It was you, wasn't it?' said Lilly-Mae. 'You killed Frank.' She sounded angry, her voice almost a whisper. Yet it cut across the room like a knife. I stopped and looked back at her, forgetting about the rifle. She was staring at Gus with an intensity which was frightening, and I turned and looked at him. He was still pointing the gun at me, but his eyes had switched to Lilly-Mae and his mouth had gone slack, as if the muscles in his face had lost all flexibility.

I thought about what she had said. It didn't seem logical. Why would Gus kill his own man? And why leave a body in his own pool, waiting to be discovered by the first person to happen along? He could have claimed it was the result of a break-in gone wrong, but why disappear, immediately throwing all the suspicion onto himself?

Gus evidently felt the same way. 'Don't be stupid, girl.' It was a warning, loud and clear.

But she wasn't listening. 'It was you,' Lilly-Mae insisted. 'There was no attacker; no men in the woods with guns. If there had been they would have come into the house for us before we even woke up.' She advanced towards him, her boots scuffing on the carpet. 'You'd been working downstairs that night. Anyone who wanted to get to you would have had hours to do it. They could have done it through the window with a squirrel-gun. Was that what you were working on, Gus? How to get out from a Federal investigation? How to get even with Selecca?'

'Honey, you're dreaming,' Gus growled. He didn't sound too convincing, but at least he wasn't concentrating on shooting me for a moment, which was something. The only problem was, I had no idea if I could do anything to stop him when he got back on track, which he was likely to do the moment Lilly-Mae stopped talking.

Or the moment she pressed the wrong button.

'No, Gus. I'm not dreaming.' Lilly-Mae stopped a couple of feet from him. She looked statuesque and imposing, and Gus backed up a few millimetres, a look of surprise on his face. Maybe he'd never seen her like this before. 'You think I'm just a pea-brained lil' girl, don't you? That I can't tell a rifle bullet from a lip gloss. I'm just a trophy you picked up along the way and kept around because it made you look good among those back-country corn-suckers you call friends. Well, I've got news for you, Gus. I'm not dumb. And just because I wasn't in the room didn't mean I never heard what was said.'

Not now, Lilly-Mae, I wanted to shout. *You've just said the wrong thing.*

'Heard?' Gus's face hardened and he glared at her as if he was talking to a backward child. 'You heard what, hon?' He lifted the gun and pointed it at her. 'You heard... exactly... what?'

'The deals. The calls late at night. I heard you getting nowhere with those gun nuts up in the hills, and those other losers who used to buy stuff from you. You think I didn't hear some of the calls from – where were they – Nicaragua? Venezuela? You've been selling to terrorists, Gus, did you know that? Those people... Jesus, how many laws have you broken? You think framing Selecca's going to get you out from that?'

'Lilly-Mae,' I tried to butt in but she had the bit between her teeth, and I guessed it was months, maybe years of tension and anger and heaven-knew-what finally coming out. She'd been living under the same roof as someone who'd been playing with matches and had finally set light to the whole box and was about to get scorched. As a time to choose to let him have a broadside, it couldn't have been worse, but it was too late now.

'Let me finish,' Lilly-Mae said with exaggerated calmness. 'Let me finish this. Gus, I didn't say anything before because I couldn't believe you were doing this. You've been dealing in guns – okay, so that's bad enough... It isn't what your average guy does for a living, but it started off legal, right? Then selling to those assholes in the hills... they never hurt anyone except themselves. But in the last – what, two months –

you've been losing it. And now you've gone over the edge. I mean, Gus, you cannot sell to those people down south and think you can get away with it. And now the cops and probably the FBI and Homeland Security have got Selecca, do you think he's going to keep quiet? Do you think he's going to protect you? Like he owes you a favour?'

'Selecca's never going to see the light of day. He's finished.' Gus spoke with quiet certainty, as if Lilly-Mae's tirade had gone right over his head. And maybe it had. Instead of the expected retort at being pinned down like that by Lilly-Mae, he didn't seem to be affected in any way. Quite the opposite, in fact. It was unnerving.

Lilly-Mae looked at him. 'Why? What did you do? What was on that stick, Gus?'

Gus grinned suddenly, as if the prize had popped out of the box for all to see. He looked from Lilly-Mae to me, and I braced myself in case he decided to start shooting. But instead he shrugged like it was a perfectly reasonable question. 'The one the boy scout from England, here, took to Palm Springs for me? Well… everything, I guess.'

'Everything?' I asked, since we all seemed to be getting on so well. Might as well join in now he'd mentioned me. It seemed only fair.

'Everything. Names, dates, amounts, shipments – the whole nine yards. Once they open that baby, they'll have enough dirt to put Selecca away for a thousand years. All linked to him, shipped by him, paid for by him.'

'The arms deals?' Lilly-Mae looked stunned, and puzzled.

'That's right. I figured if my business was going down the toilet and Selecca was moving in – 'cos that's what he was planning on doing, you know, moving in – then there was only one way to get him out of the way. Set it all up so it would look like he was top dog.' Gus looked pleased with himself, like he'd pulled a rabbit from a hat.

'It'll take 'em months, maybe years to unravel it all, by which time Selecca will be dead of frustration and I'll be… well, I'll be a long way from here.'

'You'd give up this house and everything?' I asked. I guessed he had other resources tucked away for this kind of eventuality.

He looked around at the room and shrugged. 'This isn't mine any more. I sold it months ago as collateral to set up the deal. Come another month and I'd be out of here, anyway, so what's to lose?'

'Something you forgot to mention to me, Gus?' said Lilly-Mae with heavy irony.

He gave her a look devoid of any interest. 'I'd have told you, Lilly-Mae… eventually. But hell, you'd have soon found something else, right? Let's not pretend we ever had anything going, the two of us.'

The comment was meant to be as cold as it was low, and Gus probably expected it to strike Lilly-Mae like a slap in the face. But she brushed it off without flinching.

'And Frank? What about him?' Her voice nearly cracked, and it was obvious to anyone with a brain that Frank's murder had left an indelible mark on her. Tied in with everything Gus had just said, it was the final straw.

'Frank got in the way. Turns out he was a light sleeper. He heard me on the phone to some people. He didn't like it and threatened to split. I couldn't let him do that.'

'The freezer,' I muttered. 'And the pool.'

Lilly-Mae looked at me. 'What?'

'The house near Charlotte: the air conditioning was switched on, remember? When we walked in the air was cold. And the pool heating was on. Why heat the pool in a deserted house? And why stock the freezer?' It meant Gus had been using the house as a base – and probably planned on doing so for some time. Since few people knew he owned it, it was unlikely he would have been discovered unless someone happened to stumble on the connection. Or unless Lilly-Mae returned. And perhaps even then he'd reckoned on her siding with him. Or maybe not.

'You've been to my house?' he asked softly, and looked at Lilly-Mae. 'You took him there?' His eyes swivelled towards me, and I realised that apart from everything else – as if that wasn't enough to be contending with – and in spite of his comments moments before, Gus was suffering from an acute attack of an emotion as old as the hills around us: jealousy. Insane and dangerous jealousy. And it was aimed right at me.

'Yes.' Lilly-Mae glanced at me, an urgent pleading in her eyes as if there was something I could do.

Suddenly it was as if the conversation was at an end, as if all the points had been covered, all the balls dropped into position and the explanations made. Now we were three people in a room without much to say to each other. Except Gus wasn't quite finished.

And he was holding the gun.

He turned towards me and lifted the rifle, his knuckles whitening around the stock. I saw his forearm tense with the first movement. But while he'd been exchanging confidences with Lilly-Mae, the barrel had gradually drifted away towards the floor, leaving me by a good foot and a half.

It was the only chance I was going to get.

I took my small travel flashlight out of my pocket and threw it as hard as I could straight into his face. It was barely six inches long, about an inch wide, but it was made of metal. I hurled it with desperation and fear and a sudden burst of anger, and it hit Gus right between the eyes.

I'd never hit anyone before, and I had no idea what to expect. So when Gus went down with a crash as if he'd been smacked with a brick instead of a tiny flashlight, I was nearly as stunned as he was. One second he was huge and unmoveable and thinking about killing me, the next he was stretched out on the carpet like a corpse, a small round area of vivid red skin mushrooming in the centre of his forehead. The rifle clattered to the carpet beside him.

The next moment the night was split by the wail of a police siren and I heard the roar of car engines approaching along the drive. Then I noticed a tiny red light blinking up in one corner of the room. The place had been wired with an alarm – probably activated by the lights being switched on.

'Something you forgot to mention?' I said to Lilly-Mae, picking up my flashlight.

'That's not part of the system,' she replied. 'The cops must have installed it.'

Which meant they were watching for Gus after all. So much for his being able to stay out of their hands. And we'd walked right into their trap.

'Come on!' I said. I grabbed Lilly-Mae with one hand and picked up her rucksack with the other. Waiting around to see if they would believe our story wasn't an option in my book. Had it been me in the blue uniform, I wouldn't have believed me either. It was time to be travelling.

I just hoped she remembered the way back through the trees, because I didn't.

THIRTY-THREE

We scooted across the lawn to the trees as lights flared at the front of the house and car tyres screamed along the drive in true Hollywood fashion. Luckily there were no security lights on at the back and, as we hit the wire fence and scrambled through into the undergrowth, we had darkness to swallow us.

There was a lot of shouting from inside the house, and the lights began to go on as all the rooms were searched. A couple of figures in uniform appeared by the pool and stared into the darkness towards us, but they made no move to come any further.

'Thank Christ for that,' I breathed, and sank down on one knee, drained by all the excitement and tension. Life in London NW9 just wasn't like this. 'Anyone for a walk in the woods?'

Then I heard a dog barking. That wasn't good.

'Does Gus have a dog?'

When Lilly said no, we jumped up and started running.

Whatever we had hit on the way down was small beer in comparison to our return journey. Every mud hole, every fallen branch, every obstacle nature could possibly put in our way was there for us to fall over and step in. By the time we were halfway up the hill we were both gasping and sweating, skin burning from dozens of tiny cuts and scratches. It was only adrenalin and desperation which kept us going the rest of the way.

We emerged not far from the car and clambered aboard, out of breath and looking like we'd been run over by a truck.

'What in hell,' I gasped, throwing Lilly-Mae's rucksack on the back seat, 'have you got in there?'

'Everything important that's mine,' she replied. 'You don't think I'm ever going back, do you?'

Fair comment. The way things were looking, Gus was unlikely to ever see freedom again, and anyone associated with him was in line to join him. It took me a few seconds to realise that included me.

'Is there a back way out of here?' I asked. If we went down to the main road we'd most likely find it blocked by the police. And while we both looked as if we'd been rolling in the heather, I didn't think it would convince anyone for very long that we'd been canoodling in the bushes.

Lilly-Mae nodded as I climbed behind the wheel. 'Over the top of this range. Do we risk going back to the house outside Charlotte?'

'We have to. My stuff's there – including my passport.'

Neither of us said much for the first twenty miles of winding, bumpy back road. I was too busy watching out for bears – the kind driving patrol cars, not the furry kind – and I think Lilly-Mae was trying to come to terms with what had happened with Gus and her disintegrating life. She couldn't even go back to the place she had called home.

I knew how she felt.

We hit the main road and I drove as sedately as my jangling nerves would allow all the way back to Charlotte, one eye on the rear-view mirror for signs of pursuit. There were a few other cars around, all minding their own business, and I figured as long as I didn't break a law, there was no reason why we should stand out from anyone else.

'What will you do?' I asked Lilly-Mae.

She checked her face in the visor mirror before replying. It was quite a question, and one which I guessed needed careful thought. You can't have your life turned upside down and simply rush off into the blue as if nothing had happened. I should know – I'd tried it.

'Move on, I suppose. I've done it before.' The way she said it sounded pretty desperate, and I felt for her. 'How about you?'

'I've been thinking about that. I have to go back to England at some stage. I can't keep moving around the globe in the hope it will all go away. Better to get back and sort it out. Anyway, it's not as though my problems compare with what we've just been through.'

Lilly-Mae smiled and put a hand on my arm. 'Thank you, Jake. For back there.'

'Don't thank me,' I said modestly. 'If you hadn't stood up to him I'd never have got the opportunity. Anyway, I don't think he'd have harmed you. It was me he was annoyed with.'

She shook her head and threw her half-smoked cigarette out the window. 'I think he would have – hurt me, I mean. I knew him better than he thought. He wouldn't have meant to, but it would have happened anyway. Did you see the look on his face at the end? That wasn't the Gus I used to know. I think he'd gone over the edge. We'd never have got out if it hadn't been for you.' She pushed the seat back and within minutes I could hear her breathing steadily.

A little while later, when I was sure she was in deep sleep, I took the opportunity to call Marcus. I figured he'd be up and about by now, but I had to make sure he was all right. Being woken up by me, if that's what happened, was better than having Basher kicking in his door.

Surprisingly he answered the phone sounding almost chirpy. 'What do you want?' he asked. 'I thought you'd be away longer.'

'I am,' I said. 'I just wanted to check in, see how you were doing… and ask if you'd seen Basher.'

'Basher? Hell, no – I'm relieved, to be honest. I've been hearing some strange stuff about him. I think the investment thing is off. Why do you ask?'

My relief was massive. The idea that Basher might have decided to take out his anger on Marcus hadn't occurred to me before I'd spoken to Clayton, but so far, at least, the beast had stayed in his cage. 'Same as you, really,' I said airily. 'I'd heard a couple of things and wanted to warn you to be careful.'

'Well, big brother, I'm not a kid any more, but thank you. Are you sure you're all right? You sound weird.'

'I'm fine,' I lied. 'We'll catch up when I get back.' I cut the connection before he could ask more questions, and focussed on driving.

When we arrived back at the house I half woke Lilly-Mae and helped her inside, gently lowering her onto one of the beds and covering her with a blanket. I took off her boots but that was as far as decency allowed me to go. Then I went back out for her rucksack and put it down nearby where she would see it the moment she woke.

After that I made a cup of coffee and prowled the house, staring through the large windows at the darkness outside. All I saw through my own reflection were images of Gus and his rifle, and the way he had looked at me; as if I was something about to end up on a marble slab. I realised then that Lilly-Mae had been right; Gus hadn't been sane right at that moment. He probably hadn't been for some time – certainly not the first time I met him. And in his frame of mind, whatever that was, he was unlikely to have let Lilly-Mae go, especially if he was thinking about her and me in this house together.

It made me wonder if he would tell the police about this place. If he did, they would be round there sooner or later looking for information. On the other hand, if we tried to find a hotel to stay in, two dishevelled people looking for a room at this time of the night would likely attract the attention of the cops.

I finished my coffee and took a shower in the bathroom furthest from where Lilly-Mae was sleeping. I washed off the assorted mud, grass stains and bits of undergrowth, and found some ointment to treat the scratches I'd picked up in the woods. If anyone came calling, at least I might look halfway decent instead of resembling someone who'd tangled with a bear. There wasn't much I could do about Lilly-Mae, who'd picked up her own bunch of scratches, short of dragging her into the shower with me. So I let her sleep.

By the time I tumbled into one of the other beds, I was past caring about middle-of-the-night callers and had just enough energy to drag the duvet around me before I fell into a very deep pit with no bottom.

I woke several hours later to find a mug of tea by the side of the bed and Lilly-Mae watching me from an armchair nearby, her feet curled beneath her. She was wearing a blue T-shirt and jeans and had a cleaned and scrubbed look which meant she had showered away the debris of the previous night. Once again she looked very different, and I was struck by how each new appearance made me want to see if there were any more hidden away.

She uncurled her legs and came over and sat on the bed. 'Good morning,' she said, and handed me my tea. 'You sleep very quietly, you know that?'

I grinned at her over my tea, which was surprisingly good. 'Is that so? Well, you sleep very tidily. What time is it?'

'Eleven. I took a walk earlier. No signs of anyone watching – although I guess they could be well hidden.'

'If they were interested enough to be out there, I think they'd have shown themselves by now. How are you feeling?'

She shrugged elegantly. 'Tired, still. Like I've been trampled by something big and angry.' She looked at me and prodded my leg through the duvet with the tip of one finger. 'You know, you're in good shape for a guy who doesn't take exercise. You pretty much carried me and my rucksack up that hill.'

'Good shape for a man my age, you mean?' I tried to pitch it so that it came out light but it didn't quite work. The age thing again. Then I remembered Gus must have been some years older than me.

'Just good shape is what I meant,' said Lilly-Mae reprovingly. 'You shouldn't put yourself down, Jake. Or is that the English art of understatement, and really you think you're pretty darned good?'

'Hardly that,' I said, and touched her hand where it rested on my leg. 'If I was in really good shape, I'd have been up for a jog and done twenty lengths of the pool by now.'

Lilly-Mae looked interested, 'Hey – swimming. Good idea. It'll help get rid of some of those aches and pains.' She stood up with a grin, her enthusiasm ignited. 'I'll fix a couple of pool-type drinks and see you in there.'

'Wait. I've got to get back to England.'

She turned at the door and looked back at me with a slightly sad expression. 'I know,' she said softly. 'I already checked for you. There are no available seats on flights out of here to London until late this afternoon. And the airport's less than fifteen minutes away, max. You'll find some shorts and stuff in a box by the pool.'

When she had gone I levered myself out of bed and threw on a bathrobe, then walked down to the pool. It seemed reckless to be chancing our luck by hanging around this way, especially given the way Gus was feeling. But I couldn't be bothered to argue. Anyway, right now I needed a swim.

The inflatable chair was floating in the pool, with a glass of something interesting sitting in the moulded holder on one arm. I found a pair of new shorts and put them on, then slid into the water. It was pleasantly warm and I did a couple of brisk lengths, feeling the rigours of our run the previous night beginning to make themselves known again. I didn't normally go in for swimming much, but today it seemed the right thing to do.

As I pulled myself into the chair and settled into the moulded shape, the door from the kitchen creaked open and Lilly-Mae dived smoothly into the pool wearing a flesh-coloured swimsuit. Her body was arrow-straight and slim, and sliced into the water with the stylish and elegant poise she brought to everything.

I took a sip of my drink and watched her shadow coming up the pool beneath the surface, then lost sight of her as she swam beneath the chair. She moved with a powerful stroke which spoke of good training or plenty of exercise.

Then she burst to the surface in a shower of spray and flopped against the side of the chair.

That's when I realised the flesh-coloured swimsuit wasn't a swimsuit after all.

She smiled at me and wiped away droplets of water from her face, while I tried manfully not to look at her naked breasts, which were gently nudging my arm. In the end it didn't seem to matter, so I gave up pretending while Lilly-Mae smiled some more and playfully kicked her feet behind her in the water. When I leaned over a bit, I could see she wasn't wearing anything on her bottom half, either.

'You ever skinny-dipped before?' she asked, dragging a fingernail across my arm.

'You know I have,' I replied, and shifted in the chair as my position became uncomfortable. If Lilly-Mae noticed, she pretended not to and concentrated on tracing her fingernail across my chest, leaving a faint white line behind.

'Right. You ever done… it… in a pool before?'

'No,' I gasped truthfully. 'I tried snogging in the sea once. I was only six so I suppose that doesn't count.'

'You're right. It doesn't.' Then she bobbed down for a second, before giving a powerful kick with her feet, and with a smooth movement hoisted herself upwards and out of the water. Before I could move she had flung one slim, muscular leg across me, and was straddling my lap, bouncing away happily and grinning like a kid in a playground. Then she leaned forward until the tips of her breasts were touching my chest.

'You think maybe we could do it here, Jake? Maybe help take our minds off things for a while?' She whispered it softly and settled herself into a more comfortable position by slowly and suggestively wriggling her bottom against my groin. When that got the required response, which made her eyes go wide, her grin became even broader. Then she was reaching down and somehow easing me out of my shorts. This was a tricky manoeuvre which nearly had us capsizing several times, but by skilful shifting of her balance, Lilly-Mae was soon holding up the shorts, which she threw out of my reach.

'There,' she said, and leaned against me until all I could feel was her warm, wet skin pressing me into the plastic chair. 'Now, where were we?'

We kissed each other for a while, with me enjoying the warm smell and taste of her and the feel of her body against mine. Then she lifted herself and took me in her hand, and with a quick movement, settled back against me. This time both our eyes went wide and I forgot all about everything except the feel of Lilly-Mae's body against mine.

I awoke several hours later in the comfort of Lilly-Mae's bed. I had no clear memory of getting there, but the images of the pool and the floating chair, and her entrance to the water were vivid. I turned and watched her sleep, her hair gently rumpled on the pillow and a smile on her face.

Outside a bird clattered past the window, and I eased out from beneath the bedclothes and padded over to peer through the vertical blinds and see what the day was promising.

Across the untended grass at the back, a handful of what looked like partridge were pecking at the ground, their plumage blending in with the vegetation. Simple life for a bird, I thought. Eat, fly, eat, sleep and avoid men with guns. Not unlike my life at the time, come to think of it.

Even as the thought took wing of its own, one of the birds looked up with a start and took flight in a clattering rush. The others followed suit until the grass was deserted.

I wondered what had spooked them. A cat, maybe. Did they have wild cats in this area?

Then a movement in the trees caught my eye and a man with a holster strapped to his hip stepped into view and stood looking at the house.

THIRTY-FOUR

I dived back to the bed and shook Lilly-Mae. She came awake with a start, those lovely eyes blurred by sleep.

'Jake,' she murmured and yawned, stretching beneath the bedclothes like a large cat. 'What's up?' She sat up, letting the bedclothes drop away. It left her naked and blinking seductively up at me. At any other time it would have been more than I could stand. Right then the timing was disastrous.

'Come on, Lilly-Mae,' I urged, trying not to look at her. 'There's no time for that. I think Gus must have told the police about this place; there's a man with a gun in the trees out back, watching the house.'

'What?' She came awake with a start and leapt out of bed, grabbing for her clothes. I scrambled into trousers and a shirt, and gathered together what few things I had into my bag. One legacy of a life spent travelling was the habit of keeping everything close by me. Not that I was in the habit of leaving places on the run, but I had found out many years before that, in certain parts of the world, it paid not to get too comfortable.

While Lilly-Mae finished packing I went across to the window. The man was still there, scanning the area around him but making no move to approach the house. He was dressed in a camouflage top, pants and boots, and looked as if he meant business. There was a solidity about him, a sureness of purpose which meant he was no idle weekend visitor out for a stroll in the trees to commune with nature. Not unless he hoped to shoot a sycamore, anyway.

I went through to the kitchen and peered carefully round the door frame, from where I could see another expanse of grass and trees. If there was anyone there, they were being more cautious than the other man and staying well under cover. The view from a narrow window by the front door showed the same deserted scenery along the length of track leading away towards the road. The Toyota 4WD stood where we had left it the night before, seemingly untouched.

Lilly-Mae appeared, eyes wide with apprehension, but businesslike and showing no signs of panic. Thank God for Nancy Drew, I thought, and scooped up the car keys.

'Ready?'

She nodded. 'Uh-huh. Are we just going to drive out? They could be waiting at the bottom of the road.'

'Who do you think "they" might be?' I queried. It wasn't the time for hair-splitting, but I was curious. I'd never been pursued by the police before – well, not outside NW9, anyway – but knowing how many different law enforcement agencies there were in the States, and with Gus's business being what it was, it could have been anyone from the National Guard to the Department of Homeland Security. Whoever they were, I hoped none of them had itchy trigger fingers.

Lilly-Mae was on the same wavelength. 'Take your pick,' she said briefly. 'The guy out back's got a blue shirt underneath his jacket. I'd say he's local police… maybe state.'

Okay. State police. That didn't sound too bad.

'Or he could be in a SWAT unit,' she added.

I tried to look casual, as if it didn't really matter. I could handle this, I told myself. So why did I feel like we were about to emulate Bonnie and Clyde? I balanced the car keys and my bag in one hand, and with the other eased the front door open. The click of the catch going back seemed to carry across the open space, and I hoped none of the massed ranks of state-funded gunmen in the woods had good hearing.

'When I say go,' I whispered, 'just walk to the car and get in. Don't slam the door and don't stop.' Slamming doors, I seemed to recall from films and books, sounded a lot like gunshots to people with taught nerves and itchy trigger fingers.

'Wait.' Lilly-Mae put a hand on my arm. 'Where are we going?'

Good point. 'To the airport. It's the quickest way out of here. We'll talk about it on the way.'

'Okay. But be careful, huh? Please?' She leaned close and kissed me, a gesture somehow more intimate and meaningful than anything we'd engaged in a few hours ago in the pool.

I pushed her out before my resolve wavered and closed the door quietly behind me. As I stepped across to the car, I felt the back of my neck twitch and tried not to imagine myself lined up in the sights of someone's rifle out there in the trees. It was a strange feeling.

I climbed aboard and inserted the key in the ignition, then looked across at Lilly-Mae, who was staring at me with those big, beautiful eyes. If she was frightened, she was managing to hide it remarkably well. I winked for good measure – and partly to reassure myself – then kicked off the foot brake and started the car.

The engine sounded too loud in all that silent countryside. I didn't bother checking the treeline where I'd seen the uniform, but drove away from the house and down the track as fast as I dared. Behind me a figure stepped into view and stood watching us, holding what looked like a radio to his face.

It was the man from out back.

We hit forty before losing sight of the house, the wheels drumming beneath us on the uneven track and making my teeth rattle, and the steering-wheel vibrating in my hands. I hoped nobody would step out to prevent us leaving as there was no way I could stop in time. I'd once taken part in a cross-country rally behind the wheel of a souped-up Saab, which was the extent of my experience of high-speed driving. Apart from that I'd driven the occasional 4WD vehicle in remote areas, but none of them had prepared me for this. This was a matter of jail or freedom.

As we reached the bisection with the blocked track to the other property, I caught a faint gleam of reflected light through the trees in the distance. It might have been a harmless vehicle on the main road or sunlight on a discarded bottle. Whatever it was, I didn't want to take a chance. I stamped on the brake and skewed the car round ninety degrees and headed down the overgrown track towards the next house, just managing to squeeze past the pole blocking the way. Thirty yards past it, I stopped the car and ran back, and did my best to straighten the grass flattened by our wheels. It wouldn't fool anyone for long, but at a first glance it might look as if we had continued on down the main track towards the road.

I jumped back in the car and found Lilly-Mae grinning at me.

'What?' I asked, driving off.

'You,' she said. 'You're like, different. Like you know what you're doing.'

'Don't be fooled,' I said earnestly. 'This could be a dead-end track. If it is we may have to go walkabout.'

'Okay,' she shrugged calmly. 'You lead, Ranger Sam, and I'll follow.'

The house loomed into view. I caught a glimpse of a ramshackle wooden structure badly in need of a paint job or the wrecker's ball. It didn't look as if it had been lived in for years, with that sad and dilapidated air of a building without ownership or love.

The track curved past the house, a narrow sea of long grass and wild flowers mixed with barbed weeds, and I hoped no-one had left anything large and unmoveable lying around which was now concealed by the vegetation. If they had, we were going to seriously re-arrange the front of the Toyota and end our day in the local pokey.

The building flew by in a satisfying rumble of flattened grass beneath the car body, revealing a tumbledown shack at the rear and what had once been an ordered garden, with a trace of ancient borders, a rectangle of lawn and a large oak tree complete with a rotting rope swing. Beyond it lay a few scattered trees set on a steep slope dropping away into the distance... and an old, rotten gateway sagging on rusted hinges. I couldn't see where the track went after that, only that it led us away from whoever was after us, which was good enough to be going on with.

'Hold tight!' I warned Lilly-Mae, and gripped the wheel.

We hit the gate at forty and I heard a single crack as it gave way under the bonnet of the 4WD, strips of powdery wood and splinters flicking into the air behind us. A solitary, weather-scarred cross-member hung on the windscreen for a moment, then was gone with the next jolt.

Then Lilly-Mae screamed and gripped my arm.

The track seemed to drop off the edge of the world. One second we were on it, the next someone had pulled the rug away from beneath us.

We were probably airborne for only a few seconds, but it seemed like a lifetime. The wheel became lifeless in my hands and I had that feeling of gut-lurching weightlessness beneath me that you get preceding a downwards movement you haven't been expecting. In the distance I caught a flash of open landscape with a scattering of trees and, on the horizon, the glint of sunlight off a line of moving vehicles. The main road.

Then the car nosed down and crashed to terra firma in a teeth-rattling shower of dust and enough noise to wake the dead. The horizon disappeared as we bounced upwards again for a second, then crashed back down again and resumed our crazy journey. I looked across at Lilly-Mae, who was smiling in a sickly manner. I felt like I'd shaken my brain loose under the impact.

Amazingly, we were still on the track and still moving. I stamped on the brakes, trying to control the car before we hit something large and immovable – like a tree. The suspension, as good as it was, was barely absorbing the ruts and bumps of the uneven terrain. It was like sitting atop a pneumatic drill. If this was what top-level motor-rallying was all about, they could keep it.

The car fishtailed between two trees, the gnarled trunks startlingly clear and close through the windscreen, and Lilly-Mae threw her arms up to cover her face. Then we were through and I wrestled the wheel again, and stood on the brake pedal as the track suddenly snaked off to one side like one of Marcus's video games, and we were heading straight for a vast, angled tree trunk which fate had evidently left there for us to hit.

We stopped with inches to spare and I stalled the engine.

'Shee-it!' whispered Lilly-Mae. 'What a buzz!'

There was nothing for it; I had to get out and walk around for a few seconds, even if just to convince myself I was still alive and not buried nose-deep in a tree. If my life had flashed before my eyes, the way they say it does, I'd been too busy being shit-scared to notice.

When I climbed back inside, Lilly-Mae was looking worse, her face pale and strained, as if the shock of what we'd been through had only just sunk in. I checked her face to see she hadn't bitten her tongue or broken any teeth.

'Sorry about that,' I said with feeling. 'Lost control a bit there.'

She turned to look at me, her eyes wide, then peered round back up the slope behind us, where a trail of flattened grass and gouged earth betrayed our journey. It was only when I looked further back that I realised we'd virtually come over the edge of a cliff. There had probably been a fairly steep slope there once, manageable by a tractor at best. But the earth had since slipped sideways, leaving nothing in its place. We had jumped the gap like Evel Knievel in his heyday.

'Is that all you can say?' Lilly-Mae breathed in a stunned whisper. It looked as if there was the hint of a smile playing about the corners of her mouth, but I wasn't betting a touch of hysteria wouldn't rattle along too far behind. 'Sorry and you lost control? What is that – another bit of English understatement? Jesus, Jake, what d'you do when you have a real head-on smash – apologise for the bump?'

I gave her a kiss, then re-started the car and reversed away from the tree. If she had the energy for that kind of remark, I figured she was all right. Had she been cowering in a tearful and sobbing heap in the footwell of the car and screaming for her mommy, I'd have been concerned. But Lilly-Mae was made of sterner stuff.

Thankfully everything about the car seemed to work okay, too, apart from a bit of drift in the steering. At least we weren't on foot. If we managed to make the road, which was a few hundred yards ahead, we'd be in with a chance of getting away from there.

We came to another gate, this one metal and more substantial, with a ditch running away at right angles either side, forming a natural boundary. I stopped and scrambled out, and flung the gate back on rusting hinges, then checked the track behind us. If there was any pursuit, they had evidently decided not to go flying today.

Down another short stretch of track and through a clump of trees, and we emerged onto a nice, smooth stretch of highway.

'It's the road to Charlotte,' announced Lilly-Mae excitedly. 'Turn right, Jake.'

I followed her directions, and soon began to recognise some landmarks I'd seen on the way up. Soon we entered the beginnings of the outer suburbs, with strip malls, gas stations and motels, other signs of civilisation and, more importantly, a lot of traffic in which to hide. I slowed as the build-up intensified, forcing myself to calm down after our hectic dash from the house and behave like we were two normal people out for a drive.

Ten minutes later we left the Toyota unlocked in the main airport car park and headed towards the departure terminal. The area was big enough to make spotting the Toyota difficult, and although I had given my passport details and shown my driving licence when hiring it, I hoped to be long gone before anyone found the car and caught up with us. With a bit of luck the car would be stolen, anyway, further blurring the trail.

As we crossed a pedestrian walkway to the main entrance, I saw a sign advertising an in-terminal Business Center. It gave me an idea.

'Do you have your passport?' I asked Lilly-Mae.

'Sure,' she replied. 'Always. Why?'

'Because I know where I can find somewhere to lie low for a while. Have you ever been to France?'

She didn't answer, but stared intently at the ground. I guessed it was nerves and told her to wait by the taxi rank while I checked inside. I walked past a bored and tired-looking security guard and scanned the concourse, half expecting to see a row of uniforms lined up to greet us. Surely this would be the first place they would expect us to go? On the other hand maybe that's what they would expect us to think and they'd go for blocking the roads out of the area instead. Either way, our main hope was that they really didn't know what we looked like, unless Gus had gone full bore and given them a photo of Lilly-Mae or they'd spoken to the pool guy. It was grasping at straws but I needed all the reassurance I could get.

But the only police uniforms were the one I'd passed by the entrance and a couple more seated at a bar drinking coffee and watching baseball on the TV. No wailing sirens, no quickly-averted eyes, no beefy individuals who might be cops dressed as airport workers or travellers. I was almost disappointed.

After I'd made a second tour of the concourse just to be certain, I went back to the taxi rank to collect Lilly-Mae. Once in the Business Center, I could contact some friendly faces.

But she wasn't there.

Lilly-Mae was gone.

THIRTY-FIVE

'Excuse me, sir, is your name Jake?' A baggage captain with skin like seasoned mahogany and a walrus moustache was sitting on a trolley against the wall. He was too old and fat to be a cop, and my initial jolt of nerves disappeared when I realised he must have been waiting for me. Baggage captains don't usually sit around unless they're forced to.

I agreed it was my name.

He climbed to his feet and beckoned me over. 'You lookin' for the lady you arrived with? Name of Lilly?' His voice was a low rumble and, by the look on his face, he wasn't about to give me good news and was trying to be sympathetic about it.

I nodded, a sinking feeling in my gut. Somehow I knew what was coming.

'The lady said to tell you she couldn't come with you, sir,' he intoned carefully. 'She said she was sorry 'n all, but there's things she has to do. She said to thank you and she hopes you'll understand, and you shouldn't come looking, 'cos she's gonna be movin' around a lot.' If he had any thoughts about someone being let down so openly, he kept them to himself and looked away, too seasoned in human frailty to say anything else.

I tipped him for his kindness and walked into the terminal. I felt numb, as if a lifeline had been snatched away from me. It was pointless looking for her, because the two places Lilly-Mae wouldn't go was to either of Gus's properties. I didn't know where else to even begin.

I could have rushed out into the car park looking for her, but I knew it was no good. I'd spent a while checking the terminal for police, which had given her plenty of time to prime the baggage captain on what she wanted him to tell me and get a taxi from the head of the rank. She was probably several miles away by now.

I went to the Business Center and found a spare PC. I typed in the details Dot had given me, and seconds later I was reading a message posted two days ago.

Jake. We're off to France. Left your place real tidy. Your wife came round with another woman. Man, you're best out of that. We're stopping in Brittany for a couple of weeks. Come and join us. If not, drop us a line and we'll let you know who to call if you need to crash in London. Your mug's waiting, plus coffee the way you like it.

Dot and Dash. xx

There was an address on the French coast near a small town named Sable d'Or in Brittany. I had been through the area once, a carbon copy of Cornwall's rugged beauty, with endless beaches and rocky coves, and roads where the only people who drove with any urgency were tourists. As a place to hide away for a few days, it probably couldn't be equalled.

I wondered about the 'other woman' with Susan. Juliette, was my guess. Buddies in feminist fury. No doubt she'd been persuaded to view the scene of the crime and give moral support to Susan's desire to regain possession. Along with Mrs Tree, that would have been enough to form a coven.

I logged off and went in search of a ticket counter.

Destination France.

I spent five lazily disorganised days in Brittany with Dot, Dash and a scattering of their friends, camped out in a large farmhouse owned by a local member of the group. It was rustic, charmingly derelict and isolated enough to seem like a lifetime from anywhere. I was accepted among them like an old friend, and if I needed a *laisser-passer* of any kind among the strangers in the group, my coffee mug said it all, carefully unpacked by Dot from a box in the bus and put on display.

'So, what ya bin doin', Jake?' asked Dash in his usual forthright manner. He was seated in a battered deckchair in the overgrown rear garden, where the air was abuzz with insects.

I gave them a pared-down version of events, leaving out any mention of dead bodies and making it sound like a delivery trip which had gone sour. They seemed to accept it, and soon lost interest, the talk turning to where they were planning on going next. The idea was to head south and follow the sun, taking on grape picking or other casual jobs as and when they felt like it to pay their way. Once they hit the Med, it was the end of the road for a couple of months before they decided on somewhere else. Greece seemed favourite, or Turkey, and it was obvious they were happy for me to tag along if I wished.

It was a different lifestyle from any I had known and, while it had a certain appeal, with no set agenda or responsibilities other than caring for each other, I could already sense an itch I'd soon be wanting to scratch if I went along with them. Maybe lotus-eating wasn't for me, in spite of the attractions.

For a while, though, I was happy to vegetate, enjoying the solitude on offer as well as the laid-back companionship. In no time at all I felt rested and relaxed, and had a healthy tan from lying around in the sun and going for long cliff walks. No radio, no television and no friction, and the only time I asked to use Dot's iPad was to feed in Lilly-Mae's name to see if it featured in any news items. Thankfully it didn't, which I chose to think was good. The only unsettling aspect was that looking out to sea and to the distant horizon, I kept finding myself thinking about her; about where she was and what she was doing.

In the end I had to leave.

'Take care, mate,' said Dash, clapping me on the shoulder. 'You come down south, you call us up, you hear?' I think he meant New Zealand.

'Will do,' I told him, and meant it. Whether it was because of what had happened with Susan, then Lilly-Mae, or the way I had been forced to change the way I thought, I realised I didn't want to let go of these friends too easily.

'We'll keep your mug handy,' said Dot, who gave me an embarrassingly lengthy and enthusiastic kiss, to the delight of the whole group, including Dash. 'Wow,' she added, with a look of surprise. 'You're a real good kisser.'

The sky over London was cold and grey after the warmth of Brittany. I felt depressed and wondered if I had done the right thing. I could have stayed with the group and ventured south with nobody the wiser. But even as the thought tried to assert itself, I knew I'd had no other option.

First things first; I went straight to Charles Clayton's office and was told to go right in.

He looked me over with a faintly amused air and shuffled together some papers. He made no comments about my tan or the casual clothes I was wearing, and if he was surprised at my turning up unannounced he hid it well. But then, I wasn't sure there was much that could surprise him.

'Welcome back, Jake. How was Charlotte?'

'Fine, thank you.' I gave him a brief rundown of my trip to Brittany and why I had felt the need to return. 'Was I unwise coming back?' The question had been bothering me all the way across the Channel. In spite of the rest and recuperation, after having been nearly shot by Selecca's sidekick, Paulie, then by Gus Mekashnik, I think I could have been excused for thinking someone had it in for me. All I needed was for Basher to leap out of the woodwork and I'd probably have a nervous breakdown. I was hoping Clayton wasn't about to deliver bad news.

He wasn't.

'Your problems with Mr Lyons seem to be over,' he said matter-of-factly. Then he beeped the venerable Francis on the front desk for some coffee.

'Lyons? Oh, you mean Basher.' Lyons seemed almost twee after the picture I'd built up, coloured by visions of Hackney Marshes and buried bodies.

I sat down and he explained that, among several interesting things which Francis had discovered about Basher Lyons, the Hackney Marsh roughneck was deeply in hock to HMRC, while he was currently arranging the purchase of a large villa outside Marbella, in Spain. He also had some interesting 'investments' which had gone undeclared and which flouted at least seven or eight financial regulations.

'The killer, though,' he smiled, as Francis entered with coffee on a tray, 'is that Mr Lyons recently became a father.'

'Really?' I was surprised. Jane hadn't looked pregnant.

'By a young woman in Waltham Forest,' he added, as if that was unthinkable. 'A dental assistant, apparently not his wife.'

Oops.

'His missus went ballistic when she found out,' declared Francis, his voice strangely soft. 'She liked playin' the odd away game, but was ready to cut his balls off for doing the same. You're well clear of that, Mr Foreman, you want my opinion.'

He winked and left us, sure of tread and large of presence. 'So where is Basher now?' I asked.

'Travelling,' Charles replied. 'His wife is suing for divorce and half of whatever she can get, and the Revenue is after the rest. I doubt he'll stop running for a long while yet.'

I sighed with relief. That was one problem off my back. Now all I had to worry about was Susan and her battery of lawyers. It set me wondering what Dunckley might be thinking about me. I still had in mind the last time we'd talked and the threats he'd made.

Charles must have been reading my mind. He said, 'The other business – HP&P? You'll be pleased to hear it's been resolved. There have been certain developments.'

'Really? What kind of developments?' Dunckley having forgotten I'd ever existed would be useful.

'HP&P have been put under the spotlight along with two or three other multinationals. Questions were raised on *Panorama* about bribes paid to foreign government officials in exchange for contracts. When it came to HP&P your old boss Dunckley was mentioned. He seems to have been running his own little operation within the company for some time and has since gone AWOL with a large amount of funds wired to an overseas account HP&P claim they knew nothing about.'

'That's not good.' I wondered if Susan had gone with him, and thought it was unlikely.

'Not for Dunckley, certainly.' He shot his cuffs and studied his fingernails. 'I had a word with one of their chief executives in Amsterdam. I suggested that it wouldn't be good for business if he had any intentions of pursuing former employees.'

'What did he say?' I wondered if the word had been delivered by Francis.

'He doesn't need the aggravation and agreed to forget all about you.' He gave a thin smile. 'The truth of the matter is that outwardly they'll be interested in pursuing Dunckley, although instinct tells me they might not try too hard to catch up with him. In the current business climate they can do without further publicity and court cases. They're bidding for a big government contract here at home, and having you or Dunckley hauled in front of the cameras won't help.'

'Thank you. I appreciate it.'

'Well, it wasn't entirely unselfish of me. I've got more work, if you feel up to it.' He stirred his coffee. 'A couple of my people have dropped off the payroll and I need someone… reliable.'

I nodded. 'I need a few days to sort out some stuff. Can I get back to you?'

'Of course. Take your time. I was actually thinking of something more permanent.'

'Permanent?' I had a sudden flashback to my suspicions about the kind of packages I'd been carrying so far, and wondered if I wanted to be involved further than I was.

'Yes. The business can only grow, but I need someone to open up new markets – preferably on the ethical side. Someone who can travel – spend some time overseas laying the groundwork. That someone would eventually become a full partner. What do you think?'

I was stunned. He was offering me a partnership in his business. But did I want it? I trusted him more than I had Dunckley, but wasn't this going to be more of the same?

'I have a question.'

'Go ahead.'

'Gus Mekashnik.'

He saw what was coming. 'You want to know what it was you delivered to him.'

'Yes.'

'It was a contract. I was asked by certain UK government officials to act as intermediary in the purchase of some obsolete Russian military equipment from the Cubans, being updated and revamped by North Korea for sale on the open market. It was all perfectly legal under US, UK and UN regulations but they wanted someone to monitor events, which was where I came in. For whatever reason Mekashnik was willing to pay an absurd price for you to deliver the paperwork. Unfortunately for him, he'd made one too many enemies in his own backyard and his time ran out.'

'Oh.'

He smiled. 'Don't worry – you had a right to know. Anything else?'

'Why me – with this offer? You hardly know me.'

He shrugged. 'The last time you were in this office you entrusted me with your money. I appreciated that more than I can say. Trust is important to me. I've placed the money in an account for you, incidentally. You can have it whenever you want.'

'That's very kind of you.' I really didn't know what to say.

He nodded and waved a hand. 'Let me know when you're ready. Good to have you back.'

He sounded as if he meant it, and I added another name to the growing list of people I'd become closer to recently. More than in all the preceding years.

THIRTY-SIX

I headed out into the street past a grinning Francis. It was time to face Marcus. If he'd heard from Basher that I was the mystery man at the party, then it was better to approach it head-on. It might be a shock for him but there wasn't much I could do about it other than plead innocence of Jane's identity and a complete loss of control of my unsettled hormones.

First, though, I needed to speak to Hugo. As an updater of all that was going on in my life, he would be able to provide a useful summary. That way, I might at least be prepared if Marcus asked any strange questions.

I rang him on the way, and he surprised me by saying he would meet me at his place.

'Are you sure?' I was thinking of Juliette and wondering if she would be spreading salt and garlic across the threshold before I got there and putting poison in anything I might drink.

He meant it and said so with a faint laugh in his voice. Curiouser and curiouser.

He met me at the front door and virtually dragged me into his study, where he thrust a whisky into my hand. 'Jake,' he boomed.

'Glad to see you again. Where have you been, you dog? Juliette will be down in a second.'

I took a hefty snort of the whisky. The last time I'd shown my face there Juliette had made it very clear that I should be tarred and feathered and rolled down a hill in a barrel. As far as I knew nothing had changed. So what the hell was going on?

Juliette entered with a cool smile on her face, designer-dressed from coiffed head to varnished toe, as clinically elegant as always. Then she came up and kissed me on the cheek. It was a hair-light touch, but a kiss nonetheless. Christ, this was getting spooky. I took another slug of whisky and looked for stray pieces of kitchen cutlery with sharp edges.

Once Juliette had a drink we all sat down and exchanged pleasantries. They seemed keen to know if I'd had any contact with Susan. I told them I'd been out of touch, not caring much if they thought it was deliberate or not. Then Hugo gave his wife a look, and she sat back and went silent. Stone me, this was getting better.

'Jake, old son,' he said sombrely, peering into his glass 'I've – we've got some news for you. It may come as a bit of a shock.'

I looked at them and thought that whatever it was, it had to be a belter for Juliette to have allowed me back into her Kensington pad. And with a kiss, no less.

'Go on,' I said, when he hesitated.

'Oh, for heaven's sake, Hugo,' Juliette murmured impatiently. 'You men are so hopeless.' She looked at me and took a deep breath – the sort you take when you want to get something out in a rush. 'Jake, Susan has a new person in her life. That ghastly Dunckley person seems to have disappeared, although that was probably a good thing. What she saw in him in the first place, God only knows. He was such a creep.'

'Juliette,' Hugo muttered.

'Sorry – I was merely saying. Anyway, she has a new person in her life. It looks serious.'

'Fine,' I said. 'Anyone I know?'

'I doubt it. Her name's Debbie.'

Her? I looked from one to the other. 'Say again.'

'Sorry.'

Sorry that this Debbie was a woman or sorry she had to tell me? I wasn't sure. Either way it didn't matter much. I looked at Hugo and he nodded.

'And it's a relationship?' I wasn't sure how to put it; asking if it was serious didn't sound quite right.

Susan, Juliette informed me, had decided to get fit – a change of lifestyle which went with the separation. Two days after she had walked out on me, she had joined a gym in Knightsbridge, met Debbie, one of the resident instructors, and the rest, as they say, was history. The last Juliette had heard, Susan was moving in with her new partner and saying goodbye to her old lifestyle and hello to modern exercise fabrics and a new diet.

That explained the woman Dot had seen with Susan at the house.

By the expression on Juliette's face, it was a greater shock to her than it was to me. I would love to have been a fly on the wall when she met up with her circle of girlfriends and gave them the news. Smelling salts all round, at a guess... and a new topic of conversation.

'Of course, this doesn't really help her case against you,' said Hugo the pragmatist. He jumped when Juliette punched him on the shoulder. 'Well, it's true!'

'I don't care about that,' I said, before they began fighting and rolling around on the floor. And I didn't. It was over, so whether she'd shacked up with another woman or the Dalai Lama's second cousin was immaterial.

'Don't you feel anything?' Juliette gave a shudder. 'I can't take it all in.'

'No,' I said, and drained my glass. I needed to get some fresh air. And to see Marcus.

'I'll be in touch,' I told them and headed for the door. 'Thanks for telling me.'

I left them on the doorstep and headed across town to Marcus's place. When he came to the door and smiled, I knew everything was okay.

'Jake.' He reached out to punch my shoulder. 'Why didn't you call? I've been worried. Come in.' He grabbed me by the arm. 'Come through to the kitchen.'

I wondered what was up. He seemed unsettled – as if he'd been given a surprise he didn't quite know what to do with but was determined to handle – and, at the same time, somehow grown up. No longer the kid brother.

'What's up?' I asked. 'You're not pregnant, are you?'

'Don't be daft.' His voice was pitched low, and I wondered if he'd fallen out with his flatmates. 'There's something I've got to tell you – about Susan.'

'No need. I've just seen Hugo and Juliette.'

'Oh.' He looked relieved. 'You okay with it?'

'Why not? As long as she's happy.'

'She said she won't make any demands. That's good, isn't it?'

'Yes,' I said, and clapped him on the shoulder. He needed the reassurance, if only to prove Susan and I weren't going to be at each other's throats for the rest of our lives. 'It's good.'

He sighed and whatever tension he'd been storing up in him

flooded out in a rush. 'The thing is,' he continued in a low voice, 'there's someone here to see you. She arrived a few minutes ago. She wants to talk.' He glanced towards the front room, and I felt my guts turn over. Jane, I thought. Now she's free of Basher she wants to take up where we left off. Oh, boy, this is all I need. No wonder he was rattled.

'I can explain,' I said. 'It's complicated.'

'There's no need. Really.' He surprised me by smiling. 'And I'm pleased – I really am. You did it.'

'Did what?' Had he been smoking something?

'Made a smart move. Remember, we talked about it?'

Oh, that. I waved an 'oh-that-was-nothing' hand. It seemed a long time ago and I still wasn't sure I was any smarter. Being with Lilly-Mae would be smarter. Not this.

I walked through into the front room and pulled the door closed behind me. Whatever Jane and I had to say to each other was best done without witnesses. Our brief dalliance seemed a lifetime ago, and with the threatening bulk of Basher lurking somewhere in the shadows, it was a situation which held as much promise as a snowball in hell.

I stopped in my tracks as a tall, slim figure rose from the settee. Elegant as I remembered her, eyes large and smiling, her mouth slightly open in what could have been anxious expectation, but what I hoped was something else. The room seemed to stand still and I felt a silly grin begin to spread across my face.

'Hello, Jake,' Lilly-Mae didn't so much speak the words as breathe them, and I developed a warm, fuzzy glow all over.

It took me right back to when we'd first met and the way she'd looked at me as I climbed from the pool at Cedar Point Road and...

I wondered how Charles Clayton would feel about me taking a little longer to make up my mind about joining him.

Or maybe a lot longer.

'Lilly-Mae,' I said, hopelessly relieved and delighted and tongue-tied all over again. Now I knew what Marcus had meant. He'd met her only minutes ago and already he knew – and was pleased.

Yes, Marcus, I thought. This is smart. Exceptionally so, in fact, for me.

'Charles told me where you'd be,' she explained, and put up her hand to touch my face. 'I remembered his number from when you called him from Charlotte. I was worried about meeting Marcus but he was so nice to me and told me I had to wait here for you because you needed someone.'

'He said that?' My voice sounded croaky.

'And Charles said I wasn't to bring you back for a while.'

'He said that?' I was repeating myself because I was reeling from the fact that she had managed to track me down.

'Uh-huh. R and R is what he called it. My dad calls it that, too. Rest and recreation. And I reckon we both need some R and R. Don't you?' She moved closer and breathed into me, and I could see the beginning of moisture glittering in those lovely eyes. 'Sorry I took off, Jake. I had some stuff to sort out. I went home.' She shrugged against me, soft and gentle. 'That's okay, isn't it?'

Hell, she'd come all the way over here and found me. How could it not be okay? 'It's brilliant,' I said, and kissed her.

A long while later she sighed and said, 'So you've got room in your life for a lil' ol' southern gal, then?'

'Damn right,' I said, and hugged her. Over her shoulder I saw the door open and Marcus's grinning face appear. 'How do you feel,' I whispered to her, 'about taking that R and R somewhere hot and

275

quiet? We could buy new costumes and go swimming. Although the costumes wouldn't be mandatory, of course, depending on the location.'

I was gabbling but she didn't seem to mind. She laughed and moved against me in a way that made my spirits soar. 'Costumes. You said costumes *again*! God, that's so cute! I just love your accent, Mr Foreman.'

'Tomayto, tomarto,' I said easily. 'You'll get used to it…'

Acknowledgements

To the monkey on my shoulder which made me wonder if I could try something different. David Headley, for his support and encouragement, as always. Rebecca Lloyd, for making this story so much better than it was.